TUESDAY'S CHILD

ANYA MORA

ABOUT

My daughter is dead.

My husband and I cling to what's left of our family,
desperate to make sense of the tragedy.
But when the sheriff knocks, he delivers news no
mother should ever have to hear.
Betsy was murdered.

And my son is the prime suspect.

When we adopted eleven-year-old Holden, we weren't
wearing rose-colored glasses.
But we never could have imagined this.

Did I choose my daughter's murderer?

*Tuesday's Child is a gripping domestic suspense. Doubt,
desire, and the demise of a once picture-perfect family force*

Emery, wife to a state senator, to live out a mother's worst nightmare.

DEDICATION

For Jeremy
I regret nothing.

FOUR DAYS EARLIER...

BETSY

IT'S SUPPOSED to be the best night of the year. A bucket full of candy, the costume Mom sewed, stitch by stitch.

But it's all gone so wrong. So terribly wrong.

Tears prick my eyes, Julia and Jasper's words ringing in my ears. Holden's fists raised. All of us shouting.

I run into the woods, the ground covered in pine needles, the damp air hanging heavy in the branches. It's dark and familiar. And forbidden.

I had to get away.

"Whoa, the baby is having a tantrum," Julia had laughed as everyone circled me. "Do you need a time out?"

"I'm telling my parents how mean you are," I said, eyes burning. We're in fourth grade now and I wonder if the teasing will ever end.

"Oh, you're going to go tattle-tale?" Julia sneered. "Sounds about right for a little baby."

She has always hated me. Ever since first grade when I won the school art competition and my drawing of an orca whale got me a blue ribbon and her drawing of a horse got her nothing. She's always held a grudge and I'm tired of it. Of letting her make me feel small.

"You're an awful person, Julia." I pointed at her. "I'm brave, what are you?"

I sounded so sure of myself, but now, alone, I don't feel so brave.

I try to stifle the sobs, the tears I held back when they watched me. But now I can let them fall.

My foot snaps a branch, an owl hoots in a tree, but besides that, it's silent.

Until it's not.

Until I feel someone lunge, pushing me.

Mom told me to never come to the woods alone.

Why didn't I listen? I wanted to be big. To be fearless, like her.

I squeeze my eyes shut, pretending this isn't happening. Pretending I'm in my bed, with a flashlight on, drawing my fears away with colored pencils.

A hand covers my mouth. "Don't scream."

No. This isn't right. I try to think, to understand what's happening.

I try to scream, but my voice is muffled. Lost.

I feel dizzy, like my world is spinning. It's so bright, then I'm falling.

But I don't fall against the forest floor. I don't fall into my mother's arms.

One blink, and I know -- this is the ravine.

2

PRESENT

I STARE AT THE REFRIGERATOR, transfixed by Betsy's drawing of an oak tree. Thick branches covered with leaves, roots spreading out on the crayoned green grass.

It's been four days since she died.

She'll never draw another.

Doubling over, hot tears streak my face, and I want to pull my daughter to my chest and kiss her cheeks and breathe her in. She made me a mother and now she is gone.

Wiping my eyes, I straighten myself to stand, and look out the kitchen window into the yard. The leaves from the oak tree cover the grass; the sky is streaked in grey. Outside the boy I'm raising looks past me. Through me.

I see him, though. See his eyes, fueled by rage; eyes that say I will never accept you as my mother.

Five months ago, we stood before a judge and promised to be Holden's forever family. Betsy was happier than anyone that day – she and Holden only one month apart in age. She never saw him as a threat, only as a brother.

She stood beaming as Mark and I signed the adoption papers. We were all crying happy tears, so full of nervous energy, most of the day was a blur.

Well. It was a blur for a lot of reasons. There was more than nervous energy, there was panic and doubt and terror and so, so much regret.

But by then it was too late.

Mark comes up behind me. He holds me so tightly that I can't breathe and that's how I want it. If I can't breathe, then maybe I can forget for just one second that I'm now faced with a life I don't want.

Because I don't want a life without Betsy.

"Shhhh, it's okay, it's going to be okay," Mark tells me as I take long, shaky breaths. I want to believe him. That it's going to be all right. He's been by my side for the last twelve years.

He held my hand when Betsy came into the world.

I need him to hold me as we bury her, too.

"Nothing is okay," I tell him. "Accidents like this shouldn't happen to girls like her. To anyone."

"I know, Emery. I know." Together we look out the kitchen window facing the front lawn. Holden is outside, kicking a soccer ball against the garage door. Each kick sends a boom echoing through the house, and I flinch every time.

Mark takes my arm, trying to lead me away. I keep staring out the window, looking for something I know I won't find. Her.

The doorbell rings and my eyes dart from Mark to

the door to the window. Holden keeps kicking the ball, not pausing for a second, even though a police cruiser is now parked in the driveway.

I missed it pulling in because I'm still looking out the back window, hoping to find freckles. Sunshine. Unruly golden hair and a wild heart; a girl beating her own drum.

"I need to get that," Mark tells me and it takes a moment to register. He is asking me as gently as possible to loosen my vice-like grip. My need for him is startling, but nothing should surprise me after the year we've had.

Trista says everyone grieves in their own way and it's okay to want to be in a cocoon right now. She said this yesterday as she loaded my dishwasher. As her husband, Jeff tried to engage with Holden over a game of chess. We all knew it was a fruitless endeavor. Holden does what he wants, always. He beat Jeff though, checkmate after six moves, and it made me wince. His ability to best a grown man.

Mark walks to the door. With his dark hair, chiseled jaw, and warm smile he always put people at ease. But right now, that isn't his job. Today he isn't a politician. He's a grieving father. He pulls open our front door and I follow him, reaching for a tissue on the side table, wiping my eyes, trying to pull myself together. As I walk into the living room, I see it was for naught.

"Em." Cooper looks at me, his eyes betraying nothing.

"It's Emery," I correct.

He nods a flicker of concern in his eye, stepping

aside to let Margot Smith, the officer we met the night Betsy died, walk through my front door.

Time changes things. Time gives and time takes and Betsy is dead. Right now our shared history doesn't matter.

"What's this about?" Mark's tone is clipped as he closes the door.

"Can we sit?" Cooper asks, and we move to the couch and armchairs. Betsy's comic books are still piled on the coffee table. A family photo above the mantel. Painting projects, half-finished, are on the art table in the corner, the spot where we spent our afternoons. She is here, in every inch of this home, yet she is gone. Dead.

"It isn't easy to discuss why we've come here today." Cooper's eyes travel between Mark, Margot, and me. "The coroner's report was significant. And it changes our course of action."

Blinking, I try to focus on his words, but my eyes catch on the empty stool where Betsy would perch, ink pen in hand, drawing. Drawing. Drawing until her fingers cramped. Her laughter filling the room. "Come look, Mom," she called. "It's a milkshake time machine." Holden smiling, in on a joke meant for fifth graders, not their mothers. Me, walking toward her in the living room, wiping my hands on the dishtowel, dinner almost done. She showed me her comic strip, eyes on mine, looking for affirmation. "One day I'll be just like you," she said.

I press my fingers to my temples, deep breath in, out. One day that will never come. My daughter slipped and fell into a ravine and was gone before anyone could say goodbye.

"Emery, do you need some water?" Mark asks.

Steeling myself, I shake my head, attempt to focus on the moment before me, hard as it is.

Margot's mouth is set in a tight line, her eyes are cloudy and grey, her hair cropped short. The opposite of Cooper with his light hair and open face and a heart too soft for a world where little girls die when they are playing dress-up.

Cooper never could deal with tragedy. The fact he became a police officer still catches me off guard. Yet here he is, wearing a badge in my living room with news about my daughter's death.

"What kind of developments?" Mark asks for me. He's leaning forward, present. Even if his eyes are bloodshot from so many sleepless nights, he's holding it together.

When Cooper clears his throat, my eyes dart up. "Betsy's death report has revealed something... unexpected." Cooper runs his hand over his jaw. "I hate coming here like this, but, uh..."

Margot draws a sharp breath as Cooper stammers. It's then his eyes meet mine and I know why he can't.

Because whatever he came here to say is worse than what we already know. And how can anything be worse when your daughter is dead?

"Betsy's death wasn't an accident," Cooper says, as if just now remembering he is the Deputy Sheriff. His words destroying what's left of me in one fell swoop. "Mark and Emery, your daughter was murdered."

3

ONE YEAR EARLIER

"You sure you'll be warm enough?" I ask as the SUV behind me honks aggressively. "I can go home and grab you a sweater."

I look over my shoulder and see Jenna in her new Silverado. Honking again. And again. Seriously? We live in the sleepy waterfront town of Port Windwick, not Seattle. I don't see the need to rush the morning drop-off. Taking the time to make sure my daughter gets off to school okay is an important part of my day. She's my whole world.

"I'm fine, Mom, promise," Betsy says, offering me a smile; one I hope she'll keep wearing. She could really use a friend. Or two. Fourth grade means sleepovers and play dates for most girls, but Betsy has struggled with her friends this year. It's like they've moved on without her.

But that's just Bets. She wears her heart on her sleeve, tears filling her eyes over what seems like small things. She is soft in a world that is hard and it scares me. Her innocence.

"I love you, sweet pea," I tell her, wishing I could crawl through the window and give her a hug.

"Love you more," she calls out, swinging her lunchbox as she walks toward the Montessori School House she's attended since pre-K.

I turn on my blinker, heading toward the drive-thru for a morning latte. Ten minutes later, coffee in hand, I'm exiting the Starbucks parking lot, and that's when I see Cooper.

He flags me down. And since he's in uniform, I can't exactly ignore him. I know he's been back in town a few weeks, having just taken the job as a deputy. We haven't yet come face to face and I wanted to keep it that way. So did Mark, though he'd never say it. Rehashing a long-dead love triangle isn't exactly the way I want to ring in a new school year. I roll down the window at Cooper's prodding, resolved to be totally in control of the situation. Just because we have a history doesn't mean we need any sort of future.

"Em," he says, giving me a lopsided grin. "Long time."

"You weren't ever going to come back, remember?" There's an effort on my part to keep my heart from pounding. To keep my words steady. A decade ago he left and swore he'd never return.

My life *works* because he hasn't returned.

"I couldn't pass up the gig," he says, shrugging as if this encounter is no big deal. God, his eyes are as clear blue as I remember. The last ten years don't appear to

have changed him in any way from the man I used to
know. I swallow, resenting the fact that some days I feel
like the ghost of the girl he knew.

He rests his arms on the window. We're inches
apart.

"Coop, I don't think--"

He cuts me off, pulling back. Running a hand over
the back of his neck, it's clear he refuses to make the
moment easy. "Have you missed me?"

I press my fingertips to my temple. "God, Coop.
Really?"

He smiles. "Relax, Em. I'm just messing with you."

I exhale. "Mission accomplished."

He looks me over. I'm instantly considering my
clothing choices this morning. A red cashmere sweater
over a crisp white button down. In my lap, I twist the
solitaire diamond ring around my finger. I may have on
dark denim jeans, but they cost three hundred dollars.
I'm polished in a way I never was before Mark.

"I heard you'd changed," he says, with a smirk I
know all too well.

"I heard you hadn't," I say. My words cause him to
chuckle and the sound is so familiar, I feel a pang of
nostalgia for what we shared. In truth, we shared
everything.

Waving him off, I leave the parking lot, my breath
catching as I drive away.

He'd heard I'd changed. I snort as I pull up to my
house. I bet someone like Jenna gave him that line.
She's probably fed him spoonfuls of gossip about me.
How I'm no longer the flannel shirt-wearing, picket-

sign-holding activist. How I traded my beat-up Subaru for a bells and whistles Land Rover. Now I have a gold chain around my neck and an ethically sourced diamond on my finger.

It's not fair though, to hold the money Mark came from against us. Cooper may be a good man in many ways, but Mark is too. Both of the men from my past are reputable, honest, social servants. A deputy and a senator.

Yet as I park in my driveway, I hate feeling like Cooper was judging me. Who cares if he was? My life is full. Beauty-full.

I have a daughter who is the literal light of my life. Married to a good man, who despite his insistence on things being *just so*, has mellowed out slightly over time. I have a creative outlet; I get a few freelance design jobs a month. I'd be a starving artist if it weren't for my husband's bank account.

That should be plenty. More than plenty.

Still, there's a gnawing in the pit of my stomach. Trying to ignore it, I get out of the car, pausing to post a photo of me in the front yard, golden leaves around the bright red Hunter rain boots on my feet, Starbucks cup in hand, captioning the image: #Autumnvibes #PSL #fallcolors

Before reaching for the newspaper on the front steps, I toss my phone deep inside my Hermès bag. I hate both of those two things--the iPhone and the purse. But I can't exactly ditch the 10th Anniversary gift from Mark or the device that keeps me tethered to the real world.

Real world. I don't even know what that is. I've deleted my social media accounts about fourteen times over the past year only to give up my resolve after a few weeks. Every. Single. Time.

I'll be totally committed, then Trista or Caroline will call asking why I haven't responded to the birthday party invite that I never got because I'm off Facebook, and I'll ask what they've been up to and they'll tell me they just got back from San Juan Island, didn't I see the photos? And I'll feel like a flaky friend and reinstall the apps, loathing the fact that I am forever living in the in-between. Both loving the life I've been afforded and wishing I could be living in a simpler time when people were doing more with their lives.

When I was doing more with my life.

I enter my home, kicking off the unnecessary rain boots -- the sky is blue today, dropping my purse on the table in the foyer. After setting my pumpkin spice latte on the white marble kitchen island, I spread out the paper. All the while, resenting the Cooper-sized insinuation that I've changed.

It's simply not true. I'm still the girl I once was. I've got a record player. A one-speed bicycle that I never ride. A subscription to the Port Windwick Tribune.

Now, though, I'm alone in the kitchen. Mark's at the capital, Betsy's at school, and I have the next seven hours to fill. Laundry will take an hour-ish. I can work on the new logo for the Montessori Parent Group. That can eat up two, three hours. Caro and I are meeting up to talk through the fundraiser for the women's shelter tomorrow so I can brainstorm ideas for that...

Still, I feel idle. Maybe I'll email Mrs. MacIntire and see if I can come in this month and lead an art project for Betsy's class.

I run my fingers over the black and white newsprint, scanning the articles of today's paper. I see Cooper's name in a headline—*Deputy Dawson Saves Cat.*

And I thought I was a cliché.

In the photograph, Coop has a white cat tucked under his arm, his shaggy hair and slightly askew smile a throwback to a life I could have had. A life he asked to share with me.

There is a twinge in my chest that I don't want to put words to, so I turn the page, knowing what day it is as I do.

Tuesday. And every Tuesday there's one feature I always read.

It's called *Tuesday's Child*. Each week a foster child in the region, waiting to be adopted, is highlighted. There's a photo, a short biography, and a website for more information.

I've wanted to type in the web address more times than I can count but I've always stopped myself, knowing that I'd end up in a puddle of tears if I started looking at these innocent children waiting for families.

But today feels different. It's not because I saw Cooper. It's different because the child looking back at me is different than all the others.

It's a boy I know. Not in a physical way. And it's not fair to even say it's an emotional way.

It's a maternal way. A way I understand.

Staring back at me in the photo is a ten-year-old boy with dark brown hair and darker eyes and skin the color of sand, glittering like gold, and at that moment I know.

I know that he is mine.

We don't look alike. My shoulder length hair is soft caramel-color, my eyes green, and my complexion rosy.

I read his short biography over and over again, biting my bottom lip as I do, trying to focus and not jump ten steps ahead of myself.

Holden is a fourth grader who loves reading and sports. He has been in foster care for six years and is excited to meet his forever family. He responds well to positive reinforcement and boundaries are a wonderful way for him to feel safe. Holden is loyal, resilient, and loves to be challenged.

My heartbeat quickens. This boy has captured me. It's like looking at someone I've always known. He's been in foster care for so long. His parental rights were terminated a year ago. He's legally free to be adopted and is just waiting for a family.

I swallow. Hard. I look at the clock. There are so many empty hours in my life. Hours I want to fill. I have more love in my heart to give. More money than any one family should have. More rooms than are full.

I heard you'd changed.

I want to be more than a good person. More than a generous person.

I want to be this child's mother.

————

THAT NIGHT, when Mark comes home after nine, he's loosening his tie and looking for leftovers. I've cleaned up the whirlwind of Betsy and me -- the bags on the floor, the jackets on the back of chairs. I've put up the art supplies and washed every dish in the sink.

"How did Betsy's day go?"

"She spent the afternoon making a collage with Mod Podge and fall leaves." I point to where it's drying on the kitchen table. Instead of leaves falling from the tree, they are floating upwards, to blackened clouds. Mark's eyes narrow, taking in the image. "She said it was a metaphor," I explain. Betsy had said that as if it were obvious. It wasn't.

Mark smiles tightly, taking in the eerie image. "Looks like Bets."

"She okay, you think?" I ask, wiping down the counter the way I know he likes. Meticulous is a good word for Mark. It's why he is so successful as a senator; he's thorough.

"I think Bets is like her mother. Deep and complicated and misunderstood by the masses." Mark chuckles and I feel his smile even before I see it. I wish he'd wrap his arms around me, kiss my neck. I settle for his laugh.

I spin to face him. "Ha ha," I say, deadpanned. "For the record, I'm not that complicated. And I don't need to be understood by the masses. I have Caroline and Trista. That's plenty."

"And me, right?" he asks with a smirk.

"Right, and you. Though to be fair, you and I aren't exactly two peas in a pod." It was meant to be a lighthearted comment, but Mark immediately pulls back, sitting down on a stool at the kitchen island.

He changes the subject. "So Bets is in bed?"

"Sound asleep, finally," I say. "She wanted me to read her five chapters before she'd let me out of her sight."

"You're too soft with her," he says.

I turn from Mark to set a plate of spaghetti in the microwave. "The world is cruel enough as it is. Why not be gentle?" I uncork a bottle of Pinot Noir, set it on a cloth napkin so it doesn't drip on the counter, and then reach for two glasses.

"Because her classmates will eat her alive. She needs to toughen up."

"I'm the one here with her all day, Mark, while you're at work. Can you trust my instincts on this?"

I hand him his glass of wine, and he takes it, nodding. "I know, Emery. You're an amazing mom."

"Thank you," I say, tucking a strand of hair behind my ear. "On that note..." I have so much more on my mind right now and I'm ready to launch into it. All of it.

"What is it?" he asks, a knowing smirk playing on his lips. I'm the dreamer in the house. I plan our vacations, our house renovations, our charitable causes. I bite the side of my lip as I prepare myself to present my biggest idea yet.

"Do you still ever think about having more than Betsy?" I ask, turning my back on him as I ask, suddenly scared to see if his face might break mine.

Our marriage is for Betsy. We don't sleep together more than a few times a year. When we first married it was an opposites attract kind of love... now that excitement has worn off. Now we're two adults raising our little girl. I want more.

He's caught off guard, maybe, by the way, I worded it, but then he understands.

"More?" His voice reflects surprise. "But we tried, Emery. For so long. I thought we laid that idea to rest."

I refill our glasses with wine, heavy-handed pours this time. Mark just put in a thirteen-hour day and maybe the timing isn't right. But will it ever be?

I set the warmed spaghetti on the counter in front of him. "I'm not talking about getting pregnant."

He tilts his head as I slide onto the stool next to him. "What are you talking about then?"

"Adoption."

His brows rise in surprise. "Really? I thought--"

"I know."

He'd suggested adoption several times over the years. I always resisted. "I wanted to give all of myself to Betsy -- and I have. But now Betsy is ten. And I think... No, I know, Mark. I want another child."

He leans back, mulling over the words. "What brought this on?"

I reach for my iPad on the counter and pull up the website I have been obsessing over all day. Before handing it to him, I explain *Tuesday's Child*.

"An older child? That seems..." Mark shakes his head. "It would be a lot, Emery. And with my job, you know how busy I am. I'm gone more than half the time at the capital. And I want to run for Congress next year, we've talked about this."

"I know, but just think. I'm home all day. I have time. I want to do something meaningful."

"Raising Bets isn't meaningful?"

"It is. But Mark, you're making the world a better place. You're a state senator, doing real work to change lives. You're going to be a congressman. It inspires me. I want to do more with my life too. I want to do this."

"And Bets? What about her?"

"It wouldn't change anything."

Mark rests his hand on my own. His touch familiar, but still surprising. We live like friends, but maybe with this joint endeavor, a new spark would light. "Emery, it would change everything."

"But change for the better, right? I mean, it would show her empathy. The importance of family."

"We could volunteer at the food bank with her to teach her about compassion."

I nod, understanding what he means, but also wanting this in ways I can't explain. It's like, when you know, you know. And I know this child is going to be mine.

"Just look at this boy, Mark."

I hand him the iPad and he pulls in a breath. His features relaxing as he looks at the photograph, as his eyes scan the biography.

"Why him?" Mark asks.

"He needs us. And I don't think it would hurt you, as far as your career goes."

He softens his gaze as he looks at the boy. "This doesn't have anything to do with politics. But Emery, there are fifteen hundred children on this database for Washington State alone. Why this child?"

"He has been waiting so long. He's the same age as Betsy. He loves reading and playing soccer. Just like me. Just like you."

"What if he is, you know, uh, angry? Violent?"

"Of course he's going to be angry," I say, already on the defensive for a boy I've never met. "His childhood has been a mess. But just look at that face. Don't you see a gentle lion?"

He looks at the picture of the boy, and emotion floods my husband's face. "You've always been an optimist."

"Is that a bad thing?"

Mark shakes his head, his eyes filled with understanding. "No. I love that about you. And so will this child."

"Is that a yes? Can I call for more information?"

Mark hands me the iPad. "Yes," he says, pulling a bite of spaghetti to his mouth. "Of course, you can."

4

PRESENT

MURDER?

"No," I say, looking up at Cooper and Margot. My single word is ragged and laced with shock. "No. Betsy couldn't have been. It was an accident. She tripped. She fell. She--"

Cooper reaches for me the same time Mark does and I pull back from them both. I curl into a ball on the couch, wanting to be small enough to disappear because this can't be true.

Murders happen in metropolises. In dangerous places. Not here. Not in the quiet town where I've lived most of my life. Not on a street that is safe, where children go trick-or-treating and ring the doorbells of people they've known since they were little.

"The injuries to her head don't correlate with the fall. Before she landed in the ravine, she was hit over the head multiple times with an object."

Mark scoffs. "What does that mean exactly?" His voice is so raw that I can't recognize it. I look over at him and see my strong, capable husband suddenly as breathless as me.

Margot clears her throat. "The case is now a murder investigation and her body is the evidence. The detectives we are working with have already requested an additional autopsy so they can analyze the brain injury in a more comprehensive way."

I wrap my arms around my knees, rocking and shaking and falling apart all over again.

"Of course," Mark manages. "But who..."

"The most difficult part of this conversation is what we need to say next." Cooper's words catch me off guard -- there's more? How is it possible for there to be more than this? I look up at him and try to focus, but everything around me is a whirling, blurry mess.

"I want you both to prepare yourselves for what I'm going to say. It's going to be hard to hear." Cooper speaks softly. It's a voice I know so well; a voice that comforted me when I was a little girl. When I fell off my bicycle, it was Cooper who cleaned my cuts, who kissed my bruises. Now he is going to be the one to hurt me. I know it by the way he looks at his hands. When he lifts his head, his eyes reach mine.

"There was video footage from the night, from a phone." Cooper pauses. "We have a suspect."

I feel faint. My body goes limp. I see nothing and I see everything all at once. Betsy on a carousel, her laughter filling the air. Betsy on horseback, trotting down the beach. Betsy perched on her bed, reading aloud to me from *Harry Potter and The Sorcerer's Stone,* gasping as she turns the page even though we'd practically memorized the book.

Betsy at the morgue, her skull bashed in.

No.

"Who?" Mark asks, his tone vicious and fueled with fury, there is a rage in him I've never seen. But it's a hatred I understand. What kind of monster would do this to my little girl?

Margot clears her throat. "We need to speak with Holden."

Mark and I both go still. Light blinds me even though the shades are drawn. This isn't my story. It can't be. This is not how my family falls apart.

No.

"Holden?" Mark gasps. "You think our son... You think a child could..."

The idea stuns me into silence. My body trembles, my shoulders shake. He couldn't have.

Could he?

My daughter has been murdered and her brother is the accused.

Fear winds its way up my spine.

"Emery, Mark," Cooper says. "Do you understand what we're saying?"

How could I understand anything right now when my entire life is out of control? I should answer Cooper. Tell him, yes, I understand. But also shout no, Holden is not responsible.

Because of course, he isn't.

Because little boys don't murder their sisters.

I'm gasping. He isn't *that* little.

It's hard to see anything besides her eleven-year-old body, eyes closed, heart stopped.

I should have let her put Pop-Tarts in the shopping cart. Watch *the Goonies*. Download free apps with abandon.

I always said no.

Yes. Yes. Yes. If I could have her back I would only say that one simple word. A new mantra, my prayer.

Yes.

"But the funeral," I ask. "What happens with..."

Cooper nods. "It will need to be postponed until the investigation has..." He stalls. But I understand. There needs to be an arrest before they release the body. Too many episodes of *CSI* tell me that. Why didn't I watch *The Bachelor* like the other moms on the parent association?

"Everyone is here," I say, thinking of Mark's parents who had flown in from Vermont. Family friends and college roommates all caught the first flight to Seattle, ferried over the Sound to our unsuspecting town that has been painted in a familiar grey. The rain hasn't stopped since Halloween.

Everyone is settled in hotel rooms, their luggage filled with black suit coats and modest heels, all ready to pay their respects to my daughter.

"The service is... It's--" My chest is tight and I feel the stare of the officer Cooper brought with him.

"We know," Margot says. "This isn't what anyone wants to hear. But it's necessary. Holden will need a lawyer. There will be an investigation, and your son will be brought in for questioning. Or we can do that here if you'd prefer."

I feel Mark's body stiffen next to mine as if he is reaching down, looking for strength inside himself. The strength he wasn't sure he'd find. "I'll get him representation, of course." Then he adds, sharply, "Before he is questioned."

"He didn't do it." I shake my head; my voice is rattled with fear and laced with fervor. "He didn't." My words are my conviction. My faith.

Mark reaches for my hand. Squeezes it. "I know, Em. We know."

Cooper nods slowly, and I know it's a trained maneuver. He's trying to calm me; no one wants to replay the hysteria that happened the day after All Hallows Eve.

When I fell to my knees, the rain sleeting down upon me, a cruel joke as if anything could wash this sorrow away. My sobs were etched against the morning light, my hollow heart breaking along the cracked sidewalk strewn with empty candy wrappers, and pale ghosts hung in trees. Taunting me.

Blinking, the room comes into focus. Holden. I can't cling to her because she is gone but I can cling to Holden because he is here. Because he is my child. I chose him.

I made my choice over a year ago when I picked up the phone and called the child services offices.

Now I choose to hold onto the only hope I can find in the midst of this mess. If I don't cling to saving Holden, I'll be swallowed up, whole.

Betsy's death is a cave that leaves me lost without a lantern. But I will carry a light for Holden. I just have to find the flame.

The sliding glass door opens and Holden walks into the house, his dark eyes fierce with fury, the relentless wave of rage he refuses to keep at bay, and it fills the room. Everyone feels it. Holden is not tender; if he's lionhearted it's not because he is courageous, it's because he is fearless in a way that scares most people.

In a way that, if I'm being perfectly honest, scares me.

I look at him, standing in the living room wearing his Air Jordan's and oversized tee-shirt and basketball shorts even though it's November and the air in Washington is a chilly forty degrees. Even though the rain has soaked his shoulders, streaked his face.

I look at him, wishing his cheeks were washed with tears the same as mine. This boy I hand-picked. A child I stood before a judge and promised to protect. A son whose newly issued birth certificate lists me as more than a guardian. I am his mom.

I look at my son who has become a suspect, wanting to believe that he can harness his strength and become something brave, something beautiful.

Is this grief talking or is it the cry of a desperate mother's heart?

"Holden," I whisper, inadequacy sweeping over me, knowing he may unleash on me the way he has so many times before. I walk on eggshells when he's around, but it's better than glass. He doesn't even look at me, though. What would this be like if I were more than a poor substitute?

Would Betsy be alive?

"I heard what you said," Holden says, his voice razor thin, looking at me as he speaks, never having backed down from a fight in his life. "You think I killed her."

5

ELEVEN MONTHS EARLIER

"THIS IS A TERRIBLE IDEA," Trista says as I first broached the idea of Holden over coffee. It's been a week since Mark and I first discussed adopting him, and here I am, ready to open up to my two closest friends: Caroline Caraway and Trista Brix.

Trista and I just dropped our kids off at the school-house; Trista's son Levi is a fifth grader. Caroline doesn't work and doesn't have any children, though she's married to Pete, an orthodontist in town. The three of us met in a book club years ago, hosted at the local bookstore, and our friendship has spanned several years.

"Why is it terrible?" My initial instinct is to get defensive, but I also had a feeling she'd respond this way. It's why I waited a week to mention anything. And I still haven't disclosed my Cooper encounter with either of them. I'm not a great best friend. I keep things close to my chest. I'm not as vulnerable outside the house as I am in it. Being married to a rising politician forces me to put on a polished smile even when it's hard.

Trista, on the other hand, is an open book. "Because, Emery, all you hear are the horror stories about adopted kids chopping off the heads of their new parents."

"Ouch," Caroline says, adding sugar to her skim latte. "A little harsh, Tris."

Trista shrugs. "My sister's a social worker. All I hear about are the tragic cases. It never ends well. Believe me, I have to hear about it every year at Thanksgiving dinner."

"That's not always the case," Caroline says. "I was watching *America's Got Talent* last night. This dad, a singer, he had the entire audience in tears over his story. He adopted like five kids and they love him and call him daddy. It was sweet."

"How do you even watch that kind of TV?" Trista rolls her eyes. She's judgy and honest and I envy her for saying it like it is.

Still, I share a look with Caroline. So what if she has a thing for trashy television? There is something about Caroline that is hopeful, longing. Desperate. I know she wants a child... she's been through so many rounds of IVF. The thought has me suddenly self-conscious about the conversation. What does it say about me if I want to adopt from foster care... and she doesn't? I don't want to make anyone feel bad for their own choices.

"Look," I cut in. "There will be no head chopping. And really, talk about a stereotype based on a sensationalized news story from ten years ago, Tris." I feel my voice rise, something that rarely happens. "And every child deserves a home, regardless."

Trista sets down her cup of coffee, looking me in the eyes. "Shit. You're, like, really doing this."

I nod, tears pricking the corner of my eyes. "Mark's on board. And I'm meeting the social worker to go through Holden's file tomorrow."

"Oh, my god," Caroline says. "He has a name and everything."

I take a long shaky breath. "I know it's crazy but I feel really certain. Really sure. And I want this."

"What about Bets?" Caro asks. "Does she know?"

"We told her last night. She was surprised but happy. It's been such a rocky start to the school year for her that she actually seemed excited at the prospect of a sibling. She's lonely." Trista and Caroline twist their lips, knowing something I don't. I lean in. "What?"

"Nothing, Em," Trista says. "It's just... well..." She slumps in her chair a bit, looking defeated before even speaking. "It's actually why we asked you to coffee today. Levi came home yesterday and told me there's a rumor going around."

"What rumor?"

Trista presses her lips together, clasping her hands. "It might not be true. But according to Levi, there's a club in the fourth grade."

"What kind of club?" My words come out slowly; I'm dreading the answer.

"A girls' club," Trista says.

I frown. "I haven't heard of it."

"Right," Trista says. "Because it's a club for every girl in the grade. Except for Betsy."

"What? That's absurd, that's..." I blink away the tears that started when we were discussing Holden moments ago. But now we're talking about Bets. I'm not a crier, especially over grade school drama. But a no-Betsy club? My stomach drops.

"I know, it's awful," Caroline says, worry written on her face. "I was thinking, maybe I could do something one on one with Bets? She'd probably like to spend time with her Auntie Caroline."

"Fuck," I say, seeing Cooper walk in the café. I'm royally upset over this conversation, but that's not why I swear. My friends assume the uncharacteristic expletive is because of the fourth-grade bullies but it isn't. It's Cooper.

When Caroline and Trista finally catch on, their eyebrows lift. Cooper gives me a nod, a smile that makes my heart race an embarrassing amount, and he just keeps walking.

"What the hell was that?" Trista asks, knowing enough about the history between Coop and me to know there is a story she needs to hear.

I groan. "*That* was last Thursday."

THREE WEEKS LATER, Mark and I have made a choice. He's more than agreeable and accommodating. In fact, he's dreaming about this child being ours as much as I am. His laptop was on the table last night, a browser open.

It was a blueprint for a tree house.

"Will he be nice, you think?" Betsy asks, looking up from her drawing pad, a fine tip marker in hand. I look over at Mark who's pouring the green smoothie he just prepared. He measures his caloric intake in the same way he rations his screen time. With precision. I wish I were so put together. Instead, I overslept and in lieu of a shower, I dry shampooed the heck out my hair to look presentable.

"I think he'll be nervous. I mean, I'm nervous." I reach for my coffee cup and guzzle the now lukewarm liquid. I forgot where I'd set the mug as I'd rummaged through my closet looking for my other pink flat.

"Time check," he says, looking at his watch. "We have about ten minutes before we need to leave. My girls good with that?"

Betsy rinses out her cereal bowl in the sink and Mark turns off the coffee pot. It's a normal Saturday morning. Except not. Today, we meet Holden.

"I'm fine. Just ..." Bets stops mid-sentence and bites her bottom lip.

"Just what, goose?" I ask, setting down my coffee and really look at her. She's been so on board during all of this -- the conversations, the lead-up. This choice will rock her world, as much as anyone else's.

"It's just." She blinks slowly, her long lashes sweeping against the cheeks of her heart-shaped face. "I hope he likes me."

I run my hand over her hair, look into her pale blue

eyes, now brimming with tears. "Bets, how could he not?"

She shrugs, but I see the worry. She never found out about the "girl-club," and thankfully, the entire thing was squashed the day I heard about it. We don't pay thirty grand a year for my daughter's education to have bullies take over elementary school playgrounds. The principal and teacher were rightly mortified, and Mark made it clear this would be in the papers if it happened again.

Still, as a mother, it has me on edge. Last week, I ordered parenting books for the first time since she was a baby.

Caroline says it's probably just kids stretching their wings, testing the waters. Trista calls it entitled brats at a private school who judge Betsy because I won't let my ten-year-old have a data plan.

Me? I'm somewhere in between. Wanting to believe the best in other kids but wanting to protect my little girl.

The phone thing, though -- if that's truly the root cause of her trouble at school, it isn't going to change. Mark and I are on the same page with that: no phones for anyone under eighteen in this house. Call it old school, but as a family who relies on public approval rating for our livelihood, we aren't taking any risks with unintentional texts being read the wrong way; for any adolescent glitches in judgment. One screenshot can ruin a career. We've watched it happen.

"I just want a brother who can be my best friend," Betsy says, so honestly my heart aches.

"Hey, sweetie," Mark says, resting an arm on her shoulder. "Let's not put too much pressure on him, on any of it, okay? Today is about meeting someone new, we don't know how it's gonna go."

She swallows, nodding, then wrapping her arms around her dad. "I love you," she says.

He kisses her head. "To the moon and back."

We leave the house, the three of us in Mark's BMW. The lawn crew is just arriving as we head down the drive. We have an actual white picket fence and a row of rose bushes and shutters on our windows. We have a picture-perfect family and as I look over at my husband -- hands on the steering wheel, ten and two--and back at my daughter, a smile on her rosy-cheeked face, I know it's not just a picture.

It's real.

I may hate social media for blasting fake messages to the world about how amazing everyone's lives are... but honestly? My life *is* pretty fantastic. My husband has a big charitable heart, my daughter is thoughtful and kind, and I'm at least trying to be my best self.

I've chaired committees for the school, coordinated the silent auction for the Food Shelter, held signs when the teacher's union demanded a livable wage. And now this. A step of faith, a risk with no rewards. My optimism is no act. This is the real deal.

We pull up to the Ridgedale Shopping Mall which is two towns over. We're meeting Holden and his social worker Linda at the food court. Betsy finds walking through the mall exciting. It's something we never do; I order everything online. She's fascinated by the large window displays of handbags and watches, the kiosks in the walkway selling hair straighteners and miniature drones.

When we enter the food court there's a maze of people, stale greasy air, and a toddler playland in the center full of squishy blocks and foam slides. I glance at my phone and see we're early. "Why don't you grab us a table," I tell Mark and Bets. "I'll order some..." I look around. We never eat fast food.

Betsy chirps. "Shakes and fries. I bet Holden will love that."

I nod. "Come help?"

She takes my hand and Mark smiles, telling us he'll look for a large table. As we walk through the food court, I see Caroline out of the corner of my eye. I smile, waving at her and she walks over to Bets and me, shopping bags in her hands.

"What are you doing here?" she asks, her hair looks great, her blond bob swishing as she leans over and hugs me, then Betsy. "I know how much you loathe the mall."

I know Caroline has lots of reservations about Holden, so I try to choose my words carefully. Also, I'm not exactly interested in her scoping him out. She may be one of my closest friends, but I've found myself feeling private about Holden, about his history. I'm protective of a boy I've never met.

Betsy speaks up before I can formulate a reply. "We're meeting Holden here. Isn't that awesome?"

Caroline's eyes flash with concern. I see it as she looks at my daughter "You're excited?"

Betsy beams. "I've always wanted a brother."

Caroline lifts her shoulders, a tight smile on her face. Betsy doesn't notice, but I know Caroline. I know she's holding back a well of opinions.

"Hey, why don't you head over there?" I tell Betsy. "The line is pretty long at the Burger shop. I'll be there in a sec, okay?"

She gives Caroline a hug. "Love you, Auntie Caroline."

"Love you more, sweetheart."

Betsy walks fifteen feet away, and Caroline rests a hand on my arm. "You sure about this? She seems so excited like it's a done deal. But what if he's--"

I flinch. "If he's what? God, Caroline. Do you hear yourself?"

She presses her lips together, adjusting the bags in her arms. She speaks quietly, but her words are sharp. "You're acting so cavalier about all of this. I'm worried about you. But mostly I'm worried about Bets."

"This is you being worried? Because it feels like judgment."

"I just don't want you to make a choice you'll regret for the rest of your life. Carrying guilt like that around... it could ruin you."

I scoff, incredulous. Who is she to judge? In the distance, Betsy waves to me, pointing to the line that is rapidly clearing out. "We'll finish this later," I say irritated. "But what I need right now, is your support. Nothing else."

She steps back and I feel a line between us form. The beginning of our end.

———

A FEW MINUTES LATER, red plastic tray in hand, Betsy and I navigate the crowd.

"There they are," she says, pointing to Mark who has been joined by a woman and young boy.

Swallowing, we begin making our way to them. Mark shakes their hands. I look down at Bets. "You okay?"

She nods, an innocent expression on her face. She's being so brave, so open. It makes me want to be braver, too.

As we reach the table, I notice Holden staring at the ground. I meet Mark's eyes and he takes the tray from me.

"Hello," I say reaching my hand out to Linda. "I'm Emery. And this is our daughter Betsy."

She greets me warmly, but her appearance is ragged as if she's perpetually short on time. Rumpled suit, hair falling out of its curl, worn fake-leather boots. I think of every social worker stereotype -- underpaid and over-worked -- and wonder how closely that fits the bill.

I swallow, thinking how I meticulously chose my outfit today. Pale pink Louboutin flats paired with dark denim Saint Laurent skinny jeans, a cream cashmere sweater. Shame floods me. Who the hell do I think I am to be doing this? Do I think I'm some savior for this orphaned boy? A politician's wife, through and through.

But then Holden looks up as Betsy offers him a chocolate milkshake and my worry washes away. Who cares if I'm an upper-class woman who never experienced the kind of trauma Holden has been through? I'm here, showing up. Trying.

He takes the milkshake. There isn't a thank you, but he raises his chin, and for Bets, that seems like enough. She gives him a smile.

I decide it can be enough for me too.

6

PRESENT

THEY DON'T STAY to question Holden -- Mark insists they can't until a lawyer is present. I'm grateful for his ability to navigate this because right now, I can't think clearly. I'm beyond my breaking point. Of course, Holden didn't hurt her. Kill her. He loved her in the best way he could.

"You need to breathe, girl," Trista says. She's in a pair of sweats and a stretched-out tee-shirt with the words *Not My First Rodeo* printed on it. It looks like she just rolled off the couch.

She came right over after Mark called her, filling her in on what the officers had come to share. I didn't want him to call anyone or say anything about this -- the moment the press finds out I fear they will be camped outside our home. I can see the headline, *SON OF CONGRESS CANDIDATE ACCUSED OF MURDER.*

The thought has me dry-heaving in the master bathroom, shaking and refusing Ambien, Percocet, wine. Mark knew what he was doing when he asked my only friend to show up and keep me from falling completely into the deep end.

Still, I don't want painkillers of any kind. I don't want anything to take me away from how I feel in this moment. I want to remember it. Feel it for the brittle broken day it is.

"Is Cooper still here?" I ask, knowing I could never pose the question in front of Caroline. Not that she's talking to me anymore.

God, a part of me wishes she were. Or at least, I wish things between us were like they were. I lost more than Betsy this year. Since Holden came home, I've lost nearly every shred of my old life.

So, I don't want Caroline here now, not after everything. The words she said still feel like sharp cuts. But oh, how I crave her. The familiarity of her laugh when we split a bottle of white wine during happy hour. Her texts midway through a particularly rough day, making me snort with laughter -- making me feel seen. Her stops at the house in those early months after Holden came home when she was still my best friend and not someone who took a side.

Because there were sides even then. Of course, there have always been sides in religion and politics and women's rights and border control. I just never knew there were also sides when it came to children.

My children.

"Cooper hasn't left yet," Trista tells me, pulling me back to the question at hand. She wraps an arm around me and guides me from the bathroom, forcing me in my bed. We crawl under the thick cover of the duvet and turn on our sides, facing one another.

"Why is he still here?" I ask.

The question is loaded and Trista knows why. "Still in town or still in this house?" she asks, a small smirk playing on her lips. Only Trista could find a slice of humor on a day like this.

"Both." I close my eyes, so fucking exhausted.

"Holden has Mark. He couldn't be in better hands."

"I need to see the video footage," I tell her. "What the hell was on it?"

"I don't know. We were both in the house all night, with Jeff. I honestly have no idea what the kids got up to." She rubs her temples, and I know I'm not alone in being anxious. "It could be bad, Em. They wouldn't be questioning him if it wasn't."

The words hang heavy in the air.

"He couldn't have," I say.

"I know."

But the truth lies between us. Thick and knotted, tight as a rope.

Holden is not Betsy. He is not kind and not gentle. If he holds onto hope, it's something I've only barely glimpsed, if that, in a flash of him thinking he might get what he wants. Not childlike hope, not the kind my darling girl has. Had.

"I can't live without her," I say, gasping for breath. The sobs so thick in my throat I think I might pass out.

Trista wraps her arm around me. She doesn't speak.

What can she say?

After I let every last wrecked cry out, I hear the click of the front door. Hear it close.

Cooper is gone.

I open my eyes; Trista hears what I hear. She knows what I wish for, forbidden as it is. Him.

"Did he mention anything since Halloween?" she asks.

I shake my head. "He hasn't said a word to me. And I doubt he will. We haven't been alone once. I'm guessing he wants to be on this case, wants to find out who killed Bets."

Trista turns, facing the ceiling. "What a mess."

"I know. And if Mark knew?" I sigh. "He can't know. Not now. It would devastate him."

"I agree," Trista says. "It would stir too much up."

"There's enough to deal with. People are coming into town for the service. And now I have to cancel it all."

"Let me deal with that," Trista says. "You're in no place to do that."

"You're sure?"

She nods. "Of course. That shouldn't be on your plate."

Relief washes over me. Thank God for friends. "While you're on it, can you make sure Mark's parents don't stop by the house?"

Trista looks at me, smirking. "You think they want to see you or Holden? You're both on their shit list."

"They're still holding a grudge that we didn't visit last summer. I feel bad, now. I mean, it was the last summer they would have had with Betsy."

"Stop," Trista says. "Now isn't the time to blame yourself or get all guilty. Right now, you need to survive. You need to stay strong. Rested. Hydrated. Understood?"

"I wish I could stay with Cooper," I admit.

"Stop, Em. You can't have everything. You made your choice. Holden needs stability. He needs you to be his mom. You can't go running off with your high school boyfriend."

"He's more than that."

"I know. But Em, you can't fall apart right now."

"But life without Bets... I mean, could you live without Levi?"

Trista bites her lip. "I couldn't imagine. It's a mother's worst nightmare. Still, even if you think you can't live without her, Em, you have to. For Holden."

I nod, knowing she's right. My friend, who is both crass and cruel, is also so very wise.

Trista didn't want Holden to join my family initially, but since we made the decision since he came home to us -- she's never once brought it back up.

She is loyal.

And she is right.

I sit up in my bed. I need to talk to my son.

7

ELEVEN MONTHS EARLIER

WHEN THE DOORBELL RINGS, we all start. Mark, Bets, and I have been sitting in the living room waiting for him to arrive. And now he's here.

"I'm so nervous," I admit. Mark squeezes my hand as he passes me to answer the door. He's been doing that more lately. Not kissing me or hugging me... but his fingers have brushed against mine here and there. It's reminded me how much I miss his attention, his touch.

I've hardly seen my husband all week. He's in session right now, which means he's staying at his apartment in the capital most weeknights. It's the main reason we hesitated on Holden being placed with us now, so fast.

But once Linda, his social worker explained that his current foster home was being closed down, and if he didn't move in with us, he'd have to move to yet another temporary facility, Mark had relented. After lunch at the food court, it was obvious that the foster home he was living in was doing more harm than good.

And that's putting it lightly. He had asthma because the bedroom in the foster home had walls covered in black mold. He'd never been given the diagnosis before the placement. Linda was certain it would be reversed if he were living in a home that was mold-free.

Mold-free -- that's the bar the state is reaching for when it comes to where this boy lives.

I remember so clearly Caroline and Trista's reactions after telling them about the asthma. Trista was furious. "Who approves these foster parents in the first place?" Caroline was quieter. "It's just so sad. The kids who are hurting the most and need the most help are getting such a small slice of the pie. It makes me think I'm not doing enough. I have empty rooms in my house too."

Caroline's words had grated on me. I'm already protective of Holden, not wanting to share. It made me regret telling them about the asthma in the first place.

Now, as Linda and Holden enter our home for the first time, I know that if Caroline were standing here right now she'd be in a puddle of tears.

Holden arrives with a black garbage bag holding his every possession. His eyes flare with anger as he looks around the foyer, and when Linda offers me a strained smile, I wonder what the conversation had looked like on their way to our home.

I run a finger over the gold chain around my neck, feeling self-conscious about our house. It suddenly feels overdone and forced. Like a mockery of all Holden didn't have before and everything we can give him now. As if we can sweep in with money and change this little boy's life.

I know it isn't the truth, the intent -- but it feels like that. And as Mark leads the pair into our living room, I feel more like a politician's wife than ever. Trista had cynically asked if Mark was on board because it would be a good platform for when he ran for Congress. I'd rolled my eyes at the time, thinking the question absurd -- and I still do -- but as Mark warmly welcomes Linda into our home, offering her coffee, tea, water, I see the politician in him shine.

I swallow, not liking the potential implications. If Trista jumped to that conclusion, would other people? I push it out of my mind as I head to the kitchen to get the coffee Linda requested and cans of La Croix for the kids.

Kids. That right there is the reality. Holden coming here today is our family saying yes, we can make room. In our home and also our hearts. No longer claiming Betsy as ours alone, but Holden too.

Carrying the tray into the living room, I set it on the coffee table, handing Holden a can of sparkling water.

"What's this?" He turns it around in his hand as if a foreign object. Once again that flash of shame rises up. How fucking pretentious, serving this to a ten-year-old.

"It's just sparkling water," Betsy says with a shrug, taking a seat on the grey leather sofa, the Anthropologie throw pillows propped against her back. "Mom doesn't let us have soda at home, but it kinda tastes like it."

Holden nods slowly, watching Betsy as she opens her own can, following suit. I breathe then and turn to Linda as I take a seat next to Mark in a green velvet slip chair. "Thank you for bringing Holden here today, I know the ninety-minute drive was a bit of a trek for you."

"Oh, no bother. Part of the gig." She brings the dark roast coffee to her mouth and moans in pleasure as she takes a sip. "God, I needed this. I have been shuffling kids around since seven am. By four in the afternoon, I can use a little pick me up."

"Of course," I say, thinking Linda is as much a saint as schoolteachers. "You mentioned some paperwork?"

"Right," she says, reaching for her messenger bag. She takes out a manila file folder then looks around the room. "Do you think Betsy would like to show Holden the yard while we talk some of this through? I saw a swing set as we drove in."

Holden raises an eyebrow and I turn, meeting Betsy's eye. Last weekend Betsy asked Mark if he could take it down before Holden came home.

"He might think it's babyish."

"Do *you* think it's babyish?" Mark had asked.

She hesitated before answering. "No other fourth graders play on the swings at school anymore. So maybe, yeah?"

Mark hadn't been able to dismantle Betsy's childhood jungle gym or hire anyone to do it on such short notice. And secretly, I'd been glad. I wasn't ready to tear down that piece of my only daughter's childhood on a whim. I'd need time to process. To prepare. We were experiencing enough change as it was at the moment.

And I hated the idea of Betsy feeling like the things I knew she still enjoyed were babyish. Why the need to rush childhood? Life is already on this accelerated speed that exhausts everyone I know.

Holden stands, his words clipped. "You want me gone? Fine. Whatever. I get it. You want to talk about me when I can't hear."

Betsy's eyes soften, and I watch her, trying to gauge her thoughts on the matter. My daughter is trying to figure out how to connect with Holden. She's never been a dramatic or self-serving kid -- she's soft in spots that get her heart easily bruised. She isn't weak, but she is tender. Kids at school don't understand the difference yet.

So, when she smiles up at Holden, wearing her heart on her sleeve, I feel a swell of pride at my little girl. "Holden, let's go to the swings. It's more fun outside anyways. " Betsy stands and cocks her head toward the back door.

He follows her, glaring at Linda as he passes.

Mark calls to them as they leave. "Let us know if you need anything, okay?"

"They're going to freeze out there," I say, looking out the sliding glass door. It's practically dark out, November in the Northwest means coming home from school as the sun sets. "I can just grab them coats real quick."

"They'll be fine. They've got on long sleeves," Linda

says, waving me off. "It's better than Holden snooping around inside without your supervision."

Mark frowns at this, resting his elbows on his knees as if taking Linda's comment seriously. "What do you mean, exactly? We can't watch him 24/7, that's understood, correct?"

Linda nods, lifting her hands to explain, as she begins speaking with trained authority. Not tiptoeing, she is clear and precise with her words: "I'm not talking surveillance. I'm saying you need to walk through each room with him and make sure he understands the household boundaries. His track record shows he isn't very good at those at the moment. Valuables should be in a safe," she says, eying my diamond ring, "along with medication. Don't assume the best intentions until Holden gives you a reason to trust him. Be vigilant, aware. He needs to know who's boss."

I meet Mark's eyes. Alone, I'd gone to the DSHS office last week and read through a massive file box, containing every document the state has ever made with Holden's name in it. It was a part of the pre-adoption protocol and was required to be completed before Holden could come into our care. Mark couldn't join me, he had to be at the capital for a vote. But obviously, he trusted my opinion on the matter--that I didn't believe Holden would be a threat to either Betsy or me when he wasn't home.

But now, Linda's comment on boundaries has him on edge.

"Does he want to be here?" I ask Linda the blunt question that has been on my mind since he entered my home. "We want him here, but not against his will. I don't think it will work if he resists this placement."

Linda sets down her coffee. "I understand what you're saying, but you have to understand it's a lot for Holden to process. Your lifestyle, your home, your job title, Senator, it's a blessing. Every adult in this process realizes that. You can offer Holden a life he wouldn't have had otherwise. Honestly, people in the office refer to this placement as a foster kid winning the lottery."

I cross my legs. My arms. "Okay, well, that feels slightly uncomfortable. And still doesn't address my question. Does Holden want to be here? Want to be adopted by us?"

"I understand," Linda says, frowning, considering her words. "And I don't have a clear answer for you. This has been a fast transition. We're all aware of that, and we're equally aware of why. Having Holden come here instead of another foster home helps with the compound trauma. But it's still a lot to take in, for a kid of any age, regardless of their background. I think the best thing for everyone is to take it a day at a time. Foster adoption in Washington state, as you well know, requires a nine-month waiting period before you can stand before a judge and make any promises."

"So you're saying we just see how it goes?" Mark asks.

Linda nods. "It's so wonderful what you're doing, and the fact you were able to green light the foster care course and get a home study completed in a matter of weeks is a testament to your commitment to Holden."

I'm listening for hidden meaning but hear none. I

must be missing something because when Linda and Holden came into our home, he was angry. I could feel it. And now it's as if Linda is trying to brush all that aside and focus on the positive.

"What aren't you saying, though, Linda?" I ask, leaning in.

She rubs her hands together, considering her words. "Holden has had a rough go, we all know that. But you haven't spent much time with him--only a lunch date and an afternoon at the ice rink. You've gotten to know him a bit... but..."

Mark has no patience for tiptoeing. "But what, Linda?"

She presses her lips together, her eyes moving toward the window facing the backyard. Betsy and he are on a pair of swings, their feet shuffling against the icy ground. I can't tell if they're talking. If they are, it's little more than a whisper.

Finally Linda answers. "I'm just not sure you understand what Holden is capable of."

8

PRESENT

IT's after ten at night and I've only just crawled from bed. After Trista left my room, I slept for hours, nightmares, mostly, visions of Betsy I never want to reimagine.

Now I'm showered, in pajamas, and need to find my son. Mark is at the kitchen island, laptop open, beer in hand. His eyes lift when I enter the room. It's clear he's been crying, and I'm glad to know I'm not the only one grieving in this house.

The moment he sees me he wipes his eyes, pretending he isn't utterly torn up. It's obvious he's trying to be strong for me and I appreciate the kindness. He doesn't need to pretend for me though. Our daughter is dead, if there was ever a reason to fall apart, this is it.

"You finally got some sleep."

I nod. "You should try it, I'd forgotten how it felt."

He gives me a half-hearted smile. "I've been trying to figure this all out," he says, pointing to the file on the counter. "Tom is on the case. I've spoken with him several times today. He'll be here tomorrow morning, to speak with Holden."

"I'm relieved he's taking the case."

Mark nods. "Me too."

Tom and Mark went to law school together at the University of Washington. Tom and Rose Bradshire have been family friends since Mark and I married. They have two children of their own: Lily and Logan -- Logan's the same age as Bets and Holden. I trust Tom, and so does Mark. And most of all, Holden likes him. And right now, we need people around us who can see Holden as a boy, not as a criminal.

"The police department sent him the reports already, so we're moving forward."

"The footage too?"

He shakes his head. "Not yet. They promised tomorrow. I'll get this taken care of, Emery, don't worry. I'll be Tom's right-hand man."

"Isn't that a conflict of interest?" I ask.

"Are you insinuating I don't know the law?" Mark asks eyes narrowed.

I can't do this. Fight. Not today. "No, I meant that you're emotionally invested is all. You're the father of the prosecuted and the defense. It seems messy."

"It is messy," he says tightly. "All of this. And I hate that Cooper is involved."

I've been waiting for him to say this. "I know. Should we ask to have him reassigned?"

Mark exhales as if exhausted by the mere topic. "I

don't know, maybe the fact you used to fuck him will make him more dedicated to the case."

My body tenses at his word choice. "That was so long ago. I can't do anything about the fact he moved back to town."

Mark scoffs, closes his laptop, and looks at me with so much disappointment that I can't help but wonder what exactly my husband knows. "In the end, I won the girl, didn't I? Should be solace enough."

I want to turn from him, to stop myself from saying something I'll regret. But I've never been the strong and silent type. "I'm not a prize to be had, Mark."

"Then what are you, Emery?"

"Your wife."

That seems to appease him, he takes another sip of his IPA. Tears burn my eyes but I don't want to cry. I want to argue. Fight. Let out some of the emotions building inside of me.

Besides, just like that, Mark is already moving on. Looking in the fridge and pulling out Tupperware containers. "Are you hungry? Trista brought food, I can warm it up."

"No," I say, wishing my marriage wasn't hanging on by a thread. Now more than ever, I need a partner. "I need to talk to Holden. I haven't seen him since this afternoon."

Mark stiffens.

"What?"

"Nothing," he says. "I mean, he's where he always is." He runs a hand over his jaw. "Don't expect much."

I get myself a glass of water. Food holds no appeal,

but I need to stay hydrated. Clear-headed. At least try. "You spoke with him already, then?"

"After Cooper and Margot left I tried. But you know how he gets. Totally shut down."

My first thought is *why does my husband think he'll be able to prove Holden's innocence if he can't even get him to speak*, but I hold back. I want to see if I can get Holden to tell me something without Mark refereeing.

Mark clears his throat. "And he downloaded that game you hate. Just so you can prepare yourself. I didn't want to fight with him about it, not tonight. Not after everything."

I sigh, crossing my arms. "He's in his room?"

Mark nods and I turn to go. He speaks, though, with my back turned toward him. "Do me the courtesy and don't get too close to Cooper."

I swallow, spine chilled. How much does he know? My gut tells me that he knows everything. "You are telling me how to behave?"

"Yes, Emery, I am. There's no room for error right now. The reporters will be in our driveway by tomorrow morning."

Turning to face him, I ask, "Reporters?"

"I'm running for Congress for Christ's sake. Do you understand the implications here? Our son is accused of murder."

"I get that, but God, Mark. I'm not thinking about bad publicity right now. I'm thinking about our son." I step toward him as he runs his hands through his dark hair.

"Fuck, Emery. I know. But I'm just... falling apart

here. This isn't what we, how we ever imagined things." He drops his face into his hands, his shoulders shaking as he sobs for all that we have lost. What we just might continue to lose. Everything.

Tears fall down my cheek as I grapple with his words. Mark's outburst, his requests, come from a good place, but he isn't thinking clearly. "Port Windwick is a small town, Mark. We can't hide from the press. But we can face it head on, together."

Mark wipes his eyes and I know my words help relieve some of the pressure he feels. For that, I'm grateful. God knows I've done plenty wrong. "And the thing about Cooper -- well, he's the deputy. I don't think he's going anywhere. But I will do anything that you need, anything to help with finding the truth. It's all I want."

"It's all I want too, Emery."

We don't hug, don't say I love you, but we share a look borne from determination. We will get to the bottom of this, together.

Leaving the kitchen, my bare feet plod against the bamboo floor as I pass the master bedroom on the main floor. Up the carpeted steps, down the hall, Holden's room is next to Betsy's.

I rap my knuckles to the door that has been left ajar, it opens slightly. "Holden?"

He doesn't hear me. The lights are off, but the bright television screen blasts at me. He sits on the floor, his back propped against his bed. His hands holding a controller as he is dropped in the battlefield of another round of Fortnite. I loathe the game -- and it's been strictly forbidden. It's Holden's favorite topic to argue.

But then Betsy died. And now? I try to hold back the onslaught of guilt, fear. Anger. Mark is right, fighting now won't help anything but my stomach twists as I walk into his darkened room. His avatar holds a massive cartoon version of a semi-automatic rifle. After he's just been accused of murder.

It's too much. All of this. I step toward the television, flicking it off. Holden rips off his headset, shouting. "What was that for?"

I sit down on the floor, not answering him. Still, wanting to be on his level. Wanting to meet him somewhere, somehow. "Holden."

The room is so dark now. I can't see his eyes, but I know him. I may not have brought him into this world, but I am his mother. His silky black hair hangs around his ears, his nose sharp, his mouth thin.

I reach for his hand. He pulls away. I don't let go. "Holden."

He is silent, but he trembles. When he looks up at me it's his eyes that draw me in. Deep and dark, as if they are full of secrets.

"I'm not going to talk to you," he says as I reach up to turn on the lamp beside his bed. The light sends a glow over the room, he sits opposite me with crossed arms, a deep scowl. Anger rushes off him. And the really tragic part of this moment is that my first instinct is to assume he is upset that I turned off the game -- not the fact he is accused of murdering his sister.

I won't give in to a discussion over a stupid video

game, though. Not now. Emery of a week ago would have fought tooth and nail for him to apologize for disobeying me. For intentionally going behind my back.

I'm not the same Emery.

And the woman I was, exhausts me now. I can hardly keep my head up, eyes open -- let alone lecture an eleven-year-old on the damaging effects of a third-person shooter game.

The room is silent, so still. But my heart pounds. "Holden," I say again, this time my eyes filling with tears. I want to say so much, but I don't want to burden a child with my particular brand of grief.

Instead, I simply say the truest thing that I can: "I'm so sorry." I squeeze his hand, wishing I could hug him without being shoved aside. Wish I could pull his face to my shoulder without him recoiling from my affection. We've been at this a year. I know how it goes with him. Rejecting me is his favorite game.

He pulls his hand from mine, this time harder, and I let it go. He crosses his arms, burrowing himself in a little ball. Tucked in his shell, safe there.

I stand, needing to go, not knowing how to stay. His room is still that of a child's. A quilt on the bed appliqued with soccer balls. A dresser stacked with books and comics-- just like his sister. A plastic sign with the words *KEEP OUT* leans against the bowling pin he got on his birthday. Pokémon cards in a pile. He's a boy, not a killer.

When I reach the door, he stops me. Not unlike Mark did in the kitchen. "Emery," he says, quiet. A whisper. His voice the opposite of his usual shouting and screaming matches. "I would never mean to hurt Bets."

"I know, Holden, I know you wouldn't," I say, my own voice a ragged scratch. "Try and sleep, alright? Tomorrow will be a long day."

I shut his door, and in the hall, I brace myself against the wall, my forehead falling to the framed photos lining the wall. I see my reflection in every image of Betsy through the years. My baby. Gone.

I move to my bedroom, the bathroom. I want the Vicodin that Mark left out for me. Holding the pills in my hand I contemplate swallowing them. The desire to disappear so great. Instead, I grip the sink. Holding on, to what I don't know. Maybe slipping away to sleep is the opposite of what I need right now. Maybe right now I need to be more aware than I've ever been before.

Mark isn't here. I'm guessing he'll be up all night, refreshing his email until he gets an attachment with the video footage.

Alone, I crawl into bed, shaking, shivering. My solitary thought sending shame through my blood and my bones.

Holden said he didn't mean to hurt her.

But that's not the same as saying he didn't.

9

ELEVEN MONTHS EARLIER

"I JUST DON'T THINK it's a good idea," Mark says as I rearrange the tray of crudités and the cheese board in the kitchen. "He can hardly handle family dinners let alone a group of strangers."

It's the truth. Every night at dinner, Holden chooses one of three signature moves. Refuse to eat, shovel it in his mouth like a feral animal, or argue about the food until I make him a peanut butter and jelly sandwich.

I move toward the fridge as Maria, our housekeeper enters the room with a plunger and mop.

"Emery," she says. "Holden clogged the toilet." When I frown, she continues. "I walked in while he was jamming an entire roll of toilet paper into the basin. He did the same thing on Wednesday when Caroline was coming over, remember?"

I swallow. Of course, I remember. He made the entire visit a headache, shouting at me because I said he couldn't play video games. He'd already played for two hours that day.

"Why don't I just take Bets out for some ice cream?" Caroline had eventually suggested. I watched them leave the house, grateful for a friend who could give my daughter a bit of attention. Holden's life may have just turned upside down, but so had Betsy's. So had all of ours.

"I cleaned it up," Maria said. "But you wait, he's going to make this party a nightmare."

"Don't say that," I snap at her. I'm so tired of so much negativity. Besides, I don't even want a housecleaner. I've always refused to get one, not because I'm above it -- but because I like my piles. My newspaper clippings on the dining room table, scraps of felt from after-school projects, my own version of messy. But Mark hired her when Holden came home, saying it was his gift to me. I know it's a lie. Maria cleaning the counters and floor is about him -- what he wants. He's the one who can't stand disorder.

Mark reaches for a bottle of red wine and begins to unscrew the top. "I'm telling you Em, this party is a bad idea."

"Mark," I say, my voice hushed. "Be positive. I want Holden to feel like a part of our family. We owe him a celebration in his honor. Think of the baby shower we had when Betsy was born? He deserves that too."

Mark exhales, pulling the lid back from the platter of chicken the caterer delivered. "Holden isn't a baby. And he's only been home a few weeks; it's still so early. He's going to have a meltdown and Maria won't clean that mess up. We will."

I spin to my husband, I've been trying to keep it

together for a month -- he's always in Olympia and it's me who is doing the dirty work. Not him. Not Maria. Me.

"All I'm asking for is one evening with our friends to celebrate our son," I say. "Can you please support me on this?"

Mark clenches the edge of the countertop. "All I've been doing is supporting you, Emery. I'll do whatever you ask -- I was just thinking about Holden -- what he actually needs."

I close my eyes, everything he says makes a lot of sense. "I know, I'm sure you're right. I shouldn't have planned this. Once again all I'm thinking about is what I want."

Mark uncharacteristically massages the base of my neck and I tense at his touch. It's been so long since we've been together... and now the slightest provocation surprises me. "Stop being so hard on yourself, Em. You're doing amazing."

I reach for a wine glass just as the doorbell rings. "I'll go get that," I say, giving Mark's hand a squeeze. "It will go well. Holden will like being the center of attention."

Mark heads upstairs to check on Betsy and I walk to the door. As I do, the bell keeps ringing. Repeatedly. Maybe it's Levi, Trista's son, being funny. But as I pull it open, it's Holden standing there.

"What are you doing?" I ask, trying to figure out the joke.

"Nothing."

"What do you mean, nothing? Why are you ringing the doorbell?"

He shrugs. "I didn't ring the doorbell."

I press my lips together. "No, you literally just rang the doorbell, Holden."

He looks at me blankly. "No, I didn't."

This is the way Holden likes to interact. Make me absolutely batty until I cave. Today, I don't have time for his defiance. "Okay, well, fine. You didn't ring the bell. Can you come in? I told you to change."

I step back for him to come inside, but he takes a step backward, mirroring me. Trista and Jeff's car is pulling into the driveway. Behind them, I see Caroline and Pete. Great, they can all witness the show.

"Can we please not do this? Everyone is coming over for you, Holden. To celebrate *you*. Let's have a fun time."

"I am having fun," he says with a smirk. I want to wipe it off his face and I hate my instinct. I should be gentle, calm, understanding. Instead, I'm irritated that he is trying to ruin the party.

Our friends walk up to the house. "Hey, guys," Trista says with a smile. "Levi, remember Holden?"

Levi gives Holden a big smile and hands him a wrapped gift. Holden doesn't take it. "We got this for you. It's really cool. Open it!"

"Why don't we all come inside and get something to drink?"

Caro and Pete give me hugs as Betsy jumps down the stairs. Her hair wild and her smile wide. "Hi, Auntie Caroline! Auntie Tris!" She gives them big hugs as they come into the house. In the driveway, Tom and Rose are pulling up, their kids Lily and Logan in the back of the SUV. Great, everyone is here and the guest of honor refuses to come inside.

"You need anything?" Tris asks as she takes off her coat and hangs it in the hall closet. She can see Holden and I are at a standoff. Mark comes into the foyer.

"What's going on?"

"Holden won't come in," I say, all of us watching as Tom tries to give Holden high fives, gifts in his arms, and when rejected, the family just makes their way in the house, giving me warm hugs. Mark offers everyone drinks and I step outside, giving my husband a wary look as I do. He smiles, telling me I got this. I want to believe him. I want to be the mom Holden needs. Supportive. Understanding. On his side.

"Hey," I say, crossing my arms to brace myself against the cold as I step outside, closing the door behind me. I don't want anyone to listen to my attempt at parenting. "Want to talk about it?"

Holden doesn't even reply. Instead, he picks up a rock the size of his palm and chucks it at the garage door. The bang echoes.

"Holden, don't. If you make a big scene--"

That gets his attention. "Then what? They will all leave?"

"Why do you want them to go?"

He picks up another rock. "Because I don't like them."

"You don't even know them. They brought you presents and we have a nice meal and--"

"I don't care about that."

I groan. "Then what do you care about, Holden?" That has been the crux of everything in the last few weeks. There is no carrot to tempt him with. His will is stronger than anyone's I know. Stronger than mine, that's for sure.

"Nothing. I don't care about anything."

The words send a shiver down my spine. Because his words confirm what it feels like to live with him. He grabs another rock, chucks it. Then another. And another. Finally, Mark comes out, concerned. "What's going on out here?"

Behind him, I see Pete and Tom, joining us outside. Through the living room window, I see my girlfriends. Wine glasses in hand they stand ready for the show. Everyone watches as Holden takes another rock, hurling it at the garage.

"I'm not coming to the party. It's stupid. You're all stupid."

Mark steps toward him, reaching for Holden as he bends down to grab another rock. "Careful," I say, and at that moment, I'm worried Holden will mess up. Really mess up. Not like disruptive meal times and his attitude in school. I'm scared he will cross a line. A line that will determine more than he's prepared to be held accountable for. He's a little boy. But when he holds that rock, anger in his eyes, I see that he's also danger-ous. A threat. Just how far will he go?

Thankfully, I don't have to find out. Because Betsy walks outside, her blue eyes filled with worry. She runs to him, reaching for his hand. Taking the rock from his fist.

"Holden, come in," she says. "Levi brought Pokémon cards."

Holden looks from Mark to her. I can sense his struggle. He says he doesn't care about anything.

But that isn't true.

He cares about Betsy.

10

PRESENT

MY FIRST THOUGHTS when I wake, are when can I see the footage Cooper has and how does it point to Holden?

After the eerie conversation with Holden last night, my mind is shredded. Part of me can't help but wonder what if? The other part hates that thought. That I am even considering the possibility that Holden... that Holden hurt Bets.

They loved one another.

Didn't they?

What do I really know, though, about anything? I thought for months that love was enough, that I could fit in the space of Holden's broken heart -- but I'm wiser now.

Bitter.

Jaded.

A wreck.

And missing my daughter with each breath that I breathe.

Mark is in the bathroom, brushing his teeth, in his boxer-briefs, his chest sculpted. He is slender and tall, his muscles revealing his corded strength. I wish they would wrap around me now, pull me near.

But grief is a wide chasm and Mark and I had plenty of issues before Halloween ... Now the space between us grows instead of shrinks. I wish we could go back. So far back. To the beginning.

I'd change so much.

Mark turns to me now, setting his toothbrush on the counter. "You slept hard. I'm jealous." I look over at him, his words themselves are easy enough, but his voice cracks. He looks awful, and not just sleep deprived. He's trembling -- more than exhausted -- he is brokenhearted same as me.

I wipe my face with a washcloth, trying to think of how to bridge this divide. Pull him close and apologize ... For what? Everything?

Maybe.

I wring out the washcloth. I haven't worn makeup in days but my face feels dry. My entire body is parched, too many salty tears have been shed, leaving me empty.

"Were you up pretty late?"

He nods, rubbing his temples. "Finally fell asleep around three this morning."

I turn on the water in the open double shower, hoping it will hydrate me. Pulling off my tank top, I step from my panties. Mark looks away.

Stepping under the shower head, I close my eyes, the water streaming over me.

Mark speaks. "I got the video clip."

I open my eyes, running a hand over my slick hair. "And?" I turn on the second shower head, an invitation. I steel myself for rejection.

But Mark is lost, his eyes bloodshot and his emotions raw. He joins me, adjusting the other shower head. I step back, this moment holds promise, but I also know the reality. He's only with me, here, naked, because he feels as lost as I do.

Hot water runs over my bare breasts, but I feel chilled.

"It's bad, Emery."

My chin trembles. My shoulders shake. "Bad how?"

It's strange to be here, naked with Mark. After everything.

"I need to talk to him, get his testimony," Mark says. "Until then I don't know."

"Did he... Do you think he..."

"I don't know, Emery, but I will find out."

I fall into Mark's arms then. He holds me up like he always has.

It's me who has given him reason to push away, to retreat -- to doubt all of my intentions. But if he's thinking it, he doesn't let on.

He wraps his arms around me, letting me cry against him. All those years ago, when I lost my Dad, he did the same thing; held me when I couldn't stand on my own.

This time it is different though. I'm not the only one falling apart. Mark is crying too, deep sobs escape him, and we hold on tight to one another. I've never seen my husband so vulnerable, dropping the façade and letting me in all the way. Would things have ended differently if he'd opened up a long time ago? Would I have betrayed him if he had clung to me then the way he clings to me now?

Our breathing slows, and Mark draws me to him, lifting my leg, filling me up and making me gasp. It's been so long.

"I'll find her killer, Emery," he tells me, his body slick with water, our skin hot and our hearts fueled with so much uncertainty.

The words send a deep chill through me. Killer. It's so much. The word is so exact, so horrid.

We finish quickly; this wasn't about making love, it was about Mark's pain, wrestling with the reality of our situation. And I let him have me. In truth, what else does he have?

Afterward, he washes himself, he grabs a towel, and then leaves the bathroom.

Alone, I turn the water to the hottest it can go. I fall to my knees, I pray.

For answers. For truth. For Betsy.

11

TEN MONTHS EARLIER

BETSY HASN'T BEEN SO happy in months. Christmas is always her favorite time of year, but this Christmas is different. She has Holden to share it with.

The kids are out of school for the winter break and I have on a record of Bing Crosby's favorite hits, the newspaper spread out on the cushions next to me. I'm curled up on the couch as the day begins -- making last-minute Christmas notes on my phone. I want this Christmas to be perfect. I've signed them both up for a Christmas cookie decorating party at the local bakery for this weekend. We're going to take the ferry to Seattle to look at gingerbread displays at the Four Seasons.

My note-taking is interrupted by a FaceTime phone call. It's Mark, and I answer immediately.

"Hey," I say, taking him in. "How's it going?"

He's doing some early morning, last-minute shopping. He hoped to finish up before the kids got squirrely. Which is pretty much a necessity these days. If

Holden's day isn't scheduled down to the hour, he gets a little... difficult. I need Mark around to help over the school break.

His face lights up the screen and I see that he's outside of a department store. He's in his charcoal suit and dark red tie, even on his day off. I can practically smell the leather and cinnamon that carries him wherever he goes.

"The mall's crazy, and it's only nine a.m." He lifts his eyebrows, the corners of his dark eyes crinkling.

"You should have shopped online like me," I tease.

"I know, I say that every year. But I just wanted to call and say I'm headed to my car now. Should be home in thirty minutes."

"Perfect," I say. "I guess I'll get off the couch and get showered and dressed."

Mark smiles. "You can wait and I can help, when I get home."

I smirk. "I bet you could."

The last few weeks we've bonded -- my husband and I. I would have thought the person I'd be growing close to was Holden, but it's Mark who I turn to at the end of the day. Who I can vent with, who is there to brainstorm new ways to deal with Holden's issues with... Mark and I are in this together in a way no one else on Earth could possibly understand.

It makes me hopeful for so much. For our marriage, for parenting Holden, for our family.

Just then, Betsy jumps into the living room, calling for me. "Mom!"

"Hey, I gotta go, Mark. See you soon." We hang up, and I turn to my daughter. "What's up?"

"Can we have chocolate chips in our pancakes?"

"Who's having pancakes?" I ask, having set out a box of granola, bananas and a carton of almond milk for breakfast.

Betsy scrunches up her face in confusion. "Holden is making them."

I stand, taking my coffee cup to refill it in the kitchen. Betsy trails me.

"He said he can make perfect pancakes," she says. In the kitchen, Holden is elbow deep in a box of pancake mix, flour on his cheeks, measuring cups on the counter. Eggshells on the floor. Chocolate chip bag in hand, being emptied into the batter.

"Wow, looks like someone had a fun idea," I say, keeping my voice light as I reach for the coffee pot and refill my cup. I must have been totally engrossed in Port Windwick's headlines to not hear him in here making this mess.

"Holden," Betsy says with panic. "I went to ask Mom if we can use the chocolate. We can't just take them without permission."

"Well," I say, turning to face them both. "No one asked permission to make the pancakes either."

Betsy sputters. "Holden did."

I turn to Holden, eyes drawn. He stirs the batter with intent.

"You did, didn't you?" she asks. "You told me you asked Mom."

He doesn't answer her. Betsy looks personally affronted so; I try to lighten the mood.

"I love pancakes, Holden," I say, determined to stay cool. I know Holden's history -- he was neglected by his birth mother; he was abused by his foster parents. Now, he needs to learn that adults aren't always the enemy. "And it's awesome you love to cook them. But you've got to ask, and a grown-up must be around. We have a gas range and ten-year-olds need parents around to make sure--"

He cuts me off. "You're not my parent."

I swallow, setting down my coffee mug. "Right. I'm not, but you need adult supervision when you cook."

"I didn't at Dave and Monica's."

"I understand that, but we're not Dave and Monica."

"I wish you were," he mutters.

"You do?" Betsy asks, blinking back tears.

Yeah," he says flatly, looking up, but not at her. At me. "They didn't have shitty rules."

Betsy gasps, looking to me to correct him. I falter. We have rules, sure, but I would never call myself strict by any means. We allow an hour of screen time every day -- two if Mark's been gone for a string of days and I'm tired. I always have some sort of treat for them after dinner. Yes, I insist we tidy up the house before Dad gets home; I am not militant about bedrooms. Maria has been coming twice a week to manage the changing of sheets and washing clothes. I honestly have no idea what rules annoy him.

"Hey, Holden," I say, trying to remain breezy. "Look, every family operates differently."

He smirks, his black hair falling in his eyes as they roll back. I tried to get him to get a haircut but he refused, saying he's always worn it long. I dropped the subject and never mentioned it again. The last thing I am interested in is a battle over hair. I'm trying to connect with him on any level possible.

I tense. Raising Betsy has had its challenges... but never defiance. She's her own brand of wild, bucking the system in a different way than other kids. Her compassion, her empathy -- that's what gets her into trouble. She is fearless when it comes to loving people. It's what has gotten her so hurt in the past.

"Holden, it's okay that we're different than Dave and Monica," Betsy says now, filling in the space where my silence hung. "Why did you like their house so much?"

He looks up at her, and for a moment I see a flicker of tenderness in his eyes. Betsy's tone is sweet, not dismissive. Not judgmental.

He looks at me when he answers her. "I liked that they let me play video games. Ate normal food. Didn't always hang around me. Like I was a baby."

I take a steadying breath before going into Mom-mode. "Why don't I finish these pancakes, kids? Bets, wanna grab the maple syrup?"

"Sure," she says. "Holden, this syrup is so good. Grandma and Grandpa bring it every summer from Vermont--"

He cuts her off. "I want to make them," he says to me.

"Sure," I say as I reach for a Le Creuset pan from a drawer. "Just let me get it started."

Holden grabs the pan from me before I can set it on a burner. "I can do it on my own," he says, eyes darkening, as I let go of the turquoise pan. I'm not going to get in a fight over a freaking frying pan.

"Okay, let's just wash our hands real quick and then I can--"

He cuts me off this time. "I don't want your help!" He lifts the pan over his head, but the weight of it makes it hard for him to keep it raised in the air. I reach for it, but he pulls away, hard.

"We don't need to shout over pancakes, Holden," I say, trying to defuse the situation. "I don't care that you told Betsy you had my permission to make them, we're all learning."

"I'm not learning from you. Ever."

"Cool it, Holden," I say, grinding my teeth. Betsy is frozen, unsure of what to do. To be honest, so am I.

His eyes stay locked on mine as he slams the pan to the floor. It hits my feet and I yelp, the cast-iron bashing my toes.

"This is so stupid. I hate this house. Hate your rules." He is a little boy but his voice is sharp, seasoned. He knows how to fight. He grabs the bowl of batter and throws it across the kitchen. The pancake mix spills across the counter before it falls to the floor, the ceramic bowl cracks, the floor spattered with his breakfast plans.

Betsy covers her face, scared. I reach for Holden, needing him to stop before he makes this any worse, but he pulls back, ripping himself away from me, the kitchen. He runs off, out the back door, and I turn, watching as he goes, climbing into the playhouse that is perched above the slide on the swing set.

My breath is shallow, and I grip the edge of the counter, shocked. All this, anger and hostility and harsh words over pancake batter?

Bets reaches for my hand, tucking hers in mine. She rests her head against me. The pair of us staring at the swing set.

She's trembling, scared. Tears splashing down her cheeks. Mark and I have argued, sure, but we never scream. Never push. Never run away.

I kneel on the ground, taking her face in my hands. "Bets, it's going to be okay. I know that scared you. It scared me too."

Her blue eyes glassy with tears falling down her rosy cheek. "He didn't mean it."

"Mean what?"

"That we were like Dave and Monica."

My shoulders fall. What the hell am I thinking, trying here, doing this? I feel underprepared, thrown in the deep end. I feel like a fraud-- all those foster parents at the training I attended had the experience. Knew how to handle situations that got out of hand.

"Don't, Mom," she says.

"Don't what?"

"Blame yourself."

Now I'm the one crying and I wipe my eyes, shaking my head. "I'm the adult, Betsy. The parent. I need to talk to Holden. What he did was not okay. He can't act like that when he doesn't get his way." I stand, needing to address his outburst. Make him clean up this mess. Apologize.

"Mom, it's new for him too." Betsy gives me a quick hug. Then looks up at me, smiling. "I'm Holden's sister. Let me talk to him."

I don't tell her no, don't push back. Maybe it's a mistake, letting my daughter fix this mess.

But Betsy is different from me. Soft in ways I'm not. Non-threatening and sincere. Me? I posted photos on Instagram this morning of the mantel, four stockings hung with care. #ForeverFamily #AdoptionIsLove #MomLife

One month in as if I have a fucking clue.

12

PRESENT

MARK WAS RIGHT. A van from Channel 4 is parked outside our house, a reporter knocked while I was pouring coffee. Tom stepped outside and made a brief statement. I'm not ready for the politics involved -- and not just with the media -- I'm thinking about the Mommy tribe at school, how they will have their own commentary on the boy they've hated since the day he came home.

When I enter Mark's study, his laptop is waiting for me. Tom spent all morning with Holden, and Mark was there the entire time. I was advised to let Tom get Holden's testimony, without being present. I tried not to take it personally; that I'm considered a trigger for my son, but I know I am.

This year was a mess for many reasons, and I am one of them.

Now, Holden is in the living room with Jeff, Trista's husband. Trista and Jeff are the closest thing we have to family in Port Windwick, or anywhere for that matter, and I need them; need their support.

Mark's parents Joanne and Bill are here, just not at the house. They're at the hotel -- in town for the service that is now on hold. I'm glad they aren't here for this. I can't handle much of his parents on a good day, let alone this week.

"So, what did he say?" I ask Tom, needing to know if there was some sort of confession. I stood in the kitchen with Jeff for the last hour, pacing. Wishing I were a fly on the wall.

"He said he didn't do it," Mark says.

"And you believe him, right?" I ask. Mark and Tom exchange glances. "What? What is that look?"

"His sequence of events is this," Tom says, referencing a yellow notepad in his hand. "First, Betsy and he were trick-or-treating. Then they came across the kids in the video, they were being aggressive. He used the word teasing."

"Teasing what?"

Mark's jaw tenses. "They were calling Betsy a baby. That she had a childish costume."

I remember her costume clearly. We worked on it for months. She wanted to be Dumbledore's phoenix. And we worked tirelessly on her wings. Stitching feathers to felt, gluing on beads. She put it on and her smile was so wide, so bright. So perfectly Bets.

She didn't die in it, though.

She died in Holden's costume. She took her last breath dressed as Voldemort's snake, Nagini.

"What about it?" I ask, my throat dry. It doesn't

matter how much water I drink. On Halloween, I asked Holden about why he had come home alone, wearing Betsy's costume. He said she wanted to trade.

At the time, it didn't surprise me. I was with them when they talked about switching costumes. I clearly remember him in the foyer of our home. His plastic orange jack-o-lantern filled with candy bars, his eyes fierce, as always. "You changed costumes after all," I'd said.

"So?" he'd hissed at me, snake-like. It infuriated me, but most everything about Holden did. Does.

But then I realized Bets wasn't with him. And finding her was all I cared about.

"What he says about the neighborhood kids confronting them, it adds up," Tom says.

"And what happened after?"

"He didn't say much else," Tom tells me. "He says they were together, but that he turned back around, and told her to go home. That he'd meet her there."

"Where did he go?" I ask.

Tom rubs his temple. "He wouldn't say."

"Make him," I say, directing my words to Mark. "Holden has to say everything."

"I know," Tom says gently. "We need to get more from him. But he's a kid, Emery. And his sister just died and he's been accused of her murder. We need to be patient."

My eyes flare at this -- I don't want patience. I want answers.

"Watch this," Tom says. "It might help."

He presses play on the video, and I lean in, holding

my breath. It's a phone recording; I can hear the voice of whoever's filming it, and it's childlike. High pitched laughter. The camera is reversed for a moment and I see it is Marcie Devon's son, Cory. The camera turns back to the neighborhood, but Cory must have turned the volume off because there is no longer any sound.

It's clear that the location is at the end of the cul-de-sac, one street over from our home. Where the circle of kids stand is where the trail begins -- the trail my children are never allowed to use because there is a ravine that leads to a rock basin.

The trail cuts through the neighborhood, and lots of locals use it. It leads to a dog park and other hiking paths that are frequented.

In the video, I recognize Betsy as a phoenix, and standing beside her is Holden, the snake.

What you can see, under the lamplight, is a grainy scene of Holden raising his fists, Betsy shoving another child. I startle; I have never seen my daughter be aggressive to anyone.

There are four kids circled around my children, and Cory, costumed as a skeleton, who is still recording. I see Jenna Handler's twins: Jasper and Julia-- a ninja and a mermaid. And Arie Middleton's boys are there too, Sam dressed as a football player, with black smudges under his eyes. And Pete, wearing a cowboy hat. Four boys, one girl. And Betsy and Holden. Light and dark, a snake and a bird. Who is the prey? I swallow, watching, wanting the answer.

Without sound, there's only action to follow. But it's obvious they are arguing, all of them, pointing fingers, shoving. Eventually, both Betsy and Holden start to leave, but then they stop. The filming continues, but the other kids run off. Cory, the boy filming from a distance, doesn't move -- instead, he zooms in on my children.

It shows Betsy crying, then Holden pushing her. I flinch when I see this -- my eyes meeting Mark's. This isn't good for Holden. He shoved Betsy, made her cry, minutes before her death. What else did he do?

Her arms flail and she shouts something back and I wish there was volume on the video -- a way to transport myself to the scene, the moment. He grabs her by the shoulders and drags her into the wood.

I want to see more, everything. Hear the fight. Understand why. Seven kids in a ring, on Halloween night. Costumes casting shadows, dark thoughts circling my mind.

What were they all fighting about? And more importantly, what were Holden and Betsy fighting about? Why exactly did he push her?

The video ends when you can no longer make out the pair running into the forest trail.

Holden is the suspect because he was the last person to see my daughter alive.

13

NINE MONTHS EARLIER

My hair is still dripping wet from my shower as I walk into the kitchen to get a cup of morning coffee, tripping over Betsy's tennis shoes as I do. "Goddammit!" I shout.

Betsy and Holden turn to look at me. "Mom!" Betsy is shocked at my language, and I guess so am I.

"Sorry, I didn't mean that. But you guys, this place is a mess." I look around the kitchen, the two of them on stools at the island eating bagels. My notebook is open on the counter -- my notes from last night next to my laptop. I stayed up late Googling foster-parent resources. I've got to get a grip on how to parent Holden. Grabbing the notebook, I shut it, not wanting Holden to think I'm under-qualified to take care of him. I am. I just need to learn what he needs.

"I'll clean up Mom, don't worry," Betsy says. "I should have put my stuff away."

"I can clean. I'll be home all day after you guys go to school." It's then that I look at them -- both in the pajamas. I glance at the clock. School starts in twenty minutes. "Why aren't you dressed?"

"There's no school today," Holden says with a shrug, reaching for the container of cream cheese and slathering his bagel. It's obscene, the amount he uses -- but I'm not going to call him out on that. I've learned that if I make any comment on his food consumption he goes on a hunger strike.

"No school?" I pull out my phone and open my calendar. "God, you're right. Teacher in-service day." I run my hands over my face, already tired by the day and it's not even nine am. Pouring coffee, I try to think of what the two of them will do to occupy themselves all day. "Do you guys want to go the bookstore? Maybe go downtown and --"

Holden cuts me off. "No. I'm not going anywhere."

I bite my bottom lip, looking at Betsy. She shrugs. "Holden I didn't even finish my sentence."

"I'm not going. I'm staying here."

"That's not your choice, and honestly I'm over your defiance. Can't you try?" I say lifting the mug to my lips. "Betsy, do you want to go get a new book?"

She looks at her brother as if trying to understand him. "Why don't you want to go?"

He eats his bagel, not answering her.

"I love the bookstore," she says. "They have comics there. I could show you."

He shakes his head. "No."

"Why?" she asks again, this time in a voice so soft it's almost a whisper.

"I don't deserve it."

Betsy's eyes flash to mine, concern written in them. Mine too. "What do you mean, Holden?" I ask trying to mirror my daughter's tone.

"It's too fancy. That stuff. The store." He groans, pushing his palms against his eyes. "I'm mean to you. You shouldn't be nice to me."

My chest tightens. "That's not how it works," I say. "At least, not how it works in our family."

"You don't get it," he says, sitting up straighter, finishing his bagel.

"That's true. You went through things I've never faced. But that doesn't mean you should punish yourself for what you've experienced."

"Mom," Betsy says. "We want to stay home. We have lots of books anyways."

Holden looks over at her, relieved. He doesn't say anything but he nods, agreeing.

"Alright." I pour more coffee, forcing myself to move on, but realizing Holden is more damaged than I really understand. "I guess I will tackle the house, alright? After you eat, you both need to dress for the day and tidy your rooms, okay?"

Betsy nods for them both. "I was getting used to Maria being here," she says with a smile.

"I know, I appreciate her more than I realized at the time." I leave the kitchen and head to the laundry room. That is an easy enough project to tackle. Maria quit two weeks ago after finding Holden's secret stash of food. She said I needed to deal with his hoarding, I told her she had no right to tell me how to parent.

But it was more than that. She said things I wasn't prepared to hear.

"I'm just saying, Emery, he needs help," Maria said, clucking her tongue as she folded a basket of the children's laundry in the living room. "I see how he treats you. He pushes you. And he threw those boxes down the stairwell. It could have hurt you, Emery."

"He threw LEGOs, nothing dangerous. You make it sound worse than it is." I shouldn't have gotten defensive. But she didn't know how I'd found crumbled pages from a notebook in the trashcan the morning after the LEGO incident. He'd written and rewritten apologies to me. He never gave me one -- but I still see it as a victory. He was sorry even if he couldn't bear to say the words out loud.

"You're blinded by love," Maria said, matching socks. "I found rotten food, stashed in his drawers. Under his mattress. He screams about having to take a shower. He lies to you, to me. It's not good for Betsy."

"It's how he's coping," I said, louder than usual, shocked at her critique. "God, you're being so cruel. He's a child."

I was glad the kids were still at school. The last thing Holden needed to hear was another adult judging him. The school has been on my back constantly. The moms at school have made enough comments that make me grit my teeth, and our pediatrician gave me the name of a child therapist at last week's appointment.

"He needs a psych ward," Maria said. "I see things,

Emery, being in people's homes. And I never see boys like this. He treats you--"

"I don't need you to tell me how to parent."

"He's going to hurt someone. He's not safe--"

I cut her off. "Stop. I need people around me who can support us, not tear Holden down."

Maria shook her head. The laundry was done. Her eyes told me she was done too. Later that day, she sent a text. She wasn't coming back.

Now, a few days later, as I'm starting a load of laundry, I realize just how much our housekeeper did. Apparently, Holden coming home has been taking more of a toll on me than I want to admit. In so many ways I have it easy -- too easy. I have money for take-out if I don't want to cook, and I have Amazon delivery boxes bringing me laundry detergent and shampoo. I don't hold down a job, yet I can't manage to hold down the fort that is my home. What's wrong with me?

I spend the day dealing with the kitchen sink full of dishes, mopping the floors, and sorting bills. When the kids ask me something -- to play Minecraft, to eat marshmallows from the bag, to have a Nerf gun fight in the living room -- I say yes. All day long. This no school day threw me for a loop and I just need to survive it. By late afternoon, I make the kids a frozen pizza and settle them into a movie on Netflix and tell them I'll be right back.

"Where are you going?" Betsy asks, looking up from the television screen.

"Just to the grocery store. I'll be back in thirty minutes."

"Really, you'll leave us home alone?" Holden asks.

"You're not alone, you're together." I leave the house and get into my Land Rover. Mark's at his Olympia apartment. He stays there when they're in session, and right now he's in the throes of trying to get bills passed. And I'm glad he wasn't home this morning. If he'd walked in and saw the disaster that was our house he'd be livid. As a stay at home parent, guilt gnaws at me.

Normally, I'd understand that he needed to stay in Olympia, but that was before Christmas. Before the disaster that was the holidays. Holden refused to get in the car to go to the Brightons' Christmas Party. Refused to go inside the house after we went to the tree farm. Refused to open a single gift we tried to give him on Christmas morning. Refused to eat Christmas dinner.

It was basically a two-week refusal of anything that Mark or I asked him to do.

Now, if Betsy asked him for something he'd eventually agree. Not happily, exactly, but when Betsy reached out her hand, smiled at him, whispered that it was going to be okay, he believed her.

So, I know Mark is in no hurry to get home, and I don't blame him.

But it also means I feel isolated in ways I've never been before. I need to talk to Caroline and Trista. But what am I supposed to say? I invited a monster into my house and now I don't know how to get him to leave?

This was supposed to be my way to give back, to return to the Emery I once was. Instead, it's made me question what special brand of idiot I am. Holden is making my life a living hell. Maria wasn't exaggerating.

But to say that out loud for someone to hear how I really feel about the boy I brought in to my home, promised to adopt, to mother, feels like a betrayal. Holden has no one else fighting for him -- I can't quit.

At the grocery store, I grab a cart, praying I don't see anyone from the Port Windwick Mommy Tribe. That's the group name on Facebook, I shit you not. Trista and I are the only mothers at the school who have opted out. Caroline doesn't get why we roll our eyes at the idea of the group but that's because being a part of a mommy tribe is her singular desire.

All of this is streaming through my mind as I grab organic chocolate bars, bags of artisanal crackers, and thick wedges of cheese.

"Hey, there," a familiar voice says from behind me, as a cart sidles up beside me. I turn to find Cooper standing there.

"Uh, hey," I say, swallowing.

"Not much protein in that cart," he says. He's next to me now, our hips inches apart. He smells like pine trees and wood smoke. His beard has grown and he's out of his uniform. Flannel shirt with red-laced boots.

The opposite of Mark in every way.

"You're judging my food choices?" I ask, looking in his cart. Lucky charms, a gallon of whole milk, and a frozen pizza.

"Not judging," Cooper laughs. "Noticing is all."

I keep pushing my cart, not wanting to stand next to him longer than necessary. I don't exactly trust myself around him. It's been so long, but the memories. God, they are still so fresh.

He reaches for my elbow. "Hey, what's the rush, Em?"

I turn, facing him. "It's just, I have a lot on my mind is all."

Cooper nods, blue eyes focusing on mine. "I heard you were adopting a foster child."

"Yeah. Holden," I say. "His name's Holden."

Cooper is still single. Zero responsibility -- besides making sure our town is safe. But as far as personal responsibilities, he isn't beholden to anyone.

I feel a tug of jealousy at this thought. *Do I resent my choices?*

"Same age as Betsy?" He lifts his eyebrow in question, but obviously, he already knows.

"Yeah, only a few months apart."

"They get along?"

I smile at this. For all the ways our life has gotten messy since Holden came home, the relationship between my two kids isn't one of them.

"They do," I say, my breathing returning to normal. "It's actually really sweet. On the surface, you'd think they were opposites. He's hard, she's soft. But then they play together and it's like... they meet somewhere in the middle. Like they find this balance." I shrug, feeling relief at the words I share. Every interaction with people regarding Holden has felt negative, defensive. But this feels light.

Tears fill my eyes. God, why am I crying?

"You okay, Em?" Cooper's hand rests on my wrist.

I look up at him, my heart swirling. I've held so much back. Too much.

"I'm just a little overwhelmed with life right now."

"I bet."

I wipe my eyes. "Sorry. I don't know why I'm crying."

Cooper's hand covers mine. "You're doing a big, brave thing, Em. Most people wouldn't take this on."

"I'm not a saint."

He chuckles. "I never said you were." He steps away, and I want him to stay. Is it wrong to wish his hand hadn't moved? "If you ever need anything, I'm here."

I nod, blinking the tears away. "Even after everything?'

"Always."

He keeps walking down the aisle and I force myself to turn around, not to stare. To wish. Wish. Wish for what isn't mine.

I pull out my phone, text Caroline and Trista: *I'm at Central Grocery grabbing wine. Ladies' night, my place, tonight.*

I don't trust myself to be alone with these thoughts. Right now, I need a distraction in the form of friends.

14

PRESENT

"WHY AREN'T you asking more questions?" I look at Tom and Mark, needing answers. The video has ended and I'm ready to move forward.

"We are, Emery, just one step at a time," Mark says, trying to soothe me.

"And what's the next step?" I ask, bile rising in my throat. Holden was the last person to see Betsy alive. Why isn't he talking?

"We have to consider the possibility that Holden did this," Mark says. "The video... The facts add up. Why did he come back home alone?" He asks the very question I'm grappling with. *Why weren't they together?*

After they found her body, Holden was questioned, of course. He told the officers the night of her death that he had been at the Becken House at the top of the hill. That he went there on a dare, and he went alone. That he wasn't with Betsy in the woods.

But he was.

My head throbs with possibilities. He lied, that

much is true. He undoubtedly went into the woods. What else is he lying about? "I have to talk to him."

"Emery," Tom says, asking me to wait, but I can't. Won't.

I leave the study, racing to the living room. Jeff and Holden are playing chess. Focused, silent, intent.

Not at all like me. "Holden," I say, my voice cracking. "What happened in the woods?"

He swallows, looks at the board. His eye on the pawn, reaching for it. Last minute he moves his hand, instead, taking his knight and checkmating Jeff's king. Swiftly.

"Answer me," I shout, dropping to the carpet, at the coffee table where he kneels, grabbing his hand. He pulls away. "What happened in the woods? You can tell me, trust me. Let me help you." Tears streak my cheek, panic rising. Did he kill her? Did my son kill my daughter?

No. No. No. But what if yes?

"Tell me!" My voice is no longer my own. It's a voice born from fear, desperation. Terror. Did Holden watch as Betsy died?

Mark and Tom are behind me; Jeff's trying to read the room. I can see it through their eyes, a hysterical woman, losing control. Lost control. It's gone. All of it.

"Emery," Mark says, his hand on my shoulder. Now I'm the one flinching, pulling away.

"Holden," I beg. "Just tell me. What... What did you ... What did you do?"

He glares, jaw clenched. An eleven-year-old boy with a lifetime of hurt, neglect, abuse in his eyes. I wanted to save him, but he pushed me away. Is it too late to try again?

It's never too late, Cooper told me that the night we made a mistake.

"You want to know what happened?" Holden asks, fists clenched, heat rising.

"Yes," I plead. "I need to know. Tom needs to know. Let us help you."

He stands, looking down at me. "You don't want to help me. You want to save her. But she's gone."

The words feel callous, cold, but there are tears in his eyes.

She's gone. And he loved her. I know he did. Even if no one saw them the way I did, I know. Don't I?

"Yes," I say, catching my breath, my palms wiping away my tears. "She's gone. But you're not, Holden. You're here. And you're in trouble."

"I didn't kill Betsy."

"I know," I say, grasping for his words. Needing them. My throat is so dry. His memories might be the only way to quench my thirst.

"Do you?" he asks, so plainly that shame courses through me. I am his mother yet I doubt his innocence.

I lift my chin. He was the last person to see her alive.

He is violent. Angry. Defies authority. He never shows affection. Refuses love. Does that mean he is a killer?

His eyes meet mine and I know he can see my thoughts, he can read me so well. He can get under my skin, push my buttons, identify my weakness. Point and shoot.

Can he also murder?

It doesn't matter what he is capable of.

I chose to be his mother, and I will choose him now.

He may be a terror of a child -- but he is still a child. If I'm not standing beside him, who will be?

"I believe you, Holden," I say, standing, looking at Tom, Mark, and Jeff. "We all do."

But even as I say that last part, I doubt it's true. The men have tells. Mark clenches his jaw. Tom pushes his lips forward. Jeff looks to the floor.

Me, though, I look back at my son.

He might not have a whole team of people on his side, but that's all right. Right now, he just needs one.

And he has me.

15

EIGHT MONTHS EARLIER

I'M JUST SITTING down to lunch with Trista and Caroline when my phone rings. "Shit, it's the school," I say, glancing at the number. "Let me take this."

Lowering my chin, I try to dim the noise of the boisterous restaurant, as I take the call. "I understand. All right, we'll be sure to address that tonight. Right. Yes, of course, I apologize, I really do."

I hang up as our food is being delivered. Trista and Caroline lean in, unwrapping forks and setting cloth napkins across their laps.

"What was that about?" Trista asks, her black hair twisted in a top knot, her red lipstick making her teeth extra white. She looks the part of a Seattle-born musician, black jeans and tee-shirt, leather bomber jacket. Jenna calls her a hipster mom as if it's a criticism. I call her one half of my saving grace. Caroline the other.

"It was Mr. Hopkins," I say, acutely aware of how pitched my voice is. If my friends notice, they don't say anything.

"What happened?" Caroline asks softly. She picks up her fork, but doesn't begin to eat. She's waiting for me to go on.

"Holden had an altercation with Jasper and Julia."

"Jenna's twins?" Trista asks. "What kind of altercation?"

"Apparently Holden flipped over their lunch trays. Food went flying."

"Why?" Caroline asks.

"Why what?" I ask.

"Why did he do it?"

"Hopkins didn't say." I close my eyes, pressing a hand to my forehead. "Honestly I didn't even have the energy to ask."

Caroline rests her hand on my arm. "You okay, Em?"

"Am I okay?" I give a sharp laugh, then grab my fork and shovel salad into my mouth to avoid answering.

Trista waves over the waiter and orders three glasses of Pinot Grigio. When it arrives, she tells me to take a sip. I down half the glass. "Seriously, Em. What's going on?"

Reaching for the bread on the table, I slather it with butter. "I can't..."

"Can't what?" Caroline asks.

I drop the bread, let my head fall back. I've been on the edge for weeks. Ever since Holden moved in. I knew it would be hard. But this is surreal.

"Holden is just having a hard time adjusting to life with us," I admit. "I haven't been entirely honest."

Caroline sighs, "Oh, sweetie. I knew something was off when we came over for wine a few weeks ago."

"It's just extra hard with Mark gone so much. I need him to be home. I just..."

"What?" Trista asks.

"Feel like maybe... Like it's a lot harder than I thought." Caroline and Trista exchange a glance. "What? Don't tell me there's another no-Betsy allowed club at school, I can't handle hearing that right now." I finish my wine and order another.

"There isn't another club," Trista says. "At least, none that Levi has mentioned. But he did say Holden starts a lot of fights. That he cusses and that he is a bully."

I gulp the wine the waiter brings. "I know. He's struggling. Massively." I don't say *so am I*. I'm hanging on by a thread. A thread Mark doesn't seem to realize is as frayed as it is.

Over the weekend my husband got an idea. When he came home from the capital, we tried to go out to dinner, but taking Holden to a restaurant is like going into public with a wild animal. He creates a scene everywhere we go. This time Holden started shouting when I told him he couldn't have a second soda. "You're a bitch," he muttered to me when the waiter was still in earshot. Shame flooded my face, my cheeks red with embarrassment.

Ten years old, and throwing that word around as if it's nothing.

We drove home in silence, Mark and I seethe. We

let the kids watch movies until ten at night and we stared at our own phones in silence.

I know he was happy when he returned to Olympia Monday morning.

He texted me: *Sorry for how things are going. I have a lot of stress at work -- can't handle any bad publicity right now, Em. I just need us to stay strong.*

I deleted the text without replying. Petty maybe, but looking good for reporters is literally the last thing on my mind. I was thrilled when the kids were dropped off at school. And I hate that. I used to love being a mom. It was my greatest sense of pride, my purpose -- my everything.

Having Holden home changes that. Because my confidence is shot, my ability to rein in conflict is next to nothing. If Betsy weren't here, keeping the peace, I wouldn't trust myself.

Every afternoon it's a new battle. Every night, another. Morning brings a fresh batch of complications. I'm fucking exhausted.

"Hey," Caroline says, her voice lifting. "Why don't I take Betsy on Friday for a sleepover? We can go to that ceramic place, Paintbrush? Get our nails done? What do you think?"

What I want is for someone to take Holden for the night, not my little girl who is appearing more angelic by the day. I always knew she was a sweetheart, but her patience with Holden deserves a prize.

But maybe a night with Caroline is the prize she needs.

"She would love that," I say, appreciating Caroline's

willingness to give my daughter some one-on-one attention. It's obvious I'm not up for the task right now.

"Okay, I can step up my game too," Trista says with a wry smile. "I know Holden can't do sleepovers until the adoption is final, but how about Jeff and I take him and Levi out for pizza and the arcade Friday? That way the house will be empty, and you and Mark can have a date, stay in, go out... whatever." She smiles. "And by whatever, I mean, you know, have sex. I bet with all this stress you could use a little TLC."

I roll my eyes. "Mark's been so stressed with the session; I don't think sex is on his mind." My girlfriends may know a lot about me, but they don't know everything. Sex with Mark is a subject I've never brought up with anyone.

"Sex is always on their mind," Caroline laughs.

"Agreed." Trista smiles. "But you'll let your friends take the kids off your hands for a night, won't you?"

I finish my wine, setting it down, my heart feeling all warm and fuzzy. "You guys are so good to me. I don't know what I'd do without you."

"Well, it also means you need to be more honest with us," Caroline says. "We can't help if we don't know."

Trista's phone buzzes. "Oh shit, I gotta run. I have an appointment to have my oil changed."

I bite back a smile. "Is that a euphemism for sex?"

She cackles. "I wish." She stands, and she and Caroline both set cash on the table. Trista's gold bangles jingle as she kisses my cheek. "I'll text about Friday. Love you, hang in there, okay?"

Caroline stands too. "I've gotta dash too, Lucille is done at the groomers."

"You can't make your Labradoodle wait," I say, thanking her again for offering the sleepover. "Betsy is going to be so excited."

They leave me at the table and I exhale, feeling slightly lightheaded from drinking the wine so fast. I pay the check and glance at my phone. I have ninety minutes before I have to get the kids.

Standing, I realize I'm really feeling it, and I finish my glass of water before pulling on my coat. When I step outside the bistro, I realize a coffee is probably a good idea, considering I'm buzzing. And way too emotional to do any shopping at the moment -- the town is small and I don't want to run into any other moms right now. The phone call with the principal left me doubting my ability to do this. Any of it.

Hitching my bag up onto my shoulder, I walk down the sidewalk of downtown Port Windwick. It's a destination town, waterfront, boats in the marina, boutique shops nestled between restaurants and breweries, and I know the owners of most establishments. If Trista's son Levi is talking, I'm guessing all the kids at the schoolhouse have opinions on my soon-to-be-adopted son.

As I'm walking past the yoga studio, Jenna flags me down. She's in her designer work out gear, her mat tucked under her arm. "Emery? I thought that was you!"

"Oh, hey," I say immediately regretting my wine. "I'm really sorry about what happened in the lunch room. I just spoke with the principal and I'm sure you're upset. You have every right to be."

She nods sympathetically. "Oh my gosh, it's you who's been through the wringer. I mean God bless you, Emery."

I lift my eyebrows, trying to decipher just how much bullshit the ring leader of the Mommy Tribe is flinging my way. "Holden is the one who has really been through hell and back, Jenna. Not me."

It's the truth. Even though I feel inadequate and resent the chaos that circles my house right now -- I know it is temporary. Holden has been living with trauma for a decade. Surely I can handle a few months' worth.

"Sure, but we've got to protect our own children, don't we?"

"What does that mean?"

"Well, your Betsy and my Jasper and Julia, they don't need to suffer just because Holden has."

"So, what? I should just not send him to school so we can protect the other kids from his outbursts?"

Jenna nods. "Exactly. I knew you'd see where I was coming from. A place of love, really. And the public schools in Port Windwick are amazing, you know, your husband's a senator!"

"This is love?" I ask, barely masking my disgust. "Segregating children based on the abuse they've faced? That's love?"

Jenna scoffs, waving the comment off. "That's not what I was saying. I was saying we should protect the innocent."

Rage burns inside me. Maybe it's her word choice. Maybe it's the wine. Maybe it's her perfect hair and her bright white teeth and the fact she isn't walking on eggshells every time she enters her own home. I don't know, but it doesn't bring out a pretty side of me. "Jenna, I can't do this." I think of Mark's request -- keep the family together. "I'm not fighting with you in public."

Jenna rolls her eyes. "You are so predictable, Emery. Holier than thou. Well, I have news for you. The Mommy Tribe isn't okay with bullies. And we are starting a petition--"

I walk away, not giving her the satisfaction of being heard. I'm sure she's already whipped out her phone to text her crew about how awful I am. I pass the Starbucks, heading to the end of the street, opening the door to the less frequented shop, CoffeeLove. I'm gonna keep my head down and try to take big, deep breaths until I need to leave to get the kids. Jenna is not stealing this moment from me.

I order a latte, adding a brownie to my order at the last minute. Then I find a table facing the window with a vase of flowers. Sitting with my treats, I snap a photo of the latte art and post it to Instagram. #StopAndSmellTheRoses #CoffeeBreak #MomLife.

I close the app and push my phone in my purse, hating my need to appear put together. It's totally fake. The truth is I'm near tears. I'm glad I opened up with Caroline and Trista, but it wasn't the entire truth. And now this petition? For God's sake, Jenna needs a new mantle to carry. Holden doesn't deserve to be the face of her cause.

As I'm finishing the brownie, Cooper sits down at my table, a to-go cup in hand. "Hey," I say, lifting my eyes in surprise. "You keep running into me."

"To be honest, I knew I'd find you here."

I tuck my hair behind my ears, feeling self-conscious. "How?"

He waves his phone at me. "You posted it."

"You stalking me, Deputy?"

He chuckles. "No, I mean, I look at your feed now and then."

"Why?"

He swallows, his Adam's apple bobbing. "I like seeing that you're happy."

Now it's my turn to swallow, to cast down my eyes. "You worry about me?"

"Of course I do, Em."

I look at him, I can't help it. He was all of my firsts and still holds a piece of my heart that's probably way too big. He'd hate me if he knew all my secrets. But he doesn't and that is why he's still here. He's the link to my past, a place no one else in my current life treads.

"Especially, since I saw you at the grocery store a few weeks back," he says. "I've been hearing stuff about your boy and... Well, you sure you are doing as well as the Internet would lead me to believe?"

I run my hand over the base of my neck. "You know the answer to that or you wouldn't be here."

"True."

"You alone at the house a lot?" he asks.

I stiffen. "Why?"

"Because I want you to call me if things ever get out of hand. If you feel alone. If Mark's working too much I can--"

"Mark is around plenty," I lie.

"Good." Cooper holds my gaze. "I've done a lot of training for work, Em. Learning about ACEs and trauma-informed care and I know enough to know you're putting on a brave face."

I bristle, knowing he sees me. Really sees me. He always has.

I tried to talk to Mark about Holden's ACEs -- adverse childhood experiences -- and how they are contributing to the way he's acting out right now. Mark didn't go to the foster care classes with me and managed to be working when I went through the files on Holden's time in state custody.

He listens, he does. He watches YouTube videos with me, and I forward him links on articles about different things we can try at home. A weighted blanket. Attachment therapy. Melatonin.

He reads, he replies, he cares.

But it feels like I'm the one with my hands on the wheel, looking ahead and out the rearview mirror, riding the brakes, trying to change lanes. I asked to be in the driver's seat, to take this on -- to bear the responsibility. But now I don't know. It doesn't feel like a one-person job.

"It will get better," I tell Cooper. "It's hard right now, really hard, but I have hope for Holden."

"I'm glad you have Mark to help you through this."

Cooper's eyes search mine. He knows the truth.

"Me too," I say, tears filling my eyes. Dammit, I hate Coop for this -- for getting so close with only a few conversations. Why did he come back to town now, of all times? Just as I decide to become an emotional train wreck?

The deeper truth haunts me -- maybe I've always been a mess, I just covered it up for a really long time. Life with Mark has been so easy, so perfect, that I've never had a reason to break, there was no pressure causing me to crack.

Holden changed all that.

I see Caroline pass the window, Lucille on a leash, fluffy and clean -- she pauses at the window, seeing Cooper and me. My tears. She points to herself, then to the door of the cafe, gesturing to ask if I need backup. I shake my head. She blows me a kiss, looking at Cooper one more time before walking away.

He leans in. The damn pine trees and fresh air making it hard for me to breathe. "I still love you, Em," he tells me.

He smiles softly, his breath on my ear, it's like he knows what I know. Knows that ever since I ran into him when he moved back to town I've been waiting for him to say this. He may have been the one to leave me but after all this time, his scruffy beard still makes my belly flip-flop, his bright eyes and light hair so damn familiar. I don't like it. It's too enticing. Right now my entire life is upside down -- but Cooper is the same. Steady.

"I should go," I say, breathless.

He nods. "You should."

I reach for my bag, trembling. "My life is a mess, Cooper. I can't deal with you too."

"But if you need help, cleaning up the mess, I will always be here to help you. I will always be on your side. I left you when you needed me the most. I'll never forgive myself."

I swallow, memories too close to the surface. I blink them away. "You want to help?"

He nods.

"Then you should volunteer at the kids' school," I say, joking, wanting to make my exit light and breezy. Anything to take care of the conflicting emotions inside me. "The principal is having a shit time dealing with Holden. Maybe you could give him some pointers."

Cooper nods, standing with me. "I'm on it, Em. You say the word and I got your back."

I shake my head. His loyalty is hard to accept. "Despite everything?"

He bites his bottom lip. "No, Em, because of everything."

16

PRESENT

I LEAVE THE LIVING ROOM, where Tom, Mark, and Jeff stand with Holden. Right now what I need is fresh air. But the moment I step outside, I'm reminded why I stay indoors this time of year. It's frigid, raining, and the dark sky, heavy with clouds does nothing to clear my head.

Frustrated, I return inside only to grab my coat and car keys. I haven't eaten in days and suddenly I'm famished. "I'll be right back," I call, but I don't wait for an answer. I need to leave the house. Now.

I step outside, blasted by three reporters who shove mics into my face as I try to walk to my car. Dammit, I'd forgotten they were here.

"Are the allegations true regarding Mark Gable's son, is he accused of murder?"

"Get away," I shout, covering my face with my hand. "I'm not answering your questions."

"When you adopted Holden, did you choose your daughter's murderer?" they ask. The question causes bile to rise in my throat, and I don't want to put on a show for them, but I can't help it. I throw up in the grass, heaving at the thought -- the thought of people watching this footage and thinking that of my son. I wipe my mouth, my puke having made my path to the car clear.

I jump into the Land Rover and pull out of the driveway. Making a beeline for a drive-thru line, I order burgers, cokes, fries, shakes, figuring Mark and Holden are probably hungry too. I cram a cheeseburger into my mouth as I put on my blinker. As I turn, I see a police car turning at the intersection. For a split second, I wonder if it's Cooper.

Distracted, ketchup falls in my lap, my lips wrap around a red straw, drinking the sugary sweet soda, something I haven't had in years. It burns my throat going down, and I take a handful of fries, the salty grease coating my fingers. I lick them clean.

My phone is tethered to the car, and Trista calls. I jab my thumb on the button to answer it.

"Hey," she says. "I just spoke with Jeff. You saw the video?"

"Yeah, it's a fucking mess, Trista. It's..."

"I know. I saw."

"What do you mean, you saw?"

"Marcie Devon posted it in the Mommy Tribe Facebook group."

I bristle. "And how do you know that?"

The call goes silent. Finally, she answers. "I joined."

"What do you mean, you joined?" We've made a

pact. It was an agreement made after one too many rants about those mothers and how we weren't them.

"After Halloween, everyone was talking about what happened, about Bets, and I wanted to know what people were saying. I caved."

My stomach rolls. Suddenly, I feel sick. What were these women saying about my daughter?

"It sounds worse than it is," Trista says. "And now you're pissed -- which I get -- but Em, this is intense for everyone. If Betsy was murdered that means there is a killer on the loose."

"Do people think it's Holden?" At this moment it is all I care about.

"Em," she says, so much softer than my brazen bestie usually sounds. "It doesn't matter what people think. All that matters is the truth."

"If I don't fight for him, no one will."

"I know, Em."

She does. Better than most anyone on the planet, she knows. She has been here for so much of this mess this year. This fucking catastrophe. Still, the thought of her talking to those mothers about my children, it kills me.

"I can't believe you joined that fucking group, Tris." I'm latching on to anything I can right now. Her betrayal of our sisterhood makes me wonder what else she's keeping from me.

"I get that you're pissed," she says. "And while some people might watch that video and point fingers at Holden, it tells me something else."

"What's that?" My throat is dry again. The Coca-Cola didn't seem to help.

"We need to find out what they were fighting about."

"Holden isn't talking."

"Then we need to ask someone else."

"I have to go," I say. I don't want to talk to her anymore. My heart hurts enough, I can't have Trista going behind my back right now. I need her here, on my side.

She clears her throat. "Look, I'm sorry I joined the group but I think--"

"I don't want to talk about it now, Tris. I gotta go."

WHEN I WALK in the door, my arms piled with bags of food, I feel overwhelmed with exhaustion. That outing, to the drive-thru, drained me.

"Everything alright?" Mark asks, concern in his eyes as he takes the food from my hands and sets it on the entryway table, next to a vase of pink roses. "The reporters get to you?"

I nod my head tightly, and he moves toward me in the foyer where I'm unzipping my parka. "Come here."

I let him fold me into his arms, let him run his hands over my hair. "I miss her, so much," I tell him, my tears soaking his dress shirt. "But Holden is still here and he needs us. I need you to fight for him the same you would for Betsy."

He nods, stepping back, his eyes are rimmed in red,

same as mine. "You're right, I'm a fucking monster to consider anything besides his innocence."

We say the right things, but I know we're both wrestling with the same information. We know Holden. Know what he is capable of, more than anyone else on this planet.

But we can't say it out loud.

"If you're a monster, so am I," I whisper. It feels so good to be on the same page as Mark. After so many months of fighting, what I need now is peace. Because if we don't find that common ground, then how can we do this next part? Find the person who killed our daughter.

"Tom and I are going to start making a list of other possibilities. Find out everything we can about the kids who were there on Halloween, begin piecing together the night."

I nod, understanding, thinking about Trista's words. I'm picturing myself marching over to Jenna's house and pulling her sculpted Barre body up from whatever yoga position she is in and making her force the story out of her kids.

"Before you go on a rampage all over town..."

I frown. "What now?"

"Officer Margot called, she wants to interview you about Halloween night. Me too. Apparently, everyone who might have been around Betsy that evening is getting a visit."

I nod; I'd assumed this would happen. "I get it," I say. "Honestly, I can handle that. Anything that will help us get answers."

Mark runs his hand over his jaw. "We will find answers. Tom is the best. You trust him, don't you?" I look over my shoulder, hoping he can't hear. "Don't worry, he left five minutes ago. So did Jeff."

"I trust him. Honestly, it's just... I remember their barbecue over the summer. Holden stood at the fire for hours, staring at the flames. Refused to talk or eat all night. I don't want Jeff's history with Holden to affect his opinion."

Mark's eyes crease, and I know he understands. "I get it, but I'd rather someone who empathizes with him represent him than someone who will cast blame."

Holden walks into the foyer, and I wonder how long he was behind the corner, listening.

I lift the bags of food and drink holder. "I got dinner."

Holden walks closer, takes the bag of burgers and fries. "I didn't talk that night at the BBQ because Jeff's kids suck. I hate them."

So he was listening. "Why do you hate them?"

"Logan sucks."

Interesting comment, coming from him -- a boy who has hurt so many people for so long.

"Sucks how?" Mark asks.

We walk into the kitchen and pull out the food. Holden eats fries, not looking at us. It's like he considers every single word, deciding if it's worth saying or not.

"One time we were at their house," he says. "All us kids were going down to their beach and Bets fell. She slipped. And he said she was a baby, that she couldn't walk yet. That she probably still wore diapers. When she started crying... you know, how she cries?"

I nod, knowing what he means. Betsy may be loyal to a fault, but she cries at the drop of a hat. I've never made a big deal over it, and neither has Mark. As parents, we're on the same team, and when raising Betsy, we always focused on what she needed, not what either of us wanted.

"She started crying and he just wouldn't let it go. He called her a cry baby all night."

My skin bristles at this. Betsy has never exactly fit in with her peers, but to have been called names -- especially by Logan, a boy who has known her her entire life -- is painful to hear.

"That's why I hate him. And why I'd rather stare at the stupid fire than be around him."

Holden rarely talks like this, so openly. And it makes me want to see what else he might be willing to say. I know that if he's pushed into something, he'll flat-out refuse. It has to seem like his idea. Problem is, Holden is one of the smartest people I know. And he doesn't like playing anyone's games but his own.

"Why didn't you tell us?" I ask.

"Betsy didn't want me to." He takes a bite of his burger, his eyes drawn down, not looking at me.

"Why not?"

Holden lifts his chin. "She made me promise."

My stomach drops. "Promise what?"

"Promise to keep her secret."

17

SEVEN MONTHS EARLIER

MARK and I are leaving the school, hand in hand. Holden and Betsy are ten steps ahead of us, then they are running toward the playground. Mark and I stop, watching them go.

I drag my hands through my hair. Most days I'm running on fumes. Dry shampoo barely helped my unwashed hair, I'm in yoga pants and a fleece shirt, athletic shoes even though I'm not running anywhere. What I really want is a bottle of wine and a chocolate bar. I'm frazzled. How can one ten-year-old boy manage to upend my family's ecosystem so drastically?

Mark says I should hire another housekeeper, but I refused after Maria left. The last thing I want right now is another adult having an eyewitness account of what a mess I am.

Today only drove that point home. Parent-teacher conferences officially suck when the entire school is out to get your soon-to-be-adopted son.

"I just can't stand how condescending Mr. Hopkins

is," I say, pulling down my sunglasses as Jenna, her husband Wayne, and their twins walk toward us.

"Maybe we should take him out of the Montessori School. Find a private school that has more flexibility when it comes to extra support."

"The Mommy Tribe would love that," I say under my breath. I don't know what happened with Jenna's petition, but I haven't heard anything more about it.

Jenna and Wayne's twins run to the playground and the couple stops a few feet from us. I grit my teeth; Jenna looks sparkling clean as always. Cropped white jeans, cute wedges, a fresh manicure in pale pink. She smiles broadly. Good for her.

As far as me, there is no faking it. All those pretenses -- trying to appear cool, calm, and collected have been thrown out with my clothes that Holden cut in half with a pair of scissors. Yep, he got pissed I wouldn't let him download Fortnite and he started whacking at the clothes hanging in my closet. He turned dresses into tank tops and trousers into booty shorts.

However, Mark is unaware of my silent feud with Jenna. She is everything I have never been. To be honest, she would fit better with Mark in so many ways. She looks the part. Barrel curls, toned arms and the boss of the Mommy Tribe.

Mark fell for me because I was broken; he wanted to fix me. I wonder what he wants now? He's been back home for a few weeks and I'm guessing he wants a one-way ticket to anywhere. Holden is changing everything, more than we've been able to admit out loud.

"Haven't seen you in a while," Mark says warmly to Wayne.

"Been chained to my desk, you know how it goes." Wayne works from home for Microsoft, so no, I don't think he gets *how it goes*. Mark is finally back home full time, and thank god. The session is out, and he is in our bed every night. The timing works in my favor -- I've never needed him more than I do now.

"I've heard so much from the twins about the new member of your family," Jenna says to Mark, disregarding me as she glances over at the playground. The kids are running around and I can't help but breathe a sigh of relief at the normal game of tag. Holden needs to run off his extra energy every chance he can get.

"Yeah, it's been a big adjustment," Mark says. "But we're making it through. Couldn't do it without Emery. She's our family's glue."

"Aww, that's so cute." Jenna squeezes Wayne's arm, the V of her shirt inching down as she does. I twist my lips, taking in her perky *everything*. How much work has she had done?

Mark doesn't notice, he doesn't have eyes for Jenna. He smiles at me, and it sends warmth through my belly I didn't know I was craving. We need another date night, just him and me. Maybe Trista and Caroline would be willing to help us out again. Mark and I haven't had sex since the last time they took the kids, and that was what? Eight weeks ago?

"Mom!" Jenna's daughter Julia shrieks. "Mom!" Jenna turns, we all do, and move toward the playground in a swift motion.

I scan the area for Bets and Holden and see they are standing opposite Julia and Jasper. My kids have their arms crossed, scowling at the twins.

Jenna pulls her daughter close. "What happened, sweetheart? Did that boy hurt you?"

I scowl, *that boy*? And what kind of assumption is that, anyway?

"What's going on?" Mark asks, stepping in as interference, apparently having heard the same words from Jenna.

"He told me he wishes I would die," Julia howls.

My neck jerks to Holden. "Did you say that?"

"No," Holden blurts, fists clenched. "I said I wanted her to disappear."

Jasper starts shouting. "Stop lying! Dad, he's a liar."

Betsy stands, stunned. Her lips trembling. I want to pull her in my arms, but I don't want to take sides.

"Betsy, what did Holden say?" I ask, feeling a pinprick of hope in my chest. Maybe this time he isn't at fault. I'm so tired of Holden messing things up -- not just at school. He threw a fit two days ago when he punched his fist through every window screen on the first floor of our house.

"Holden," she says softly. "You did say you wanted her to die. I think you just forgot."

Blood drains from my face. This is not what I need today. I can already feel Mark tensing up beside me. He misses most of the drama with Holden, but there is no hiding from this.

"Apologize, Holden. Now, " Mark says tightly.

"You need to say you're sorry," I tell Holden. "I mean it, make things right."

He shakes his head, eyes narrowed and dark. "No."

"Mom, can we just go?" Betsy asks. "Please?"

"We're so sorry," Mark says to Jenna and Wayne. "Honestly, we're trying here. There is no excuse for this behavior."

Wayne nods. "We understand, we do."

But I can't help but wonder if Mark is wrong. Can't there sometimes be justification for hurtful words? What if all you've been taught is to fight?

Jenna huffs, her arms around her children's shoulders, leading them away. "Teach him some manners, Emery. Seriously, God knows you have plenty of time on your hands."

I lift my eyebrows. "What does that mean?"

Jenna pastes on her smile. Fake. Fake. Fake. "I just mean you haven't volunteered at the school in months. What exactly is your excuse?"

"Jesus, Jenna." My mouth drops open in shock. Is this what people are saying about me behind my back? I haven't volunteered since Holden came home because I'm trying to keep my family in one piece. "Mind your own fucking business."

My word choice wasn't the best. I can admit that. But, in my defense, I just went through a horrendous parent-teacher conference, was cornered by the principal and am apparently being judged by Jenna's Mommy Tribe all the ding-dong day. I've had enough.

Mark lifts his hands in defense to the perfect family opposite us and then ushers us to the car. We walk silently, each of us stewing for a different reason. I can take a guess at all of them: Mark is probably angry over my public approval rating. Betsy is most likely upset that we forced her to speak out against Holden. I'd guess Holden is mad that he was called out on his behavior.

Me? I'm just tired. So, damn tired.

When we get home, the kids stalk off to their rooms. "Just go do something quiet for an hour. Please," I say. I don't have the energy to negotiate a single thing.

"Let's watch *Stranger Things*," I hear Holden tell Bets.

The comment agitates me beyond belief. That boy will push *every single* boundary if left unchecked. I holler, "Not that show, Holden. We've been over that."

"Fine," he groans, climbing the stairs with Betsy.

"Let's play Minecraft," Bets suggests, choosing Holden's parent-approved game of choice. They can spend hours lost in the worlds they create-- tunnels and caves and underwater realms. It satiates Betsy's creativity and Holden's desire to get lost. To disappear. To hide.

Right now, I can totally relate to his escapist fantasies. Maybe it isn't Mark longing for the one-way ticket -- maybe it's me.

I follow my husband into the kitchen where he grabs a beer from the fridge. "I took the afternoon off work to deal with that bullshit? What got into you?"

He doesn't swear often. When he does, I know he's mad. Join the club.

"I just need a breather," I tell him, not at all

ashamed to admit defeat. "I'm spent, Mark. And the social worker is coming for the visit tomorrow and look at this place. It's a train wreck."

"Let's not blame your outburst on the state of the house."

I drop my face into my hands. "This is too hard. It's more than I thought it would be. I'm not strong enough, Mark."

Mark steps behind me, wraps his arms around my shoulders, brushing back my hair. "Emery, maybe we should consider Holden needing more than we can give him."

My heart stills as I absorb what he's just said. I turn, facing him, my meltdown capsized by his words. I need his touch, to sink against him, to feel anything other than the way I feel right now. Lost at sea without a buoy

"What does that mean, Mark? We're his family."

"Nothing is official yet."

"You don't believe in me?"

Mark shakes his head, cups my cheek with his hand. Touch is what I crave. I feel like such a mess but Mark is steady. Sensible. Sound.

"I believe in you, Em. I always have. But right now you and Bets are my family."

"He has no one else," I say. "We promised him."

"I know."

"Your campaign is already running with this as your platform."

"It's just politics, Em. This is our family."

"I don't want to quit. Maybe I'm too proud. I want to see this through."

"At any cost?" Mark asks.

"If we don't fight for him, who will?"

"You were always too good for me," Mark says, pulling me to him. In his arms, I let my shoulders fall. There is no perfect-Jenna and her Mommy Tribe watching me. I can let down my guard here, in my home.

"I miss you, Mark. You've been gone so much." I pull his dress shirt from his slacks, running my hands over his muscular torso. I whimper with want -- my body not-so-silently screaming to get me out of my own goddamn head.

I'm a wreck and he knows it and this is how our love story began. A fragile girl and the hero who rescued her.

I need him to save me now.

His lip turns up, not a smile -- more a desire, and he takes my hand, dragging me to our room at the end of the hall. I close the door. Lock it. Let him drag me to bed. To strip me of my clothes, to lay claim to what is his.

He knows how to make me turn off my mind. It's what he did when I was a college student, grieving the loss of my father. When our relationship began, I'd just been hurt by the person I loved the most.

Mark found me and changed the trajectory of my entire life.

When Mark entered my life, Cooper and I had just broken up after being together for years. Since we were sophomores in high school, Coop and I had plans. So many plans -- to conquer the world together.

How, we never exactly discussed that -- but we were kids, young and in love, and felt so secure in our devotion.

My dad was an alcoholic at best, and he raised me on his own. Cooper's single mom was a pill-popping nurse who lost everything. We didn't have a lot of outside support. We only had one another. Coop loved my dad like a son and dad loved him right back. My dad was a nice drunk. The nicest drunk in the whole wide world. But he lived his life with highs and lows. One low got the best of him and he was gone.

Grief does strange things to a person. It can make them shrug off the religion they've always clung to. It can create an entirely new moral compass or convince them they are all alone in the world. In Cooper's case, the idea of being around me, constantly reminded of my father was more than he could bear. And every time he looked in my eyes, he saw memories.

But they were my memories too.

Dad, Coop, and I crabbing in the Sound, in Dad's old dinghy. The three of us camping on the coast in August, sand in our hair, our eyes. Salty waves licking our toes. Bonfires in the backyard, drinking Dad's Rainier when we were still teenagers. Dad telling stories, flicking his joint in the flames when he smoked it through.

Later, Cooper's eyes filled with water when we walked into Dad's cabin, finding him in his recliner -- dead. A heart attack took his life, and in his wake, it reshaped mine. My heart twisted and changed. I couldn't look at Cooper without seeing my father. But I wanted to see. Cooper didn't. Couldn't. He left when I needed him most.

Mark's eyes were different. Dark instead of light; deep, understanding, possessive. Not in a cruel way, in a way that told me I didn't need to fear to be alone in my sadness. Eyes that said, 'I am here, tell me your stories.' So, I did.

He was a grad student, and I needed a tutor. My grades were slipping in the wake of Dad's death. He taught me more than the textbook. He taught me that if Cooper didn't want me, there was another man who did.

After I told Mark my stories, tear-stained eyes hidden by long strands of hair, he slipped the locks behind my ear, lifted my chin and kissed me.

Similar to the way he kisses me now. Long and with intent, as if he knows I need him, this. Now.

It feels good to be known like this by another person. We don't make love often, but when we do, I'm transported in time. Back to the time when I was alone and he arrived in my life and somehow, the pain of Cooper leaving me, wasn't so raw.

Mark tugs off my jeans, unhooks my bra, kisses me until I'm gasping, panting, his.

After Cooper ended things, I gave into Mark's promises. Mark and I didn't have many shared memories, but he was offering me a future that was free of the pain of the past.

Now, as Mark makes love to me, our love has changed again. Evolving and shifting, turning into something I can't exactly recognize.

Cooper has always had a hold on my heart, in ways that would slay Mark if he knew.

Mark, though, isn't thinking of Cooper, of my regrets, mistakes, or broken vows. He is thinking of my future.

He always has.

"You're right, Emery," he says after we finish, his arms wrapped around me tightly, holding on as if he will never, ever let go. "You can't give up."

"Why not?" I ask.

"You'll hate yourself if you do."

"I hate myself already."

"Shh," he says, kissing me again, raking his fingers through my hair. "Don't say that. We knew this would be hard. But we chose him. I was thinking: I can be around more, sign him up for indoor soccer and help coach the team."

"You'd do that?"

"For our family? Emery, I'd do anything."

18

PRESENT

WHAT DOES HOLDEN MEAN, he made a promise to keep her secret?

"What secret?" I ask, near hysterics.

But Holden clenches his jaw. Shuffles his feet. Steps away.

"Make him tell us," I shout at Mark. "Make him tell us now."

But Holden walks away, and the louder I get, the more he retreats.

"Babe, we can't force something," Mark tells me. "It's been a big day, let's all just take a breather, okay?" His phone starts buzzing, and he reaches for it, reading the text. "It's Tom. He needs me to come over to his office. Do you mind?"

I scowl. "You're going to leave me, now?"

"What the hell do you want, Emery? To rule out possibilities with our son's attorney or to convince a stubborn eleven-year-old to open his mouth?"

"Fine, go." I pour myself a glass of water wishing I

could have something stronger. Betsy's body is still at the morgue. Her funeral has been postponed. We can't mourn for her properly until we have answers. Logically, I know Mark needs to go. But my heart pleads with him to stay.

"I love you, Emery." He squeezes my arm. "Maybe rest for a while? You look exhausted."

I nod numbly, then sip the water. My gut is wrecked from all the greasy food I inhaled. I follow Mark to the foyer, watch as he grabs his keys, his coat.

"I've asked my parents to make calls, to explain the situation. I don't want you to have to talk to any more people than you already have to."

"Thanks," I say in half a whisper.

"We'll find out who did this. Honestly, it could be an accident." But his eyes tell me something else.

"He loved her Mark. He would never have..."

Mark nods. "I know. And now we just need to prove that he didn't."

He leaves the house and I climb the stairs, looking for Holden. Wanting to apologize. If he thinks I'm angry with him, he will never fill in the blanks.

I look into his bedroom. He's not here. "Holden?" I call, he doesn't answer. I pull back his blankets, knowing he likes to burrow away from the real world, but there is nothing but rumpled sheets, a Percy Jackson book. Dirty socks kicked off during restless sleep. His PlayStation controller is on the floor, I stoop down to pick it up, my anger over him playing Fortnite flashing for a moment, but I push it aside. There isn't time to dwell on that. Right now, I need to know what secret my little girl asked him to keep. Why would she tell him, and not me?

I stand, wrestling with self-doubt, calling for Holden again. Still, no answer and a shiver runs up my spine. What if he did kill his sister, and is coming for me next? I spin around tightly, imagining him with the raised Le Creuset pan -- not for pancakes, but this time to bash in my head. Same as Betsy.

No one is there, certainly not a child, and shame fills me as I try to erase the images I've just created. Right now, I feel like the real monster in the house.

He's sitting on the floor in Betsy's room, and I close my eyes, dizzy at the sight of my daughter's mint green and pale pink space. I lean against the doorframe for balance. Holden is sitting on the cream carpet, his fingers running over the spines of the books on her shelves.

He hears me and turns as I sink to the floor, crawling toward him like a submissive dog, cowering to him. I don't want to be a threat, but in a deeper, animalistic way, I feel like I'm losing all sense of my humanity. I'm becoming a shell of a woman. Turning into a wild hog, a scavenging lion -- willing to take anything tossed my way. But I don't want pieces of meat, I want information. I need words, need explanations. Answers.

I watch as Holden pulls out a composition book, tucked between her thick tomes set in fantasy worlds. She and Holden shared a love for reading. I didn't know most of Holden's love languages, but I learned early on new books were one of them. I scoured the bookstore for new releases. The glossy hardbacks with thick cream paper. Betsy shared all her titles and they would watch movie versions of their favorite stories, arguing the same side -- the book was always better.

People rarely saw this side of Holden. I'm his mother and I rarely see it myself. Now, I realize with a hollow guttural noise, as I crawl toward him, that I will never see this side again. The pair of them holed up on the couch, the gas fireplace blazing, hot cocoa at their side. My records playing softly, their eyes scanning the pages as they each read in silence, as I sat with a sketch pad trying to draw them. Capture the moment with pen and paper. I hadn't sold a comic strip to a magazine in months – *years*, but I still turned to ink and paper in quiet moments.

It took several months to get to that place -- a sliver of peace in a home fractured with heartbreak -- but we found it in small and simple ways. And when we held it in the palm of our hands, we made a silent promise to stay in the cocoon. Summer days were spent like this, trading cocoa for lemonade, the fireplace for sunshine. We'd go to the beach, I'd pack a cooler and chairs and books and they would read, side by side. I would walk along the water's edge, collecting broken shells, tucking them in my bag to take home. I didn't need whole, perfect shells. My life was cracked, ragged, flawed. And in those moments, with windswept hair and freckled cheeks, I didn't care. I loved it for exactly what it was. Mine.

Now, I sit beside Holden, staring at the notebook in his hand. Holden flips through the pages. Betsy's drawings in pencil. Dragons. Fairies. A phoenix, a snake.

I trace the drawings, and he doesn't shove me away. The moment feels electric, charged. A teardrop falls to the page. It's not mine. I'm not the only one grieving.

"I love this one," I whisper, my fingers on a falcon. Large wings, soaring, a scroll tucked in its beak. Unable to imagine a life where she wouldn't be perched on a stool at the kitchen island while I made dinner. Unable to see a life where she didn't flip the pages of one of her drawing pads, showing me her newest incantation.

"She didn't like it."

I swallow, still. "No?"

Holden shakes his head. "She said a bird's face was the hardest. Harder than people even."

"She never drew people, though," I say, cross-legged now, beside him.

"Yeah, she did," he says plainly, closing the notebook, tucking it back on the shelf.

"I never saw one."

"She didn't show you."

"But she showed you?" Jealousy surges in my chest. The monster inside me is talking. Loud. I need to shut it up.

Holden doesn't seem to notice, he simply nods.

"I want to see."

He doesn't answer, letting the silence do the talking.

"Holden, show me."

He looks at me with eyes full of shadows. "She'd be so mad."

"She isn't here. People think that you... We have to prove your innocence. And Holden, her secrets, whatever you're protecting her from, might hurt you. Do you understand?"

He shakes his head sharply. "I didn't kill Betsy. She was my sister. She was my..." He starts shaking now, tears streaking his cheeks and I pull him into my arms. Hold him tight. Realizing with disgust that I haven't done this since the day my daughter died. Since his sister died. Holden pushes everyone away, all the time, and it leaves little space for intimacy. But he's still a boy who lost his sister. He's still my son, aching for what is gone.

We may not have a lot of common ground, but we share a love for Bets. Right now, that is more than enough.

When his shoulders stop shaking, when he pulls back, wiping his face, he reaches under her bed, pulling out the vintage suitcase that she always used to store her American Girl dolls. Silently, he unlatches it. I lean in, aware of every detail. His shallow breathing, his trembling lip. It's clear he feels like this is a betrayal of Betsy's trust.

"She'd be so mad," he says again, setting a doll aside, pushing beneath the tiny clothes and pulling out a journal. I resist the urge to grab it from him, to pore over the pages alone. He's offering this to me and I will share it with him. He holds the key to something that is locked away and I want access to it more than anything else in the world.

He opens it, flipping to the first page. It's immediately obvious what it is -- a comic book. Hand drawn by Betsy.

"This was the secret?" I ask as he hands it to me solemnly as if it's the most precious thing he's ever held.

"It's her life story," he tells me. "From her side. She didn't want anyone to know, about the other kids and how they treated her and stuff until it was over. Until she ended it."

Blood drains from my head. "Until she ended it?" Thoughts pound at my skull. Did she want to die? Did my eleven-year-old daughter want to end her life? Did she...

I feel sick, and I lean over, retching the burger and fries and fucking cola on the carpet. My daughter's carpet. She is dead and I am desecrating her room and I hold her secrets in my hand and did she do this to herself? Did she want to end her own life, finish her story? She was eleven years old. She couldn't have done it. Besides... she didn't go into the forest alone.

The coroner said someone did this to her.

Oh god.

Holden is frozen, scared. His eyes panicked and so are mine. I need to understand.

He seems to know I am weak and he stands, quickly, darting from the room. He returns a few seconds later. I'm still gasping for breath as he uses a spray cleaner to deal with my vomit, silently cleaning it up, covering the spot with a towel. He shoves a glass of water in my hand.

I'm shaking as I try to drink it, it sloshes on my shirt. I set it down, it falls. Holden leaps to catch it. One step ahead. In control.

"What did she do?" I ask. My voice a moan, a desperate plea.

He shakes his head, nostrils flared, fear coursing through his face. Refusing to answer. Taking control by refusing to speak.

And I shudder. Because what if I've been all wrong?

19

SIX MONTHS EARLIER

LINDA, Holden's social worker is so pleased, her voice bubbly and optimistic over the phone.

"It's just so wonderful," Linda says. "For so many children it doesn't end on a happy note. But Holden, that boy has been through so much. I remember when we first met, you were so sweet, so patient. So open-hearted to him and his needs. And to see it turn out like this, it's just such a lovely thing to witness."

I swallow, running a sponge over the white marble countertop. "So what happens next?"

"Well let's see," she says, clucking her tongue. "I'll set a date with the judge. You'll need to go to the courthouse in Seattle. Is that a problem?"

"Not a problem," I say, even though I'm thinking about the last time we took a ferry to the city. We went to the Science Museum at the Seattle Center and Holden decided it would be awesome to stay in a bathroom for an hour while we were frantically looking for him.

"It's usually pretty quick," Linda says. "As a family, you'll go before a judge and they will ask you a few questions -- all of you. Your daughter will need to be there too. Of course, you'd want her there. It's a sweet time for family photos with the judge who finalizes the adoption."

"And then?"

Linda laughs warmly. "Then it's signed, sealed, delivered. You'll be sent Holden's new birth certificate, listing you as his mother, in a few months."

"Simple enough," I say, my hands shaking. I should say something. But what? After Mark's public appearance, touting us as adoptive parents, it would be more than a little awkward to back out now. It's all too late.

"I wanted to mention, it was so good to see you at this month's Adoption Support group."

"We enjoyed it," I tell her. "Or at least, we were glad to have gone."

"Oh, good. You know, everyone at the office gushed over Mark's speech that was televised from Olympia. You must be so proud."

I nod. She can't see me, but I *am* smiling, so proud of Mark. He is using his power for good, to enact change. He's taking a play from Gandhi -- *be the change you wish to see in the world.*

"Yes, it was such a special day," I agree. "And the initiatives he worked to pass will do so much for kids like Holden."

"It's all so wonderful. Especially, for a boy with so many behavioral issues. But I know you and Mark are committed to helping him through those."

I swallow. "Right, we're totally committed. We have a Reactive Attachment Disorder specialist we're set to see in a few weeks. I got the name from another parent at the support group."

"See," Linda says. "That's why it's so important to attend those meetings. So you don't feel alone."

We spent ninety minutes with other parents, who live all across Western Washington, giving brief glimpses into one another's struggles -- but there were no true connections. How could there be? Every person sitting in that room, drinking lukewarm coffee and eating store-bought cookies, were all hanging on by a thread. You can't make friends when you're in survival mode -- or if you can, I haven't figured out how.

I can hardly keep things in a good place with my longtime friends, let alone new ones.

On the hour-long drive home from the group, Mark and I vented about Holden. We knew he'd had serious trauma from being left alone in a double-wide for nearly two weeks when he was six. When he'd finally been found by a neighbor. His aunt was dead inside the house, a needle still in her arm. She'd overdosed and just how much of that he'd seen is unknown. But everyone knew he'd seen more than any child ever should. After that, he was put into state custody.

It's been six years.

We refuse to undermine his pain... but now we've taken that pain on for ourselves. And we go in circles -- blaming the system, blaming his birth mom, blaming ourselves, wanting to quit. But by the time we got home, we were back where we started.

We were doing this. Holden deserved a second chance at a forever family. Betsy loved him. And we wanted to learn *how* to love him -- really love him. We'd gotten out of the car at Trista and Jeff's house to pick up the kids, in a positive place. Hopeful. We held hands. Smiling. We could do this, *we're* doing this.

Holden was outside Jeff and Trista's large bungalow. A giant stick in his hand, lashing against the trunk of their cedar tree. His eyes were narrowed, black rings, hollow.

"Hey, buddy," Mark said, stepping toward him, hands raised, both of us on immediate high alert, wanting to deescalate whatever was going on.

The moment Holden saw Mark, he dropped the stick. Relief on his face -- the kind we never, ever see.

"We can go now," Mark said. "We don't have to stay here."

Holden huffed, walked toward us. "Good. I want to go home."

Mark and I looked at one another, my chest pounding.

Home. Holden called our house home for the very first time.

The arguing on the car ride home from the adoption support meeting felt miles away, the struggle forgotten.

Home.

Holden didn't hate us. He wanted to go home.

"Okay," I said, breathless. "We just need to go inside and talk to Jeff and Trista, and get Betsy. Then we can stop and grab ice cream on the way home.

That sound good?" I was going to celebrate this victory and I wasn't going to let anything get in my way.

Holden's face fell. "I'll just wait out here."

"Why?" Mark asked, but immediately I knew something had happened. Holden made a one-eighty in two seconds flat.

In Trista and Jeff's house, the energy was off and alarm bells started ringing in my mind. Trista was frazzled, her normally shiny hair was in a messy bun, her kitchen was a tornado and I could smell burned grilled cheese in the air.

"You're back," she said eyes wide with relief, pouring a glass of red wine as she said hello.

"Sorry, did something happen?" I asked, hugging Betsy, who grimaced - telling me that yes, something *had* happened.

"Hey, kids," Mark said, stepping in just like he had promised to do after the student conference last month. "Let's get your stuff and head to the car, let Mom say goodbye."

"Thanks, Trista," Betsy said, giving my dear friend a warm hug. I didn't see her husband or son anywhere. "Tell Levi I hope he's feeling better."

"I will, sweetheart." She kissed Betsy's head.

Betsy ran out of the house with Mark and I took a deep breath. "What happened?"

"There was a *thing*. Levi and Holden got in a fight over the PlayStation. Holden threw his controller at Levi."

"Oh shit, I'm so sorry."

Trista's features were smooth, expressionless. "It broke his nose. The controller. Jeff took him to the ER."

At that moment, I wanted to hide. An ache was growing in the back of my throat. Couldn't we just have five minutes to celebrate Holden calling our house his home? Couldn't we just sit with that for a hot second?

The answer was no. Trista wasn't having any of it -- her face was stony, the half-empty bottle of wine told me she wanted to drink her feelings right now, not talk them out.

We'd never fought, never felt a divide. Now, though, she wouldn't even look at me.

I left, tears stinging my eyes. When I jumped out of the car at Central Grocers and filled a basket with quarts of ice cream, hot fudge, bright red maraschino cherries and a can of whipped cream -- I remembered something someone at the adoption support meeting had said.

A woman who had adopted a sibling group clasped her hands and spoke solemnly. It was like a prayer, the way she said it. Reverent.

"The old life is over," she said, head bowed. "The friends I had moved on. This choice we've made costs so much. It's not for the faint of heart. But sometimes, my heart still feels like it's breaking. After all this time. Not just for myself, not just for my kids. But for all of it. The beautiful mess that is unconventional love."

She wasn't someone I would have thought I had much in common with. She was fifteen years older than me, short hair, no makeup, wearing sweatpants, a plastic watch. But she was eloquent. She was strong.

She was a veteran and I was so, so new. I hadn't earned many badges yet. This woman had wisdom dripping from her and I sat up straighter, looked closer. Wished my life didn't feel so messy, so I had space for her, wished she had space for me.

I watched her drive away after the meeting in a fifteen-passenger van, bumper stickers covering the back doors. Coexist. Think Globally, Act Locally. Love Is Love.

As I watched my celebratory sundae toppings roll down the conveyor belt, I thought of the woman's words. Her friends were gone. This choice had cost so much.

Was Trista gone? Was this choice Mark and I had made too much for our friendship to withstand?

I paid for the groceries, blinked my tears away. I didn't know where things would land with Trista -- but tonight I was choosing my family. And Holden was my family now. We chose him.

Linda is still on the phone, asking if I have any more questions about the adoption proceedings.

"No, Linda, I'm good. I know we're in for a lot with Holden, but we're committed to this. To him." I look around the kitchen, seeing the newspaper reminding me of something else. "Oh, Linda, I wanted to mention. The *Seattle Times* contacted us about running a story once the adoption is final."

"Wow, that's amazing."

"Mark's speech got great feedback from so many people and when the *Times* called, I was really pleased. The first time I saw Holden's face was in the Tuesday's

Child article. So to give back like this, share our story, feels really great."

Linda congratulates us once more before hanging up. I set down my phone with unfamiliar warmth spreading through me.

I understand the cost. The weight of this choice. I'm not making it blindly. I'm going in with my eyes wide open. Broken noses heal. Friendships can be rekindled. School drama can be dealt with.

After all, what is the worst thing that can happen?

20

PRESENT

HOLDEN IS STANDING, paralyzed. The journal is in my hand, his words hanging like a noose around my neck. *Until she ended it.*

"Please, I need you to talk to me Holden, okay?" I lift my eyebrows, walking slowly but deliberately toward him. "What did you mean when you said she didn't want anyone to know until she ended it?"

Holden's eyes are hollow and dark. Bruised. Like a grave. "She wanted to finish the story before she showed you. Explained it to you."

"Why?" I'm careful here, don't want to scare him away. Mark is at Tom's office. Right now, we're alone. And I need answers.

"She thought... She was scared that if you knew, you'd..."

I drop my head back, wanting to shake him by the shoulders and make him speed it up, his story. The memories. Whatever he knows about my daughter.

"Scared I'd what?"

He looks in my eyes. "Scared you'd send me away."

"I don't understand."

Holden clenches his fist, breathing heavy. He steps toward me, grabbing the journal from my hand. Flipping the colorful pages. "She thought... She thought you'd think it was my fault."

"Was it?" I ask, my words like venom and I know the moment I speak them they were the wrong ones. I am so stupid, so damn flawed. Weak. Not a strong mother who earned her badges. My daughter is dead and this boy -- my son-- is looking at me with piercing eyes as if he wants to stab me with his truth.

He knows whatever he is holding back will hurt me. Will make me bleed. But I left my heart on the floor of the trail a week ago, when Betsy's body was found at the bottom of the ravine. There is nothing left to hurt. It's all gone, washed away with the rain.

"She thought if you knew how bad it was, you'd think... you'd think I was taking too much attention from her. Making things too hard. That it would make you take back the adoption."

My stomach drops. "Holden, you can't take back adoptions. This is final. Forever. You are my son and I don't know what you did, or she did, but tell me, tell me you didn't do something... Something that hurt her."

Holden starts sobbing, his shoulders wracked and he falls to the floor, his arms and face buried in the blankets on her bed. He pounds his fists against her mattress, angry and broken and I sit down, beside him. I may not know what he needs ninety percent of the time, but right now I know he needs boundaries. To be wrapped in arms that will steady him. Ground him. Remind him that he isn't lost in the world, alone anymore. He is here. Here. *Home.*

"I did hurt her, Em. I hurt her," he sobs. "It's my fault. All of it."

I'm shaking, heart pounding, terrified and yet feeling so close to an answer, a reason. Some sort of sense in this mess. I force myself to speak in measured breaths. "What do you mean, your fault?" I ask, dizzy at the possibility. That I am wrong. That the world at large is right. That my son is a murderer.

"If you hadn't brought me home," he says, trembling, "she would never have been so sad. So bullied."

"What do you mean? Bullied?"

Holden looks up, wiping his eyes. They are rimmed in red, the eyes of a boy, not a killer. A boy who is as lost as me.

"After we got in the fight with Jasper and Julia, on Halloween, I went into the woods," he tells me. It's really a plea. "With her. But then I left. I went to the stupid haunted house on a dare. And she was going home. She promised she'd go right home."

"What are you saying?" I ask him, blood coursing through my veins.

"Read it," he says, pointing to the journal that I've dropped on the bed. "It says everything."

I reach for it, shaking, scared. "Just read this?"

Holden nods. There is a knock on the door.

I exhale. I don't have the energy for anyone right now. Holden senses this. He stands and walks to the bedroom window.

"It's Cooper's cruiser," he says. He looks at me then, like he knows. Everything. Not possible, not even Cooper knows everything.

"Are you going to be okay if I go down there and get the door?"

Holden nods. "I'll just go to my room."

I want to say *No Fortnite*, but right now I don't care. It's too late to care about brain damage from addictive video games. His brain is already wired to assume the worst.

Journal in hand, I walk downstairs, open the door. Cooper is alone, and I am alone and he walks in. In my foyer, I fall against him and I know it's wrong. Clinging to him, the past, the things that we said goodbye to. But do you ever really say goodbye to your first love? To the person who helped write your story, pen in hand, the lines so perfect. The history there for anyone to read. You can see it in his eyes, and you can see it in...

I stop thinking those things because if I do, I will fall apart all over again, shatter on this floor, and I need to be strong. Strong for Holden. For Betsy's memory. I need to find the truth and I won't if I collapse. If I crawl into bed and pull back the sheets and hide.

Cooper won't let me fall anyway. He holds me. Tight. So tightly I can feel his palms on my back, five fingers on each hand, holding me in place.

Then his hands are on my face, holding me. My salty tears fall on my lips and I breathe him in and I remember. Everything. I want to turn back time, so much time. I want to start over, go to the beginning. The woman at the adoption group said our old life was over and she was right. It is over. But not Cooper and me. We are a flame that will not die. I won't let it. Neither will he.

I'm shaking so much it scares him, he pulls back, searching my eyes and he is crying too. Cooper's blue eyes are clouded with tears and he has lost so much, but I want him to know he hasn't lost me. I am still here, barely standing, but I am.

"Em," he groans. "Fuck. Em."

Is there such a thing as wrong when your daughter is dead? Is there such a thing as inappropriate when everything has already fallen apart?

"The kids at school killed her," I tell him.

He closes his eyes, steps back. Presses his hands on both my arms as if forcing me to stay put. As if he knows if I had my way, I'd wrap my body around him and my emotions would strangle his heart. I would claw my way back to where we once were.

"Why do you say that?" he asks.

I hold up the journal. "I have proof."

Proof is a strong word. But I need him to listen. "Holden says she was bullied, that she was keeping it a secret so Mark and I wouldn't blame the problems on Holden. He says she was protecting him."

"And what's this?" Cooper asks, listening closely.

"Her journal." I swallow, already regretting that I handed it over. I should read it first, cover to cover, memorizing everything. "Holden says she was wanting to finish it before she showed me."

"You believe him?"

I bite my bottom lip, nodding. "I do."

"Have you read this?" he asks.

I shake my head.

"Fuck, Em."

My chin trembles. Betsy is dead. She drew in this journal, the one Cooper holds, and she is dead. I don't want a life without my baby girl and what am I supposed to do now?

"I suppose we ought to read it then," he says, taking my hand in his, walking to the stairs.

"Where are we going?"

"Her bedroom." Cooper's voice reveals everything.

"You want to go there?"

He nods. "It's time, isn't it, Em?"

I let him lead me, one step at a time.

21

FIVE MONTHS EARLIER

"I JUST CAN'T BELIEVE Trista isn't going to be there," I tell Mark. "I really thought we'd be over this by now."

Mark is fixing the collar on his dress shirt in the bathroom mirror. When he finishes, he moves behind me, helping me with the zipper on my navy dress.

"We knew this was going to change things, Emery," he says, kissing my neck. "But you're right, it's bullshit that she is still angry over the broken nose."

I reach for my lipstick, leaning away from Mark and running a pale pink shade over my lips. "I got a text from Caroline. She said she wanted to talk this morning." I roll my eyes. "My friends are so clueless. They have no idea what my life is like."

"What did you tell her?"

"I said I'd talk to her on the ferry. She and Pete will be on the eleven a.m. too."

"It's gonna be an interesting afternoon." Mark chuckles, shaking his head. "Tom and Rose will be on the boat too."

"You think Holden will hang in there?" I ask.

"It's gonna be a lot," Mark says. "Especially with the *Times* photographer coming."

I twist my lips, suppressing my pride. *The Seattle Times* is going to cover our family today, when the judge bangs his gavel, announcing us an official family when we walk out of the courthouse, the four of us promised to one another forever. It's the day I dreamed about all those months ago when we first brought Holden home. It's all been building up to today.

Finally, we can stop doubting our choice -- once we are committed, there will be no going back. We can stop debating this decision and move on with our life. Everyone in this house is ready for that -- to take a sure step forward.

And we will be getting coverage in the newspaper, our story a beacon of light for all those kids waiting for a family.

"It's going to be great, Em," Mark says, opening the top drawer of his dresser. Turning to me, he adds, "You've been incredible this entire journey, Emery. Your open heart is the reason I've made the initiatives for foster kids in the state. You inspire me, so much. And the kids are so lucky to have you as their mom." He opens a black box, inside rests a ring with two diamonds. "One for Betsy, one for Holden. They are your light, after all."

"Oh, Mark," I say, overwhelmed at his gesture. "This is so unexpected."

He smiles. "That means I did a good job." He slips

the band on my right ring finger and I pull him into a hug.

"Thank you," I say. "For seeing me."

"Always."

Outside we hear Betsy shouting for us. "Mom, Dad, we're gonna be late!"

I look at my watch, we have plenty of time, but I know Betsy has a lot riding on today. She's so anxious to get this over with. She made a countdown out of construction paper rings.

"Sweetie, we're fine," I tell her, walking into the foyer where she waits with Holden. "We'll make the ferry, I promise."

She nods, looking at Holden. "Good, we just want to be sure you aren't canceling anything."

"What would we cancel?" I ask. Holden and Betsy's eye lock. "What is it?" I ask.

"We want to be sure you won't change your mind," she says at last.

"Bets, of course not," I say, pulling both of them into my arms. "We're stuck with one another, for better or for worse."

"Till death do us part," she adds, smiling up at me.

"Little morbid, Bets," I say with a laugh.

"Okay, crew, who is ready to go and do the damn thing?" Mark asks, coming into the foyer, car keys in hand.

"Dad!" Betsy shrieks. "You can't say that word."

But Holden has a small smile on his face and I laugh, feeling a surge of love for everyone in this space.

I wanted our family to catch a break, and finally, today, it looks like we have.

———

ON THE FERRY, Mark takes the kids to get popcorn and I excuse myself to find Caroline. My stomach twists every time I think about the fact that Trista isn't here.

"There you are," Caroline says, finding me on the stairwell leading to the upper deck. "Pete is with Mark and the kids." She gives me a hug when we reach the top of the stairs, the wind whipping at us as we step outside.

"You look great," I tell her.

"Thanks." She grins. "I actually wanted to talk to you about that."

I laugh. "About how great you look? You're crazy, Caroline." I shake my head. Her face is so bright. Glowing. "Oh shit, are you pregnant?"

She claps her hands together. "Yes! I am. Crazy right? I mean it's still early, only eight weeks, but we heard the heartbeat and everything. It's like, really happening."

"Wow, that's amazing," I say, knowing she and Pete have been trying for two years. She's only thirty-one, two years younger than me, so she said she wasn't worried yet about it taking a while. But she is so ready to start this phase of her life.

"That's why I wanted to talk to you," she says, leading me to a row of chairs on the deck. "Not about the pregnancy, but about motherhood."

"What do you mean?" No one ever asks me for parenting advice, but maybe now that my family is growing she sees me in a different light. Less a mess and more a master.

"Well." She rests her hand on mine. "It's just that now that I'm going to be a mother, too, I feel like it's my duty to say something. Talk about the thing no one else wants to say."

I shake my head, not following.

"Look, I know you love Betsy, but whenever I've been with her the last few months, she seems to be closing herself up more and more."

"What do you mean?"

"You know how she struggles with friends, I know you do. But with Holden living with you, it seems to make her more anxious than ever. Jumpier. Less free."

I stiffen at this line of conversation.

"I know I'm not an expert on Betsy--"

I cut her off. "Right, you aren't."

"Maybe not, but I know she is hurting, Em. And it started when that boy came to you."

"When you say 'that boy', are you referring to my son?" I ask, my heart pounding, my eyes tight.

"That's the thing, he doesn't have to be. You can be the mom you always wanted to be if you put a stop to all this," she says.

I gasp, incredulous. "Are you kidding me right now?"

"No, Em. I'm not. I know you don't want to hear this, but it's my job as your friend to tell you what everyone is thinking. What everyone is too scared to say to your face. You're making a mistake."

"A mistake? You think Holden is a mistake?" Tears fill my eyes, anger blooms in my chest. "He may have his flaws, but so do I, Caroline. So do all of us. Give the poor boy a break."

"He doesn't need a break," she says coolly. "He needs to be in a mental institution. He broke Levi's nose."

"It was an accident," I seethe.

She rolls her eyes, resting her hand on her flat belly as if there is a bump. "He never even apologized. You never did either, for that matter. Aren't you ashamed?"

"Damn right we didn't apologize. We won't apologize for what happened. Of course, I wish Levi hadn't gotten hurt and I wish Holden wouldn't have thrown the controller. But Holden's trauma surfaces in all kinds of ways. And stress is a trigger, it might always be that way. And apologizing for it feels like I'd be apologizing for the person he is. And I won't do that."

Caroline looks at me as if she's never seen me before. "You know what is the saddest part of you ruining your life?"

I glare at her. This woman I thought was my ally, my friend. "Try me."

"It's not Holden that will suffer. Not you or Mark. It's Betsy who will pay for this. And you'll have to live with that fact for the rest of your life."

I want to slap her. To shake her. To tell her she is a bitchy friend and a shitty person. But I don't have the energy to fight. I already lost Trista and now I've lost

Caroline and who else am I going to lose before this whole thing is over?

Over.

The truth is it will never, ever be over. We are going to the courthouse to make sure of it.

How dare she.

Holden and Betsy come bounding up the stairwell then, a bag of popcorn in their hands, shrieking with laughter as they throw kernels to the seagulls sweeping toward them, they don't see Caroline or me.

"You know what they say, a bird in the hand is worth two in the bush." Her voice is severe, this woman I would have described as maternal I now see as nothing but ice cold. "You have Betsy, and you're willing to risk it for what? Him?"

Holden runs the length of the ferry, and I know I should tell him to stop running so fast, that he'll get hurt. But the ferry captain does it for me, a voice booming over the speakers. "No running on the vessel."

Holden stops in his tracks, Betsy laughing and reaching for the bag of popcorn, she kneels down, offering pieces to the bird a few feet away. My breath stills as I watch the bird move toward her, eating out of her hand.

"You're running the chance of losing her to attain a boy who should be sent to live at a military camp."

"How dare you," I seethe. I should walk away from Caroline. And I don't want to yell or scream. That is what I've been doing for months with Holden.

But my hand slaps cold against her cheek before I can edit myself. And I'm glad.

Her palm is on her red cheek, my hand stings.

My children see. They step close enough to see the tears in my eyes. Caroline's eyes are slits, her body shakes as Holden steps toward me. Moves in front of me. A single stride and he takes the place as my protector.

"You little shit," Caroline snorts, her words directed at him. "You really have her fooled, don't you?"

Placing my hand on Holden's shoulder, Betsy moves beside me, slipping her hand in mine. I just slapped my best friend across the face in front of my children and I don't give a fuck. Not at all.

We've already been through so much just bringing Holden into our life; I can't handle more drama from the people I think are my friends. I don't have space in my heart to fight.

I need people to wrap me in their arms, to hold me tight. To say I've got this. Chin up, buttercup. Keep on keepin' on.

Right now, Caroline isn't for me. She's against me.

———

SITTING OUTSIDE THE COURTROOM, I refuse to feel sorry for myself -- for what happened with Caroline on the ferry. She isn't here, of course. I don't think I will be seeing her anytime soon. If ever again.

What kind of person says that on the day of their child's adoption? And what, she carries a fetus for a few weeks and now she has the authority to offer me parenting advice?

"It's okay," Mark says, rubbing his thumb over mine, holding my hand tightly. "Try and forget it," he tells me.

After Caroline and I had our conversation on the boat, I pulled Mark aside on the ferry and told him the cliff notes' version of the conversation. He moved quickly, not wanting disagreements to be witnessed in a public place, with cameras on us. "I'll tell Pete they aren't welcome at the courthouse."

"Thank you," I say, wiping my eyes.

"Why did you hit Auntie Caroline?" Betsy asks now, her voice soft, looking around the hallway where we're waiting. Tom and Rose are here, but Caroline and Pete are nowhere to be found.

"Turns out she wasn't a friend, after all."

Holden lifts his chin, nods. He is used to being let down, and I always had a feeling he wasn't the biggest fan of Caroline. Now I understand why. He can read people better than anyone else.

"Should just be ten more minutes," Mark says.

Just then the sound of quickly moving heels click-clacking across the polished floor get our attention. I lift my head in the direction of the noise just as Trista, Jeff, and Levi rush toward us. Carrying bouquets of balloons and flowers.

"Are we too late?" Trista asks. "Did we miss it?"

Levi's nose is still bandaged, Jeff has sweat on his forehead, he mops it away and Trista is gasping for breath.

"Not yet," Bets says. "Ten more minutes."

"Oh, thank god," Trista groans. She walks to Holden, tugging his shoulder to get him to stand.

When he does, she wraps her arms around his stiff body. "I know you might hate me. Might think I'm a wreck. Might think I am too emotional. Too whatever -- but you're stuck with me Holden Gable. For life. Because I'm not going anywhere." She kisses his cheeks and I wipe my eyes and my best friend is here. Here when I need her most.

She pulls Betsy into a hug next. "Look at you, a little sister!"

Betsy laughs. "Only by a month!"

Holden smirks and shrugs. "A month is a month, Bets."

Trista hugs Mark, squeezing his cheeks in a way only she can get away with.

Jeff looks at me his eyebrows raised. "We wouldn't have missed this for the world, Emery. Your bestie just needed to recover."

I nod, and when Trista reaches me. "Family is family," she says. "And I'm sorry I'm not as perfect as Caroline. I screwed up. And I'm sorry. But I love you, Emery. And I think you're the best mom in the whole fucking world."

Holden and Levi laugh, Betsy drops her head in her hands, laughing and slightly mortified. Tom and Rose don't know the drama but are smiling, recognizing that this moment is a tender one, swearwords and all.

"What happens next?" Jeff asks.

A clerk steps into the hall. "The Gable family? Judge is ready for you."

So that is what is next. Promising the things that are already cemented in our hearts.

We stand before the judge, the photographer from the *Seattle Times* in the room, our friends sitting in the old wooden pews of the courtroom. Mark's hand rests on Holden's shoulder, I'm holding the hand of my little girl.

Betsy is in a pale green dress with a full skirt. Holden wears a plaid shirt, untucked, sleeves rolled up. Mark is in his suit and tie. I'm wearing a dress, my new diamond ring glittering. But those things never get noticed in that photograph that runs on the front page of the *Seattle Times*.

In that photo, all you see is a happy family.

A family that came together against all odds.

A family that decided to throw caution to the wind and take a chance. A leap of faith.

A family that said yes instead of no.

Bird in the hand be damned.

22

PRESENT

"JUST LIKE HER MOM," Cooper says, sitting on the floor where Holden and I sat such a short time ago. My vomit is still covered by a towel on the floor. "She is an incredible artist."

"Was," I correct.

"Right, was." Cooper nods, running a hand over his beard. "Where is Holden?"

"Next door, in his room. Playing Fortnite."

He raises his eyebrows. I'm sure he's surprised that I have a video game system in my house. I used to be so old school. That girl seems to have been gone for so long.

I flip through the pages, reading her comic book stories. Trying not to get my wet tears all over the pages.

It's hard. Hard to read. Hard to imagine. Hard to accept. She held so much back, and why?

There are frames of Julia Handler calling her a loser in front of the other girls. Another of Jasper Handler stealing her homework and crumpling it up, putting it in the dumpster behind the school. There is an especially difficult scene where Sam Middleton pushes her to the ground, Holden helping her up, Sam pushing her down again. In one, with the date of Valentine's Day, the illustration is of Cory Devon writing a note at his school desk, with Holden and Betsy's name on it, a heart between them.

"What assholes," Cooper says, clenching his fists as if trying to gain control. "And I mean, I get that drawing and writing can be therapeutic, but why not tell you and Mark? Why keep it hidden?"

I run my hand over the pages, equally confused. "Holden said she was scared if we knew, we'd send Holden away. That we'd worry we weren't giving her enough attention."

"But after the adoption was finalized, why not tell you then?"

I blow out the air, lost on that one. But Holden clears his throat, standing in the doorway. A shiver runs over me. How long has he been there, listening? Watching.

"She didn't tell you because that's when you and Mark started..." Holden tugs at his hair. "That's when you guys ...."

I exhale, feeling like this is all my fault somehow. "That's when we started fighting."

Holden nods. "She thought you guys were going to get a divorce."

I feel Cooper stiffen beside me. I can't bear to look at him. But I know he feels what I feel. Shame. Regret. Desire.

Not wanting to think about that with my son and ex here, I close the journal, hold it up. "These kids, they have something to do with Betsy's death. I know they do."

Cooper shakes his head. "I know you want to blame someone -- but Em, it wasn't them. It wasn't some group plot against her."

"What?" I scoff. "Did you not read her stories? Didn't you see the video? They were bullying her the night of her death. They were the reason she went into the woods. The reason she's gone!" I'm shrieking now, verging on hysterical and I don't care. These kids need to pay for what they did to my little girl. How dare they treat her this way?

"Emery," Cooper says, grabbing me by the shoulders. The journal falls, Holden scoops it up. "They have alibis. Their stories check out. There was surveillance that proves it."

"Proves what?" I ask, the hair on my body sticking straight up like a dog on high alert.

"Proves these kids went home, most of them at least."

"What do you mean, most of them?"

"The Handlers' and Middletons' homes have security cameras. The recording shows the kids at home minutes after the video was taken on the phone."

"And Cory Devon? Marcie's son. What about him?"

"We don't know yet, Emery. But we'll know more soon enough."

"Know more how?"

Cooper clenches his jaw, runs his palms on his pants. "There was skin under her nails, Em."

Holden moans, and so do I.

"No." I shake my head, not wanting to believe it. That she struggled. That she fought back. That she tried to get away from the person who murdered her.

"I'm so sorry, Em," Cooper says, standing.

"Where are you going?" I ask, grasping for him.

"I have to get to work on this. Officers will be bringing everyone who could possibly be involved into the station to collect samples. It's going to be a long few days."

"We'll have to give samples?" Holden asks, eyes widening, voice panicked. My heart quickens. Why does he fear that? What does he have to hide?

"Yeah, Holden, it's protocol. It doesn't mean anyone thinks you're guilty. Your mom and dad have to do it as well. Okay?"

He nods, then with a shaky breath he adds, "Okay. I just really hate police stations."

I close my eyes, knowing his story. That he sat in a station for hours the night he was found abandoned. They couldn't get a social worker to come in for half the night and Holden, a six-year-old boy at the time, sat waiting for someone to take care of him. Every therapist and psychiatrist he's ever seen says this is his trigger story. The thing that always comes up when talking about his past. A sterile office, a cold chair. A loud clock ticking.

He doesn't want to go to the station, not because he is scared of the DNA results -- but because the station itself scares him. He is still a little boy. Only eleven. Fragile and alone and I doubt him at every turn.

I am the real monster here.

No. I'm not. I'm not the one who committed a crime.

But someone did. And that someone will pay.

"Just tell us when we need to come in," I tell Cooper, leading him downstairs and to the front door.

"I'll be in touch, Em," he says, aware of Holden a few feet away.

He leaves and I turn to Holden. "You want to go with me to get dinner?"

"More burgers and fries?"

I shake my head. "How about Chinese?" I place an order before we leave the house.

We get in the car, and I text Mark from the car. *Where are you? We're headed to Royal Palace to get food to go. See you soon, I hope.*

We get to the restaurant quickly, and when I get out of the car, I ask Holden if he wants to come in with me. He shakes his head. "I'll wait here. I don't want to see people. They think I'm a killer."

I flinch at his honesty. "Okay, I'll just be a sec."

As I walk through the parking lot, I notice a car in the distance, across the street at a motel. It's a car I know well because it is my husband's. I frown, looking at my phone. Mark didn't text me back. My phone settings tell me when someone has received a message. He hasn't. He has no idea I am here, getting dinner with Holden.

I stop, looking around for him. I see him at a hotel room door, the last room on the bottom floor, his hand on the doorknob as if trying to force it open. The four-lane highway separates us, and he won't hear me if I call out his name.

My phone buzzes, scaring me. I look at the number. It's Royal Palace. "Hello?"

"Yes, Ma'am. Your food is ready."

I pull open the door of the restaurant, I quickly get the food, but when I get back outside, I see Mark's car peeling away in the distance. In my own car, I try to focus on getting back to the house. But what the hell was that about? What was Mark doing at a seedy hotel? My eyes blur with tears as I consider the options, does he have a lead on who may have killed Betsy? But if so, why wasn't he with the police?

"That was Mark across the street, wasn't it?" Holden asks, his words shocking me out of my thoughts.

I look ahead, turning on the ignition. "I didn't see anything."

"Yes, you did," Holden says. "What was he doing there?"

Turning to him, I try to see the situation from his eyes. His sister is gone, the accusations against him are horrific. His life has always been chaos and for this to be added to it feels too cruel. He is just a boy.

"I don't know why he was there, Holden," I admit. "Right now, I don't think I know much of anything."

"Maybe it's a lead. Maybe he knows something. We should go look."

I shake my head. "No, we're not doing that. I could call Cooper, but I want to talk to Mark first."

"You love him, don't you?" Holden asks.

"Who?"

"Cooper."

I turn on the blinker, avoiding the question. Finally, the silence hangs too heavy. "Why do you say that?"

"You look at him like you love him."

"You pay attention to everything, don't you?" I silently hope he hadn't just seen whatever that was across the street. He adjusts the seatbelt in the passenger seat.

"Cooper and I used to date, for a lot of years," I tell Holden.

"Why did you break up?"

"My dad died. And sometimes when you lose people you love, it changes you."

Holden unrolls the window. The frosty December air sweeping over us. "That's what's happening to me."

I grip my steering wheel. "What do you mean?"

"Losing Bets. It's changing me."

I reach over and clasp his hand. My first instinct is to agree, to say that it's changing me too. But is it?

"Holden, maybe losing Bets is actually revealing your true colors. Showing you who you really are."

Holden sighs, still looking out the window. "Then I've always been a lot braver than I thought I was."

"Yeah, Holden, I think that's true. I think you are."

23

FIVE MONTHS EARLIER

SITTING IN MY CAR, in the pick-up lane at the Montessori school, I scroll through my phone. I'm desperate to numb myself from what I found earlier this afternoon in Holden's room. I'm going to pretend it was nothing more than a blip. Not my reality. Denial has become my coping mechanism.

My fingernail polish chipped and in desperate need of a manicure. I have been gaining new followers on my Instagram account every day due to my hashtags -- #adoptionjourney #adoptionrocks #dailymotherhood -- among others. People love a happy ending.

But I know this isn't the end. Our honeymoon period never really began and it's certainly over if it had. Holden is pushing every single button of mine in an effort to drive me up the freaking wall. It's working. Leaving the shower running for an hour after he steps out of it. Misplacing his homework every day. Ignoring me when I come to the school to volunteer for the end of year school day.

Now it's the last day of school -- the start of summer begins in thirty minutes when the end of the day bell rings. I'm extra early, but it beats being late, and right now, every parent at this school is watching me. Waiting for me to fail. And God, it's like they are vultures circling. Like they can smell my defeat.

Caroline ran into me last week as I was walking into the café we used to frequent. She was leaving with Jenna and Arie Middleton. Jenna rested a hand on my arm. "We were just talking about Mark's feature in the *Seattle Times*. Such a surprise."

I swallowed, not knowing what angle they were going to take with this. "What do you mean, Jenna?" I asked, not wanting to look at Caroline. Not having spoken to her since the adoption day.

"Everyone is just kind of surprised is all."

I shake my head, wanting a latte so much more than I want to be having this conversation. "Stop being cryptic. What's your point?"

"Holden joining your family seemed surprising at the time," Arie says. "But now we understand."

"Understand what?" I ask, my voice turning icy as the conversation continues.

"That it was about publicity," Jenna says with a saccharine sweet voice. "For Mark's campaign."

"Fuck you," I say under my breath. "Seriously, you know nothing about my family."

Arie's lips twist, her eyes meeting Caroline's as if they have already discussed this at length. "At least if he wins the seat, you'll move to DC."

I just turned, looking at Caroline. The woman who

has seen my life up close and personal in ways few people have. And this is how the friendship ends. "You're better than this, Caroline."

She pursed her lips, adjusting the purse on her shoulder. The confidence of the Mommy Tribe beside her. Her eyes though tell a different story. Deep down she is a good person. I know she is. But I can't rely on shared history anymore. I don't have time for that. Not when my life is built on shifting sand. I wish I could brave the rising tide with her, but right now I'm struggling to keep my own head above water.

They left without another word and I went into the restroom, splashing cold water on my face, my hands gripping the counter. Their words reinforcing my own doubt.

Now, as I wait in the school pick up line, Jenna and Arie are in the distance with the other Mommy Tribe mothers and I'm here, replaying the conversation at the café in my mind. How the hell am I going to get through this summer? Betsy and Holden are signed up for summer sleepaway camp, Cabo for a week, another week on Orcas Island in the San Juans, headed to Vermont for another... but all of it makes me want to take a nap. A very long nap.

And I resent that. Holden turns eleven in July and Betsy turns eleven in August. She's growing up. And I want to treasure these moments, the amazing trips we have planned but with Holden there, it won't be the same. It's not that he ruins everything... he just makes everything really fucking difficult.

So yes, maybe he does ruin things. With him, even

the simplest event becomes a thing. He won't leave the car. He won't talk. Won't eat. Won't make eye contact.

It makes everything dramatic. And it's so tiring, always waiting for him to explode or implode. His tactics depend on his mood and I can never ever seem to anticipate which it's going to be.

His behavior makes me want to take Betsy and grab last-minute plane tickets and fly to Paris and never look back until September. To walk through the Louvre with my little girl and eat frites and smile and laugh and take selfies on the Eiffel tower. It makes me want to make memories I know I could treasure. Why spend the summer months traveling when the memories will be filled with regret? Why do it at all? Why not just ship Holden off to a camp for three months and call it a day?

Even contemplating or dreaming that makes me feel disgusting. What kind of mother would prefer her son absent than at home?

The adoption was finalized such a short while ago, but ever since then, things have changed.

Holden is temperamental.

Betsy is withdrawn.

Mark is absent.

It's like everything has been run through a paper shredder, becoming slivers of what they were supposed to be. I thought the *Seattle Times* feature on us would make everyone feel more connected, more together, but ever since we left the courthouse, it's like we're on edge.

A different kind than before. An edge that is fragile, that could be ripped in half. An edge that has me sitting in the car scrolling through an Instagram feed on my phone of perfect families and perfect vacations and perfect lives. Snapshots that capture some version of perfection I am also guilty of trying to attain.

I never will. I'm one selfie away from revealing the truth. My handbags may be designer, but my perfect family is fake. My house may be lovely, but my heart is cold and cruel.

I'm a mother but I feel like a monster.

Trista bangs on my car window. I press the button and it slides down. "What's up?"

I wonder how critically she will look at me. I have coffee stains on my tank top, my car is a mess -- to-go cups piling up. Not a stitch of makeup, and I think I needed something stronger than my organic deodorant today. If Mark walked into the house right now he'd have an OCD meltdown, spraying every surface with Clorox. But bleach can't fix anything right now. You can't wipe this mess away.

The mess happening at my house is not surface level; it's deep in our bones, our marrow, our blood. You can't clean it. You can't fix it. It's all too broken. Holden is too broken.

"Did you hear?" she asks.

I haven't heard a single thing about anything. I spent the morning removing a cache of special treasures from under Holden's bed. Four screwdrivers, two pocket knives, a broken mirror from an old compact of mine, and a package of razor blades.

Welcome to summer!

"Hear what?" I ask.

Trista winces. "It's Caroline. She lost the baby."

"Oh, shit," I say, my shoulders falling. I may be angry with her, over the friendship but a miscarriage isn't something I'd wish on any woman.

"I guess you haven't spoken to her?"

"Not since I saw her at the café."

"I wish you'd make up."

I shake my head. "It's over. She thinks Holden was a mistake. That Mark and I did this as a publicity stunt. She's a fucking bitch, Tris."

Trista lowers her chin to her chest. "I miss the old days -- when we'd all go to get coffee, the group chats -- the regular stuff."

"Me too," I say quietly. "You know she sent Betsy a gift card to the bookstore to buy some books for summer reading. Right after I saw her at the café last week. Isn't that weird?"

Trista shrugs. "Does it feel weird? Maybe it's her olive branch."

"I just hate how she chooses who gets her attention. With kids, it should be equal. It's not that I don't appreciate her sending Bets things, but she didn't send Holden a gift card, which really pisses me off. I know he notices that stuff. "

Trista exhales. "I think she just loves Betsy and can't see beyond that. I don't think she is trying to hurt Holden."

"I think she's jealous of me, for having Betsy. I think she wanted her for her own." The sentence is painful to say because my own grasp on Betsy seems to be slipping. She's been in a puddle of tears as often as Holden has been shouting. Everyone is falling apart.

"That's kind of dark," Trista says, with a sharp laugh.

"I guess I've gone dark, Tris. Can you handle it?" I lift my eyebrows, smirking. "It doesn't matter, I don't want to talk to Caroline now anyways."

"She called so very upset about the miscarriage." Trista pushes her sunglasses to the top of her head. "She was so ready to be a mom."

I remember the day of the adoption so vividly when she told me her news. It changed everything between Caroline and me. "I know I should be sad, but I still feel so raw about the whole thing."

"Maybe I shouldn't have told you about her losing the baby."

"It's fine, Trista. I mean getting a call like that *is* intense. I bet you're drained."

She twists her lips. "I can't believe how shitty she was to Holden."

My eye catches someone in the distance. Cooper. He's walking toward my car. I lick my lips. Exhale.

Trista notices. "Shit, you still have a thing for him, don't you?"

"It's not like that."

She lifts an eyebrow. "Like what?"

"Like... anything."

Cooper taps on the passenger window. I open it.

"Hey there, Deputy," Trista says, leaning further into my car through the driver's window.

"Hey, Trista."

"You know my name, I feel so fancy."

I look at her with wide eyes that say shut up.

Cooper grins. "I volunteer at the school. I knew you were Levi's mom."

"You volunteer here?" Trista asks, pursing her lips.

Cooper nods. "Yeah, I've been doing lessons in the classes on bullying, safety, how to ask for help. It was Em who suggested I volunteer."

Trista nods. "Oh, yeah, of course. Levi mentioned those. Just didn't realize it was you." She smirks playfully. "He said this cool police officer came to school. Had no idea he meant Em's Coop."

"Haha," Cooper deadpans. But her words, *Em's Coop* don't go unnoticed by him. I think we all realize it at the same time. The simple truth.

"Anyways, I'll leave you two to it. I gotta go drop off a form at the office." Trista kisses my cheek. "Love you."

"Love you more," I call after her. With her gone, my attention turns to Cooper. He looks so handsome with the afternoon sun filtering through his light hair, his eyes blue as the sky. So clear. So off-limits. "What's up?"

"I wanted to check to see how you were. Haven't seen you around in a while."

I run a hand through my greasy hair. "Things are fine."

"Well, that's shitty."

"I said things are fine."

He cocks an eyebrow at me. "Em, I know what your fines mean."

I swallow. He knows me too well. "What do they mean?"

"It means you're in survival mode."

"What do you know about my survival mode?"

Cooper's eyes rest on mine. Memories of us walking into my father's house. Finding him in a bathrobe, an empty bottle of whiskey at his side. The remote control in his lap. The television blaring the news. "I know you, Em. I know that when things are rocky you bite your nails. You forget to shower. You lose sleep."

"At least we know you're not in survival mode," I say the edge in my voice so obvious.

"Right." He runs a hand through his hair. "Because if it were me holding on by a thread, I'd already be pushing everyone away, running."

After Dad died, Cooper fell apart. When I needed him most. He got a job as a police officer across the state, in Spokane. He came back once, six months after he ended things -- and I thought... I thought maybe he was coming back for me. He came to Seattle for training for the police department. I knew that. That he came for work, not for me, but still. I hoped.

So, we shared one night. One night where I offered him everything, all over again. I remember rolling over in my bed the next morning, I'd only gone on a few dates with Mark at this point. And yes, I liked Mark's company, but I loved Cooper's. Cooper knew me in ways no one else did and it made me feel safe.

But the bed was empty. He left only a note.

I'm sorry Em. I'm just not ready to go back to the past.

That night I went out with Mark and decided he would be my future.

I instinctively run my fingers under my eyes. "Our history is old, Coop. Maybe I've changed."

"People don't change."

I bite my lip. "You've never adopted a child if you think that. Holden has changed me. And losing my Dad changed me, too."

He doesn't buy it. "No. Those things just reveal who you really are. Who you've always been."

I want to gloss over the sentiment. I don't like the implications. But I can't let it go. "If people don't change, why did you come back to town?"

Cooper runs a hand over his beard. "I ran because I was scared not because I didn't want you. Want us. "

"I needed you then."

"Do you still need me?" His voice is raw, the way my heart feels and still, after everything, I know he understands me in a way no one else ever will.

"I've always needed you."

"Can you ever forgive me?"

My heart stops on his words because I know what I have done. He isn't the only person here who needs forgiveness.

Shakily, I look in his eyes. "I forgave you a long time ago."

He exhales. "Fuck, Em. I love you. Even if I don't deserve you."

I press my fingers to my temples. The kids will be out soon. "Why?"

"Why do I love you?" Cooper gives me a half smile so full my heart aches. Mark is so distant. So reserved. So intense. "God, Em. Don't ask things that will make this harder for me than it already is."

"Why did you move back?"

He leans into the car. "For you, Em. It's all for you."

My chest tightens. There's a thickness in my throat and I prepare for an onslaught of tears. "Things aren't fine."

"I know." Cooper's eyes stay fixed on me.

"Holden is a mess." Admitting it to him now allows the emotions I pushed down to surface. My hands shake from the coffee I've been chugging all day. My voice, when I try to speak, sounds choked, rattled. "He had all these ... these weapons, under his bed. Under his mattress."

Cooper's eyes narrow. "What do you mean, weapons?"

"Like weird stuff. It was really ... God, I don't even know how to say it. I just got really overwhelmed and decided it wasn't a big deal. But like..." Tears fill my eyes. I press my palm to my throbbing forehead. I held it back with Tris, my best friend -- I've been holding so much back for so long. The weight of Holden. He's such a heavy burden and yet I can hardly admit it to anyone. "It was freaky, Coop."

"What did you find, Em," he says, his voice so calm it scares me.

I wipe my eyes, meeting his gaze, forcing myself to speak without shaking. "Screwdrivers and broken glass and razor blades." Saying it aloud makes me realize that it's actually a really big deal.

But everything with Holden is a big deal. Nothing is simple when it comes to him.

"When did you find this?" Cooper asks, face tight.

"An hour ago? I was cleaning the house and changing his sheets and stumbled on it." Tears streak my face and I brush them away. The schoolhouse bell rings. Welcome to summer. "I tried to call Mark but he didn't answer. I just." I shake my head. "What am I supposed to do?"

"You need to take him to the hospital. The ER. He needs a psych evaluation, Emery."

My lips tremble. "I don't think he's dangerous. I'm not scared of him, I mean, I don't think he'd hurt me."

"I know, Em. But this isn't about what you think. It's what professionals think. Maybe he won't hurt anyone else, but he might hurt himself."

I blink back tears. When did this become my life?

"I love him," I tell Cooper.

"I know you do, Em," he says calmly. Steady. Safe. "That's why you're going to let me take Betsy over to Trista's, where she'll wait for you until you are ready to come to get her. And you're going to take your son to the hospital. You'll sit with him. And wait for him. Because you love him."

"I do, Cooper. I love him."

Cooper smiles, not a half smile and not a full smile. It's a smile that says he understands. That he sees. That he knows. Knows me.

I see the kids running toward my car and Cooper stands, eyes locked on me. "You love him because you're his mom, Em. He needs you to fight for him. If you don't, who will?"

24

PRESENT

IT'S BEEN two days since everyone gave their DNA samples at the police station. Two days of pacing. Anxiously waiting. Feeling like no one is doing enough. Anything.

I need answers.

When I asked Mark why he was at the hotel, he explained he was there to meet with his manager, Ryan. I felt stupid the moment he said his name. Ryan was often coming to town for a night or two to meet Mark at his local office. "We were going over some statements for the press. I didn't tell you because the last thing you want to think about right now is PR."

It's a relief, that he can handle all of this. Articles seem to be updating on the hour about the investigation. And it feels like news sources had a better pulse on the situation than I did. Not that they are reporting anything factual. This morning I read an online interview that Jenna gave the local station, saying that at times like this, mothers needed to stick together. I turned off my phone and shoved it in my purse. Now though, I reach for it, switching it on.

No one is moving fast enough for me, including Tom, our attorney. I text him, asking for an update, and he calls back right away.

"Hey, Emery," he says. "You were the next person on my list of people to call."

"My daughter's body is sitting at the morgue," I tell him. "She needs to be buried." We need to mourn her -- not bite our nails to the quick, waiting for someone to be arrested.

"I know, and I wish I had better news."

"That means you have something? A lead?"

"Not exactly, but I was wondering if you could tell me about Holden's history a bit more. I have his files from DSHS, and it's clear his biological aunt died years ago. His only other known living blood relative is his mother then, correct?"

"Right."

"And have you had any contact with her?"

"Not directly."

"What do you mean, not directly?"

"She sent Holden a package a month ago. There was a letter in it."

"And did you tell anyone about that? The police?"

"No. When we finalized the adoption, we forwarded our PO Box to his social worker. We wanted his birth mom to send him letters if she wanted to. But it was strange."

"What was?"

I swallow. "She sent it to our house."

"Do you still have the letter?"

"Holden threw it away. He wasn't interested in it."

"Alright, did it have a forwarding address?"

"No, not that I remember. It was a really stressful time when I got it and I didn't even really think much about it. Should I have? Is she connected somehow?"

"No, not at all, Emery. I'm just trying to check every possibility out and make sure Holden's case is strong."

"Alright," I say shakily. "And the DNA results will prove his innocence."

"Right. But Emery," Tom says gently. "Prepare yourself."

"For what?"

"The results might show something you don't want to see."

"Holden is innocent. The results will prove that."

"I know," Tom backtracks. But it's too late. I hear his voice crack, his doubt.

I hang up the phone, searching the house for Mark. I find him in the kitchen. Officer Margot is here, outside with Holden, playing basketball. I'm grateful for the support of the local precinct. Everyone is on edge and having their help is a relief.

"We need a new attorney," I say.

"What?" Mark looks up from his laptop. "Em, Tom is the best man for this."

"He doesn't believe in Holden. He thinks..." I shake my head, tears filling my eyes. "He thinks it's Holden."

Mark frowns. "Have you spoken with him recently?"

I hold up my phone. "We just talked. He was going

on about Holden's birth mom and wanting to know anything about her."

Mark closes his computer, nodding tightly. "That's good. Maybe she's a lead, Emery."

"It's going to be another dead end," I say frustrated at the lack of progress. "Everyone's testimony is checking out," I say to Mark. "The DNA will show Holden's innocence and then what?"

"We need to keep an open mind, Emery. I know it's not what you want to hear."

"Maybe there was an unidentified lunatic roaming the woods on Halloween."

"Maybe, Emery. But we both know that idea is slim to none." Mark's eyes sear into mine. His level of agitation has grown over the last two days. Everyone has been on edge since we went to the police station for the DNA swabs. Holden was shaking the entire time, Mark was crying silently, same as me. We're all doing a shit job of holding it together. Someone killed Betsy and no one knows who. It's tearing us all up inside.

"I don't think it was a psychopath on the loose, Emery," Mark says flatly. "I think it was Holden."

I gasp. "What? No. We've been over this."

He raises his hands, and I shake my head, angry that he would entertain this now. "His story is the only one with zero alibi. You were at the house with Trista and Jeff. I was in Olympia. No one was unaccounted for."

I know those facts are true enough. Trista and Jeff had finished off a bottle of white wine, I was nursing seltzer and lime, and we're laughing over a trashy show on Bravo, Jeff happily manning the door when kids rang the doorbell asking for candy. Levi was out with the fifth and sixth graders from the Montessori school, my kids were trick or treating as a pair, something they had begged us to allow.

Then Holden came home without his sister. Mark drove like a madman when Cooper called to tell him what had been discovered. Our daughter's body. Mark had been at the capital and when he came home, he ran into the woods, finding me on the trail with Jeff and the officers. The rain had started by then and I wanted it to wash me away. Mark helped me stand, letting me fall against him. Cooper was behind him and I hated myself. Hate myself, for not pushing Mark aside, for not going to Cooper.

"It couldn't have been him, Mark. He went to the abandoned house on Perry after the fight at the edge of the woods."

Mark's eyes are red, bloodshot, and I know he's as exhausted as me. "No one saw him, Emery. And everyone else, everyone who was close to our family, is accounted for."

"Not everyone." I glare, hating him for assuming the worst with our son. "What was Caroline doing?"

Mark pulls back, clearly not expecting me to say her name. "Caroline?"

"Yeah, I was thinking... She's always been so intense with Betsy, maybe she got..."

"What? Careful, now, with what you're implying."

"Maybe it got twisted into something *strange*."

"You think Caroline went into the woods on

Halloween night and smashed a rock against your daughter's head? Caroline, who wears a strand of pearls and walks a poodle."

"It's a Labradoodle, and not everyone is what they seem on the surface."

Mark snorts, setting down his coffee. "That's the goddamn truth."

I scoff. "What does that mean?"

"It means you sure weren't what you were selling." Mark crosses his arms, smug with disgust. "When we met it was all an act. You flaunted your sexuality until I took the bait. Once I did, it was hook, line, and sinker. You played me, Emery."

My body tenses. Mark and I don't do this. Lay it all out there -- but we are now. "It was not an act. I loved you, Mark."

"Loved." He scoffs. "That's what this is to you? Our daughter being in the past tense isn't enough -- you want our marriage to be relegated there too?"

Tears well, fear pools in my belly. "That isn't what I meant."

"Isn't it though? Aren't you just waiting for me to go, to give up on us? To let you have the life you really want with him?"

I shake my head; my fingers grip the countertop. "I didn't say that."

"You didn't have to, Emery." He shoves away from the counter and my body shakes, coursing with heat. He made love to me in the shower only a few days ago, now he is looking at me as if I'm disgusting. But was it me who played him?

I run my hand over my eyes, wiping the tears aside. "I think Caroline was mad I wouldn't let Betsy sleep-over at her house," I say, my breath shaky and voice small. "I think she lost it."

"You really think Caroline killed Betsy?" Mark looks at me like I'm a monster. But isn't that what I already think I am?

"Yes."

"I'm leaving, I'm going to stay at the Cottage Inn, where my parents are staying. I need space, Emery. You've lost... You've lost all control. It's time you took a hard look at Holden and really think his motives through. Because blaming a sweetheart like Caroline when you're living with the enemy is just fucked up."

"You're really leaving me?" I ask. Our daughter isn't even buried.

"Isn't that what you wanted?"

Mark tucks a strand of hair behind my ear. "I thought you were a girl who was nostalgic for the past. I was the fool who never made the connection." Mark shakes his head. "You wanted to rewind time and go back to before you met me. You wanted Cooper. You've always wanted him, Emery."

I shake my head, reaching for him, but he is already gone. And really, when was he here? For months before Betsy died, he pulled further and further away, leaving everything to rest on my shoulders -- on my conscience.

The only reason we've been close this last week is that our daughter died. Her death drew us together but the threads are already being tugged loose.

Ready to unravel.

25

FOUR MONTHS EARLIER

CABO WAS A DISASTER. Seven days at a resort and no quantity of margaritas could drown out the reality. Traveling to another country was way too much for Holden. He craves routine. Regular. Familiar.

He needs a plan and he needs us to stick to it. Lounging at the beach, with books and crossword puzzles, sunscreen and swimming pools, seashells and salt water was too much. By the end of the trip, he was in shutdown mode.

And we all paid for it.

Lesson learned.

Mark is over it -- all of it. He shouted at Holden in customs, snapped at all of us on the drive home, and when we finally got back to the house in Port Windwick he said, and I quote, "I'll never go on another trip with that child again."

So. Real happy memories there.

The day after we get home, I cancel Orcas Island

and the trip to Vermont. Sleep away camp can wait for a year when we aren't all hanging on by a thread.

Betsy is devastated. Which hurts more than I can say aloud. All year she's been the trouper, the one who is patient and kind -- but her tear-streaked cheeks remind me that everyone is suffering. Not just Holden. Not just me. My daughter who has always worn her heart on her sleeve is starting to crack.

"I love Orcas," she cries against my shoulder, her little arms wrapped around me. She has been my entire world for so long and the idea that I am letting her down cuts deep. "It's my favorite, Mom." She sniffles, looking up at me, her breath shaky. "The bonfires and the fireworks and flashlight tag."

"I know, Bets. Maybe next year." Orcas has always been our thing. A week each summer over the Fourth of July, spent with our closest friends. We'd each rent a house at a resort and relax with stacks of books, a chessboard and card games, hiking in Moran State Park. The mossy trails leading us to waterfalls, tree branches covered in bright green leaves that filtered the sun as we walked through the familiar forest. Mark brings his fishing poles and it's the one time a year he goes fishing, catching trout from the lake, grilling it over the charcoal grill.

"I want it *this* year." It pains me to not give her what she wants. If anyone deserves a break from Holden, it's her. Betsy loves him -- it's obvious -- but she's still a little girl who deserves a happy childhood. Has adopting Holden cost her that? Her innocence?

"I'm sorry, Bets, but it's just not going to happen." I

look around the living room, wishing I weren't navigating this conversation by myself. But Mark is already at the office, he practically ran out the door, before coffee even finished brewing. He's that anxious to get away from us.

"I know, but is Auntie Caroline still going? And the Brixes?"

I exhale, setting down my phone. "I know the Brixes are. But I don't know about Auntie Caroline and Pete. I haven't been talking to Caroline, Bets, you know that."

Holden walks in, asking what's up. And that's when Betsy runs from the kitchen, crying, running upstairs. Holden watches from the hallway as I race after my daughter. He doesn't say anything, but he watches. Listens.

"Betsy, can we talk, please?" I walk into her room, stepping over her drawing pencils and sketchbooks that lay on her pink carpet. Gently closing her bedroom door, I look at my darling girl. The quilt is pulled back and is rumpled, there's a half full glass of water on the bedside table, next to an empty bag of chips from yesterday. Mark would hate the state of her room if he paused at home long enough to notice. The house is not the pristine place he used to insist upon. It's like he's realized achieving that level of order is no longer an option. He's given up on that... what else has he given up on?

"Bets," I say, stepping toward her bed. "I know you love Orcas and are upset but --"

"No, Mom, it's not that," she sobs. "I just hate myself."

"Sweetie, what?" I drop to my knees next to her bed. "What are you talking about?"

She rolls to her side, looking at me with her big blue eyes, filled with tears. "I'm a bad sister. I know he heard what I said. This is hard for Holden, it's not his fault. And I'm so mean. It's like, I don't care about anyone but myself."

Tears splash down her cheek and I pull her to me. "Oh, sweetie," I say, kissing her cheek. "You care. You care so much that you're crying."

"Holden would never act like this to me. Be mad that I couldn't do something he wanted."

I sigh, listening to my little girl, on the cusp of her eleventh birthday, so close to leaving her childhood behind her, and entering her teenage years. Years where she would be stretched and pulled in ways she can't yet anticipate. But she didn't anticipate this either. Her parents adopting a brother so different, so damaged.

She's already so strong, so resilient, so compassionate. I'm not worried about her being a teenager. She reveals who she is every day. And that person is beautiful.

Her door opens and Holden steps in, his basketball shorts hanging low to his knees, his tank top revealing muscles in his arms that weren't there six months ago. He is growing too.

"Em?" he asks me. "I was wondering..."

"Yeah?" I ask, resting my hand on Betsy's cheek.

"I was thinking, maybe Bets could go. With you or with Mark? We don't all have to take the trip." He looks at the floor. "I know I'm ruining everything, but maybe this doesn't have to be ruined for her too."

"Oh, Holden, you aren't ruining anything," I tell him. "It's okay for us to change plans. Change is good."

"I know, but Betsy loves it there." Holden looks past me, to her. "She talks about it all the time. I don't want to ruin something else for her too."

At the psych evaluation a month ago, I thought I was going to break. That this life I had chosen was too much.

But then he was cleared, not considered a risk to himself or to others, and given mandatory counseling appointments, twice weekly. And once a month overnight at the mental health hospital, so Mark, Betsy, and I can have a respite.

His secret cache under the mattress rattled me. Made me wonder just how well I knew him -- knew anyone. But then he does things like this, sees beyond himself, considers others, and I know his heart is pure.

Betsy knows it too. She leaps from the bed and wraps her brother in a big hug. "I love you, Holden." Then she looks over at me. "Daddy loves to fish," Betsy says, hopeful. "Maybe he'll want to take me."

———

A FEW DAYS LATER, Betsy and Mark are loading the Land Rover. Heading North to the island we've claimed as our own since before Betsy was born.

Mark jumped at the chance to get away with his daughter. And I was relieved to know it isn't the entire family he was rejecting. God, that sounds so awful, but I no longer know how to sugarcoat the truth.

He comes and finds me in the kitchen. I'm loading the dishwasher when he tells me that they're off.

"Okay, have fun," I say. "Send me photos."

I'm waiting for him to ask if I'll be okay, here alone with Holden. But he doesn't. He's so closed off, and I feel so guilty for my role in that. In everything. I pushed for this life and now we're all paying for it. Will it get worse before it gets better, or will this be our new normal?

"Trista said Caroline and Pete are still going. Can you just make sure Bets doesn't spend too much time with her?"

Mark snorts. "God, you want me to tell Caroline -- someone Betsy adores-- that she can't make s'mores with our daughter?"

I lift my eyebrows, remembering my conversation on the ferry as if it just happened. "Yeah, Mark. That's exactly what I'm saying."

"A little intense, Emery. Maybe you can take this week to chill the hell out."

"Right, that's gonna happen with the spawn of Satan being fifty feet away."

Mark shakes his head. Probably as disgusted with my outburst as I am. My true colors aren't pretty. I am so fucking flawed -- so on edge -- and Mark could at least show me some grace. Be gentle instead of being so insanely hard on me. On us. Always.

"He has the overnight, right?" he asks. "While I'm gone?"

"Yeah, tomorrow. And he has counseling on Tuesday and Friday."

Mark nods, his jaw tightening. "Just maybe use that time to relax. To remember who you were before Holden came home."

"Right." My tone is tight. Who I was before Holden came home? I was a leaf, blowing in the wind.

And not in a poetic way. I was flailing. Holden was supposed to ground me. Give me meaning. Purpose.

Instead, I've become his hostage.

———

I DRIVE Holden to his overnight, wondering what I'll do with my time with him gone. Trista's out of town, and I've isolated myself from any other connection I might have had. I'm annoyed by the text Mark sent this morning. Photos of Betsy with Caroline, at the beach, the pair of them grinning ear to ear. The blue ocean behind them, morning fog hanging in the sky. Why the hell would he send this except to piss me off?

When I pull up at the parking lot, walking with Holden to the front desk, his backpack on his shoulder, I try to focus on him. But I feel angry. Jealous. If I had never invited him into my life, never become his mother, I'd be at Orcas right now with my daughter and husband.

It's not fair. It's ugly. It's not the kind of thing I could ever, ever say out loud but it's how I feel.

I wish. I wish. I wish for things to go back to

normal. I don't know how to reconcile myself with the choices I've made.

"I'll see you tomorrow afternoon, okay?" I say to him. The social worker is waiting for him behind a locked security door.

"I bet you're happy I'll be gone tonight," he says, his voice low, mumbling. But I hear him. "I bet you wish you never met me, huh?"

"I don't think that, Holden," I tell him. Urging my words to be even, gentle. Honest. "I love you. And I just want to make sure you're healthy. That we're all healthy."

"Right, by sending me to the hospital for crazy people."

I sigh, resting my hand on his shoulder. He pulls away. "Don't, Holden."

"Why not? Maybe it would be better if I was gone. If I was dead."

"Holden," I gasp. "Don't talk like that, no one wishes that."

"Whatever you say." His eyes are so dark, so familiar. Haunting me. He leaves, without looking back and I press my knuckles to my mouth. I wish. I wish.

In the car, I turn on Counting Crows, 'A Long December' blaring as I try to figure out what the hell I am doing.

With Holden.

With Mark.

With my life.

It's not just Holden I regret on lonely nights like this.

I drive to Central Grocers, feeling embarrassingly sorry for myself. I decide a pint of ice cream, crisp white wine, and a long bath will be the quickest way to get me to full-on sob. And a good cry is exactly what I need right now.

But in the parking lot, I see Cooper's classic Wagoner. The wood-paneled sides making me bite down on my bottom lip. I'm used to seeing him in his police cruiser... not this car. The car where we lost our virginity. The car he used to teach me to drive a stick shift. The car we rode to the funeral in after we found my father dead.

If I'm nostalgic for things of the past, then so is Coop.

I pull up next to his empty car. Put my car in park. A few minutes later he comes out of the grocery store, brown paper sack in hand.

He sees me. Smiles in a way that makes my heart blossom with longing.

Maybe a good cry isn't what I need tonight.

Maybe tonight what I need is Cooper.

26

PRESENT

TRISTA COMES OVER WITH COFFEE, pastries, and hot cocoa for Holden. As I let her inside the house, the reporters shout at me to come out and explain the situation with my husband. Mark would never have decided to stay at the Cottage Inn unless he was really over me. Over us. This kind of press is going to be hard to recover from and he had to know that when he made his choice. Now, I'm the one, alone at the house, dealing with aggressive journalists.

"Holy shit," Trista says as I lock the door behind her. "It's getting worse."

I nod, agreeing as the two of us walk to the kitchen. "Thankfully, Margot has been here most days. Having the police cruiser in the driveway helps keep their invasion to a minimum."

Holden enters the kitchen, and when Trista hands him the hot cocoa, he gives her a half-smile. Hey, I'll take it. So will she.

"Of course, honey," she says, ruffling his hair. "Your

mom tells me she caved and let you download Fortnite. That right?" Trista knows very well that is not how it went down.

"Uh, yeah." Holden looks at me as if waiting for me to deny Trista's claim. I sip my latte silently.

"Well, I know for a fact Levi is online right now. You should hook up with him, or whatever it is you guys do." She jots a username on a napkin and slides it to him. "He told me to tell you."

"Really?" Holden lifts his eyebrows. Always assuming kindness has ulterior motives.

"Yep. Now go, let your mom and me talk." Trista waves him away, laughing. God, she is being so cool and collected, considering. Considering everything.

Holden looks to me to make sure it's alright. Something he's never, ever done before. He never checks in with me to get the okay. Then again, the last few days have changed things between us. Sharpened and softened them at the same time.

"Go have fun, Holden," I say. After he leaves, I break a croissant in half, sitting on a stool at the kitchen island. "Thanks for that."

"Always." Trista taps her nails on the marble. "So, I kinda need to tell you something."

I grimace. "What thing?"

"Well, actually show you." Trista reaches into her black leather purse and pulls out her tablet. "I know you hate the Mommy Tribe, but I think you should know what people are saying."

I sit up straighter. "Why? Is it bad?"

"It's not good."

"I can't do this, Tris. I'm already a mess. I don't need another reason to fall apart." I've filled her in on the journal, the reason Betsy didn't want me to know about the bullies, that she thought Mark and I were getting a divorce.

Trista knows everything. My secrets. My lies. She knows about Cooper.

Last night, I had terrible nightmares of Betsy, Cooper, and me. All three of us caught in the roots of a tree that kept pulling us tighter, strangling us. I woke up in a cold sweat, knowing exactly what the dream meant.

"I know," Trista says. "But it's getting vicious. I'll say something -- anything you want -- I just want to know what your official statement is before I go all vigilante on their asses."

"Fine, show me."

She opens the Facebook group and hands me the device. I press my lips together, trying to read the page with measured breaths. One thread in and I'm shaking. "They think I'm... Do they think I have something to do with this? With Betsy's death?"

"I know, it's twisted, Em. Everyone is saying that Mark left you. That's why he's staying at a hotel. And they are making guesses about why that might have happened."

"Right," I say, reading on. "Because what kind of wife drives her husband away a week after her daughter was found murdered?"

"They don't know the whole story. Maybe if they understood that you guys were having problems--"

I cut her off. "Trista, it doesn't work that way. This entire story is getting too much coverage already. It's all over the news, on Twitter. On this stupid message group. Mark's job is too high profile for gossip," I say. "He's running for Congress, his image matters. Matters more than what these yummy mummies think of me. He's doing really good work at the capital. I'm not going to ruin that."

"This is about more than initiatives, Em. This is your life."

I shake my head. No. I have such little control as it is. "I don't care about my reputation, what people think of me. I care about finding Betsy's murderer. I care about protecting Holden. I care about --"

"Coop?"

I shake my head. "Tris... That part is irrelevant."

"Is it?"

"What does that mean?" I ask, wondering what she isn't saying.

Tris swallows, tucking a loose strand of hair behind her ear. "I mean, is that why Mark left?"

"Why are you asking this?" Suddenly, I have a flash of terror. I cover my mouth, fear winding its way up my belly. "Are you out to break my heart? Just like Caroline? Do you want to get information from me so you can tell those mothers?"

"What?" Trista's mouth drops open. "What the hell are you talking about? I'm asking because I'm worried about you, Em. Your daughter just died. Your husband just left you. Your son--" She shakes her head, tears filling her eyes. "He might go to trial. He might be charged with murder, Emery. So forgive me for wanting to come over here and check in on you." She looks around the empty kitchen, arms wide. "Who else is here? No one. It's just me. Me! So, fuck you for thinking I'd try to..." She wipes her eyes, shoulders shaking. "Thinking I'd want to hurt you."

Tears run down my face and my skin is hot and tight and I know I've screwed another thing up.

She grips the counter, her hair long bangs in her eyes. "You lost everything, everyone. But you haven't lost me. So don't push me away. Don't assume the worst."

"I'm sorry," I say, gasping for words. "I'm so sorry, Tris. I'm just..." I shake my head, slipping, hard. To the floor, crumbling. "I just don't know what I'm going to do. I'm so fucked up right now, I actually told Mark I thought it was Caroline who did this. Caroline. What is happening to me? My mind is mush. I'm so lost."

"I heard that," Trista says, grabbing the coffees before sitting on the hardwood floor, cross-legged, across from me. "Apparently, the police went to her house, got her DNA, an alibi. All of it."

I drop my head against the cupboard. "Shit. She probably thinks I'm a monster."

"No, I don't think she connects it to the police visit. And to be honest, she was happy to help. She loved Betsy, even if she was a little intense about her. She's pretty broken up about everything."

"You've seen her?"

Trista shakes her head. "No, I wouldn't do that to

you. But she posted in the Mommy Tribe about it. It seemed really sincere."

"Why is *she* in the Mommy Tribe?"

Tris shakes her head. "You're going to need something stronger for that story."

I lift my eyebrows then pull myself up, reaching for a bottle of whiskey in the pantry. Then I put the Jameson back. No. I can't have that now. I don't want to numb myself.

"Fair enough," she says.

I sit back down on the floor as Trista hands me my coffee. I lean against the cupboards and take a sip. "Hit me."

"She's adopting a baby girl. From Uganda. They're on a waitlist, but it could be as soon as three months."

Blood drains from my face. "Really?"

Shouldn't I be happy? Excited for another child to have a forever family?

Maybe. But my thoughts on adoption are so different than what they were a year ago.

I thought... I thought I could save Holden. Bring him home and heal those broken bits and help him become whole. I was so naive. I didn't understand that adoption is born from loss. So much loss. No one comes out whole when children get new mothers.

And the loss can be seen in all different ways because everyone's story is different. But it's there. At the root. At the core. Starting in the womb.

It's not a pretty picture. Not a part of the story that's easy to hear -- but it's true. People want to believe that adoption is a happy ending to a sad start. But it's not as simple as that.

And my Instagram account just perpetuates that myth.

The side of the story I share is all glory, no pain.

"I guess that's good? I mean she's always wanted to be a mom."

Trista and I drink our coffee in silence. Heartache so fully formed in my chest that it's become a physical thing.

"I hope her baby..." I don't know how to finish that sentence. I hope her daughter isn't damaged? Doesn't have Reactive Attachment Disorder? Doesn't horde food or hide sharp objects under her bed? Doesn't get accused of murder a year into their lives together?

I don't want to hope for those things... It feels like a betrayal to Holden to want that for another child. Would I change who he is to make it easier for someone else?

I realize I don't hope those things so it would be easier for someone else.

I want those things so it would be easier for Holden.

I made the decision to be Holden's mother. But he never had a choice. In any of this. In his life.

So yes, he is out of control. Angry. Unhinged. Because the world has taught him that it can't be trusted. Tears prick my eyes and I wipe them away. The agony in all of this so wrought, so heavy. So fucking sad.

"I hope her baby knows how wanted she is," I say finally finding words that are true.

Trista squeezes my hand. "I'm sorry it's gone down like this."

I blow air out of my cheeks. I can move past Caroline. Past my feelings over Jenna and her Mommy Tribe. But I can't gloss over the deeper issue here. An issue that hangs between the narrow gap of life and death. It can all change so fast. In the blink of an eye. She is gone.

"Who did this, Trista? Who killed my daughter?"

Before she can answer, there's a knock on the door. We stand, brushing away the tears from our eyes. I set down my coffee, wiping my hands on my jeans. Deep breaths. After the visit from Cooper and Margot a few days ago when they told us that Betsy was murdered, I doubt I'll ever be able to answer the door again without shaking. I'll never know who might be waiting, who might be preparing themselves to tell me news that will rattle me to my core.

I open the door, finding Cooper standing there. It looks like he hasn't slept in days, and I doubt he has. How could he sleep at a time like this? When Betsy is gone.

He's in his uniform, here on official business. Good. I need solid facts I can lean on. God knows there is nothing else to hold me up right now.

I invite him in, hopeful that he has an update.

"What? What's happened?" I ask. My voice revealing all my hope. My fear. Trista is behind me, hand on my shoulder. My hand closing the door as he steps into my foyer. I hear the cameras snapping photos, the flash blurring my vision.

"I wanted to come and let you know a few more people were cleared from the investigation. Marcie Devon's son, Cory, was playing Fortnite at the time of the murder. There's a timestamp on his console."

Fucking Fortnite.

"And Caroline was with her husband Pete at his office's Halloween party. We have several witnesses claiming she was playing Pictionary when --"

"Right, I get it," I say my voice tightening. Knowing it was never Caroline anyway. Fuck. We're still running in circles. "So, we're back to square one. Is that what you're here to say?" My words are clipped, tense. I need someone to blame right now. Maybe that person is Cooper.

Cooper's eyes meet mine and I know he hates this too. Coming here with this news and I know it's not fair but I hit him. I do. I press my fists against his big solid chest and I pound them. Because I can't believe this is happening. I won't accept it.

Fists flying. Screaming. Crying. I'm so damn mad. "Betsy deserves better than this," I sob. "Cooper, do something!"

Trista is walking up the stairs. She isn't abandoning me. She's giving me space to be alone with the man who has changed my world again. And again. "I'm gonna go check on Holden," she says.

She doesn't wait for a reply and it's a good thing because Cooper has his arms around me now, holding me tight. I'm no longer hitting him, now I am clinging to him. He holds me. Close. Letting me cry, but not letting me fall.

"Em," he says, his tears on my cheek, my lips. Salt. Life. He is an ocean and I could drown in him right now. I could dive into the waves and be swept away because how can I live without her?

Cooper won't let me down. He looks in my eyes and pulls me back to the land of the living and he won't let me sink to the bottom of the sea. No. He is bringing me to the surface. I gulp in the seaweed tinged air and I breathe. I breathe. He has me.

"Em," he tells me, eyes locking on mine. As if begging me to hold on. And if he is the one holding me up, I won't let go. "We will find the person who did this," he says. "I swear to you. We will."

I'm so lost in my emotions that I don't hear a car pull into the driveway. Don't hear a door slam. But he's here, in the foyer.

"I'm so sorry, Em," he cries, tears I rarely see filling his eyes. "I never should have--" He stops talking as he looks us over. Seeing it all so clear. Cooper's hands on my face, tears streaming down our cheeks. I'm sure my husband can hear the pounding of our hearts. Boom. Boom. Crash.

He came to apologize and I've ruined it all. Again. Mark runs a hand through his hair, anger blossoming. Anger with me. With Cooper. He's been with Tom all morning trying to make a case and if Cooper has no leads, then I don't think Mark has any prospects either.

Mark looks wounded, hit in the gut. As if I've just punched him with my fists instead of Coop.

"Emery, are you fucking serious? You're doing this to me right now?"

Cooper runs his hands over my arms, stepping back. "She was upset."

Mark gives a sharp laugh. I deserve it. I deserve so much more. "Well, good thing you were here to comfort her, Deputy Dawson."

I swallow, lost for words. Because the truth is I'm sick of pretending. Pretending like things are better or more perfect than they really are. I'm going to delete the stupid Instagram account today, but before that, I'm going to be honest with my husband.

It's time he knew the truth.

27

FOUR MONTHS EARLIER

I DON'T PLAN IT. But he pulls out a bottle of wine from his paper bag, a pint of caramel ice cream and it was like he has read my mind.

It's been a long time coming. And now I'm following Cooper home, knowing full well that this will change everything. When we pull up to his house I'm not nervous. I don't care that my bikini line is unwaxed. That my thighs touch. That the last time we made love I was over a decade younger.

Cooper never cared about those things. He cared about me. Plain and simple. He still does.

I still love you, he told me.

I believe him.

Stepping from my car, I grab my purse, my phone. Shove my keys in my bag. He's waiting for me at his front door and I lick my lips, the summer air breezy, cool. I blink slowly, memorizing Cooper under the porch, looking at me like I'm the only thing that matters.

He doesn't apologize for the mess that is his place. It's a small cabin, but it's waterfront property, and I know he always dreamed of having a place on the water.

"It looks like you," I say, turning to him. Worn brown leather furniture, a bottle of whiskey on the counter. A bike propped in the corner of the room. A record player on a side table, albums are strewn about.

Cooper is a rewind button to the girl I once was. I want to linger there. Wanting it. Him. This. Us.

He doesn't speak as I poke around his space. Taking in the photographs propped on a table. He and his mom, Elizabeth. He and my dad. Him and me. Me. Me. Me.

He puts the ice cream in his freezer, uncorks the bottle of wine. Grabs a pair of mason jars, laughing as he takes them off the open shelving. "Not fancy like you're used to."

"I don't need fancy, Cooper. I never did."

"What do you need, Em?" He steps close, hand on my waist, thumb under my blouse. My skin prickling at his touch, my belly warm. His palm hot. Hot. Hot. Yes.

I forgive him, but will he forgive me?

I whimper then, soft and weak. He kisses my ear. Barely. Enough for my body to pulse with want.

Cooper knows what I need.

He steps back. It's agonizing, but we've waited this long. I don't suppose I could expect him to just rip off my clothes within ten minutes of being alone.

If he did though, I wouldn't mind. I would give in. I would ask for more. For everything.

He takes the wine glasses from the counter and carries them to the back door. He tells me to grab the Pendleton blanket that rests on the back of the couch.

I do as he asks, following him outside. A summer night, stolen. Ours. No one knows where I am. No one needs me. Not Mark. Not Betsy. Not Holden. I am at the mercy of my own choices and I am guilty of many things but I refuse to let guilt eat away at my heart tonight. This is who I am. I will not apologize. Under no pretense of perfection. I'm flawed, sure. But right now I am also living.

We walk to the beach, the rocky shore glistening, the sun setting, the sky painted in pastels. Pink. Purple. Coral. I'd hashtag it perfection because it is. This moment, with Cooper looking back at me, his smile easy, his blue eyes bright. Hope. Hope. I carry hope for him, for us, still. After all this time.

He broke my heart and yet, being with him now is healing it.

Maybe it's my way to justify what I'm doing here. Breaking vows. But I made those promises a lifetime ago. I was a different woman.

Now? Now I just want to be his.

Am I weak for wanting the man who left me or am I strong for giving into the second chance I always wanted?

"What have you been doing all this time?" I ask, both of us sitting in Adirondack chairs. "Before coming back to Port Windwick?"

He hands me a glass of wine, taking his time to

answer. "I was in Spokane for most of it. It was a good job, a good life."

"You hate the snow though."

He laughs. "Sure, but that's not why I came back."

"Then why?"

He tenses, looking at me. Time stops and I know. I know the reason I am here. His eyes reveal everything. His need to understand. It's not about sex. It's about the truth.

Shit. Shit. Shit.

Finally, he speaks, slowly. Measured. "Em, is she mine?"

My jaw sets firm. Tears in my eyes. My chin quivers. Shakes. Shit.

"I don't know."

"Yes, you do."

I exhale. There is no guidebook for this. No parenting manual. This, right here, isn't a reality anyone would admit to, let alone write about.

"Why now?" I ask. "Why come back and ask now?"

"I saw her photo, Em." Cooper emits a long, deep breath. It's more than a sigh. It's a longing. "I know I have no right to come back. Not after I left the way I did. With a note and nothing more. You deserve more than what I gave you. So, I get it. Your marriage, Mark, the house, and fucking picket fence. I get it."

I don't speak, I just listen. Because if he's sorry for how things ended, I am even sorrier. He may feel bad for walking away from me, but the guilt I've carried all these years doesn't come close to comparing.

"I wasn't going to come back," he says. "Don't have

family here, not after your dad died. I've never done the whole social media thing, don't talk to guys from high school, college, any of that shit. And besides, I didn't want to see you. See how you turned out. It was hard enough to lose you because of my own fucking fear. I didn't want to add salt to the wound. My heart couldn't take it."

I swirl the wine in my glass. I knew my reckoning would come one day. But I hoped to put it off. When the rest of my life wasn't such a mess.

I'm so fucking selfish.

I know the truth and I've hidden it. He was scared then but I'm scared now. At this rate, I'll end up causing even more people pain in the end.

"Then I got lonely," he says softly. "You know how it goes? I was going through this stack of old photos. You, your dad and me. Pictures of when I was a kid, my mom before she died. Anyways, it was bumming me out that I didn't know what you looked like now. So, I looked you up on Instagram."

I can't bear to look in his eyes so instead, I look for a word. Something that can explain. But what can I say? Everything will make this worse than it already is.

"It was a funny thing, actually. Because I had this stack of photos of me as a kid right next to me. And then there I was looking at this picture, this tiny square photo on my phone screen, and the little girl looking back at me was my duplicate. My mini-me." He looks at me then, dead on. "My daughter."

"Coop," I try, my voice catching. Torn.

"I know why you did it, Em. I do. I left you for a

second time. You'd married Mark. Why ruin what you'd put together for a broken man like me?"

"You weren't..." I blink back tears.

"What? Wasn't broken?" Cooper scoffs, fully admitting to his failures. "We both know I was. Your father's death killed me. I was a mess."

"No, I mean you weren't supposed to..." I cover my face with my hands.

"Wasn't supposed to ever find out? Em, you had family photos blasted all over the Internet. It was only a matter of time."

"Why did you come here like you did, if you knew? Why tell me you loved me? Why make me think ..."

"Think what?" Cooper's eyes are on me now. Hard.

"That we had a chance."

"I want you now more than ever, Emery."

I shake my head. I don't deserve his love, his forgiveness. I'm a mess. A wreck. A ruin. Just like he was eleven years ago. We both break things.

"You're too good for me now. Your life is all sorted out and mine is just falling apart."

He sets his wine in the sand, stands, pulls me to him. "Don't tell me what I deserve, Em."

I gasp, he draws me to him. I close my eyes, my heart pounding as he runs his hands to the waistband of my skirt. As he unzips it, letting it slip past my hips. My top is pulled off. I am there, vulnerable. Exactly as it should be.

He drags his mouth over my neck, my collarbone. Tasting me. I whimper, his grip on my flesh strong. Sure. He knows what he is doing.

"She is beautiful," he tells me, and I tremble, tears falling down my cheek. "She is part you, part me. Ours."

I'm shaking, cold and scared. Scared of the way Cooper is touching me. Like this time, he will not walk away. I saw his worst and now he is seeing mine.

"You named her after my mother," he says and my knees give out and he catches me. "All bets are off."

I squeeze my eyes shut.

"Bet your bottom dollar," he says, his thumb running over the bridge of my nose, my upper lip, holding me by the base of my neck. I can't breathe. He knows. "Bet your life."

Cooper's mother, Elizabeth, was called Betsy by everyone who loved her, me included. We always used those terms when talking to her, she'd laugh, drunk or high, and toss the words right back at us. She loved Cooper and me. She would make our Halloween costumes every year because God knows my single father couldn't have managed. We were a motley pair, Coop and I. But Elizabeth and my father weren't ones to judge. They loved us the best way they could.

She died our sophomore year of college. She was an alcoholic, just like my dad, and she had a brain aneurysm. Gone in the blink of an eye.

"Bet your life," I whisper. We'd always say those lines to his mom, dashing in her house so Cooper could grab a change of clothes, his fishing pole. Later, it was a set of car keys, a case of beer -- that is one thing she always had, just like my dad.

"Why don't you hate me?" I ask as he unhooks my

bra. As he pushes down my panties. As he touches me the way I remember. The way I have imagined for eleven years. I lied to him about his daughter and still he touches me the way I crave.

"Because, Em, I love you too much."

He unbuttons his shirt, and I lay out the wool blanket. It isn't warm, the sun has set, but our bodies are hot and my heart pounds hard and his eyes meet mine.

We move in a rhythm that two people as close as we were could never forget. Muscle memory, maybe. His body firm and mine soft, his hands sure and my transparency a film over me that only he can seem to lift. A curtain he chooses to raise. He wants to see the good, the bad, the broken. He wants me the way I want him.

He fills me up and takes me away, and after, he cradles me in his arms, looking past my flaws.

"You're a good mother, Em," he tells me. "I watch you with her."

"What do you see?"

"Love."

"She's my whole world, Cooper. And I think I messed everything up by choosing Holden."

He runs his hand through my hair, understanding. "No. He needs you, and I think you need him, too."

"It's so hard."

He kisses my forehead. "The people who make it look easy are lying. Don't be like them."

I kiss him, his lips so warm and inviting. "I don't think I could be if I tried."

"I don't want her to know," he says.

I falter. "No?"

He shakes her head. "I want her to be happy. Her childhood should be easy. The rest of her life will be full of hard stuff -- let these years be full of good memories."

It's too much, his generosity. He's letting me off the hook of doing the hard thing -- telling Mark the truth. But more than that... He is forfeiting his role in her life. It takes my breath away.

"That... Cooper." I shake my head. "Why?"

He gives me his half-smile that's so full of forever. "Because I'm Betsy's father, I can't give her everything, but let me give her this."

28

PRESENT

WE STAND IN THE FOYER, Cooper, Mark, me. The words are on the tip of my tongue. I can taste them, the sweet relief of honesty.

When Cooper looks at me as if terrified I am going to say the one thing that will change our lives forever. That Mark isn't actually Betsy's father. That Cooper is.

But then Cooper's eyes sear into mine and I understand. If we confessed this truth, then Cooper would no longer be able to work on this case. And right now, I need Cooper on it more than I need anything else in the whole wide world. If anyone will find Betsy's murderer, it's him.

He is her father, after all.

Still, this tension is wrong, and it's too hard for all of us with this elephant in the room.

"Mark, I have to be honest with you."

Mark's eyes meet mine. I see our wedding day. Our first kiss as man and wife. Cutting the cake. My belly already carrying a child. Cooper's child.

Mark stiffens, and I wonder where we went wrong -- or was it wrong from the start? A girl like me could never measure up to a man like him.

He at least deserves one half of the truth.

"Cooper and I slept together," I tell him, the honesty swallowing me up.

Mark looks at me like I'm crazy. "You don't think I know that?"

I shake my head, confused. "What, you knew?"

His face fills with disappointment. "Of course, I knew."

"How?" I want to look at Cooper, but I can't. My eyes are fixed on my husband. The man I betrayed.

"I came back from Orcas this summer and you were a mess," Mark explains. "I didn't know it was Cooper at first, I just knew you had a secret. But I figured it out after I saw you two talking at the school one morning." He runs his hand over his jaw, pained at the memory. "I'd still been at the house, and saw that Holden had forgotten his lunch bag. So I stopped at the school to drop it off before going to Olympia."

I press my knuckles to my mouth. He knew.

"I saw you together, in the parking lot. It was pretty clear what was going on."

"Mark," Cooper says. "I'm sorry, I--"

"Don't. I'm glad you finally admitted it. And I don't want you anywhere near my family," he says to Cooper, coldly. "Now I can get you off the case."

"No, Mark, just--" Cooper tries but Mark is already gone. He's turned on his heels, walking away, leaving me with my lover.

It's not satisfying, not like I hoped. A confession that would release the weight on my shoulders. It does the opposite. I close my eyes, knowing I've just fucked everything up all over again.

"I'm so sorry, Cooper," I start.

But he shakes his head. "Fuck, I've gotta get ahead of this, Em. I gotta go into the station, tell them before Mark does."

"What does this change?"

"Everything."

———

AFTER COOPER LEAVES, Trista makes her exit, using an umbrella to shield her face from the reporters. "Call me if you need anything after the appointment, okay?"

"Thanks for everything," I say. "I owe you."

"Never."

With everyone gone, I look at the clock. It's only ten am, but it feels like it's been the longest morning of my life. Jogging upstairs, I call for Holden. He rips off his headset and I tell him we're leaving in half an hour.

His psych evaluation is an important piece to the puzzle, as far as Tom is concerned. And it makes sense. He hasn't had one in months since I found his questionable stash. His therapist, Dana will be there, and that means Holden is less apprehensive about attending. He likes Dana, and I'm grateful she can calm his nerves. Anything with the word *evaluation* or *test* usually spins Holden up. But today, he seems oddly chill.

After I shower and dress, we get in the car. The photographers are insistent on taking my son's picture - - and for what? A salacious article on the Senator's son? My daughter is dead. A killer is on the loose. There's a better story out there than a mother and son trying to get to the hospital.

As I drive, I try to understand why Holden isn't tapping the dash incessantly or clenching and unclenching his fists. "You doing okay?" I ask, turning onto the highway.

He shrugs, changing the music on Spotify. He puts on *Benny and the Jets* and a surge of love runs through me. We may not be alike in lots of ways, but my taste in music has definitely rubbed off on him.

Dana meets us in the waiting room, and she gives me a warm hug. "I'm so sorry for your loss, Emery."

I nod, trying to put on a brave face. "Right now we just need answers. And hopefully, this can help clear Holden's name."

Holden looks up at me, dark eyes full of shadows, secrets, stories.

"I'll tell them the truth," he tells me. "Don't worry, Em."

With a heaviness in my limbs, I sit in a plastic chair, watching them leave behind the security door. I hope whatever tests the psychologists give him, reveal his true character.

I pull out my phone, my thumbs hovering over the keyboard. There is so much I want to say, to so many people. It's only been three days since Cooper and Margot came to my house, saying they thought it was

Holden. It feels so much longer; each hour is filled with memories that seem to stretch time.

I want to text Jenna Handler and tell her that her kids are assholes. Text Marcie Devon and tell her to take her son's iPhone away -- he's in grade school for Christ's sake -- and he's using it to take videos of himself bullying other kids. I want to message Arie Middleton and ask if she knows how badly her son's traumatized my now dead daughter.

I want to call Caroline. I want us to go back to before when her true colors weren't so damn vivid -- blinding.

Instead, I text Mark. *I'm at the hospital. Holden's getting the eval now.*

He doesn't reply. Why would he? He is a man who has spent his adult life taking care of me, making sure I was strong, happy, taken care of -- and how do I repay him?

By sleeping with the one man he doesn't trust. By having an affair, when I could have poured my heart into our own marriage, looking for ways to fix it instead of breaking it beyond repair.

And then I told him about it. On the most stressful and horrific week of our lives.

If I'd wondered if I was a monster, I know the truth beyond a shadow of a doubt.

It hurt Cooper, devastated Mark.

And for what? I wanted to feel better, let go of the burden I'd been carrying. It only served me.

I pull out a tissue and wipe my nose. My phone buzzes. Mark. He leaves a voicemail and I press play.

I don't know how to move forward with us -- but I do need closure on Bets. We need to know who did this to her. And Cooper is the deputy for a reason. He's already been working on the case.

I'm not going to the station. It's his career and none of my business. I may hate the fucker -- but I love you. Em, I always have.

Pressing the phone to my forehead, I try to breathe as relief washes over me.

I text Cooper, asking him to call me as soon as possible. When he doesn't call back right away, I text him another message. *Mark isn't telling anyone about us. You have to stay on the case. We need you. I'll be at Port Windwick General for the next hour.*

Feeling anxious, I decide to walk to the cafe outside the hospital and get a mint tea -- hoping it might settle my stomach. I'm a basket of nerves right now.

After getting my tea, I step outside on the sidewalk, the December chill harsh on my cheeks. But it feels good -- my eyes being forced open, my hands holding the to-go cup tight, warmth seeping through the cardboard sleeve.

On the street, I see Jenna, alone. Shopping bags in her arms, a red scarf around her neck, blond hair curled and draping around her shoulders. Her eyebrows jump in surprise when she sees me.

I resist the temptation to look down at myself, to see what she sees. I already know. Eyes so heavy it's hard to keep them open. Hair unwashed and untamed, wild and loose. Body is so brittle it won't take much for her to make me snap.

"Oh, Emery, you poor thing," she says her vowels long and drawn. I look past her and see Marcie and Arie on her heels. Of course, they are.

"We did not expect to see you out and about, I mean, not with everything going on in your home." Arie gives an exaggerated grimace. "We heard about Mark leaving you. How awful. I can't imagine, losing him on top of everything."

Other days I might back down, step away. I spent the last few months refusing to give into the bitchiness whenever we crossed paths at the school, but that was before I knew these women raised children who wanted to make my daughter retreat. Hide.

"You want to comment on my marriage before offering your condolences? My daughter is dead, I think it takes precedence."

The trio purses their lips. Shaking their heads at me. "Of course, we're sorry," Jenna says. "That's why we've set up the vigil for tomorrow night. We all loved Betsy so much."

I inhale, refusing to scream at them, not wanting to waste my precious energy. The energy I need to devote to finding Bets' killer -- on them. Still, I have to say something.

"You set up a vigil in my daughter's name?"

Jenna nods, eyes dripping with insincere sympathy. "The Port Windwick Mommy Tribe coordinated it. It was a group effort, truly. We need more security in our neighborhoods, Emery. We need more surveillance cameras in our town. For our protection. For the protection of our children. We demand it, and it's all because of Betsy."

"Fuck you," I say, my voice trembling, pointing my finger in Jenna's face. Seething and shocked and just so exhausted. "Fuck you and your vigil. Do you know what this town really needs? It needs mothers who raise their children to be kind. To be generous. To be brave--not assholes."

Arms wrap around me, pulling me away. Cooper. Here. He has me, but I don't want to back away. I shout at them as he pulls me into his cruiser, "Not children like what you've created. Not what--"

Cooper slams the door on my face, silencing me. The women stand, horrified and I can already see them rewriting the script to fit their own version of the story. *Emery lost it, poor thing. Her daughter dead and her husband left her. I heard the adoption was a ploy for him to get elected into Congress. Can you imagine? And her son? Well, he's the killer.*

I can see the Facebook group now, the spin on my tragic situation. How I had a public meltdown. How they are holding the vigil with more compassion than ever.

Cooper sits in the driver's seat. "What the fuck, Em?"

"Please, Coop. I can't. Just let me go to the hospital and wait for Holden. I've ruined your life how many times exactly? Just let me go. Let me run away. Let me. Let me... Let."

I can't see straight, can't think clearly. Everything is

a blur. A puddle. A river. I want to lie down in the icy water and get swept away.

Cooper grabs my wrists, sees my face is red, with tears dripping down my face, my nose running, and I'm hysterical, shaking and uncontrollable. He tries. He tries to make me stop. He holds me until I'm done shaking and kicking and screaming. Begging to be let go. Let go. Begging for him to stop loving me. I lied to him for a decade and now our daughter is dead.

He won't. I see it in his eyes and I can't accept it. He needs to hate me. To be disgusted by me. To want me gone.

He doesn't.

"Calm the fuck down, Em. You've got to cool it."

I gulp in air, trying so hard to stop the buzzing in my ears. The pounding in my heart. The blood pulsing in my veins. I want it to stop. All of it.

I look at him and I'm a little girl all over again. Small. So small and so desperate for someone to never leave my side -- not like Mom who left when I was little. Not like Dad who was hanging on by a thread every day of his life. Not like Mark who wanted to fix me and make me whole.

I want to be loved for the broken mess I am.

He takes hold of my face, hands on both my cheeks. "I love you, Emery and I'm not letting you go."

In his eyes, I see it. For the first time.

He is here and this time he won't say goodbye and so, I silently beg him to stay.

Because deep down that is what I really want. What

I've always wanted. Cooper is my unconditional everything.

My shoulders fall and my eyes bleed tears of understanding.

I'm a lost cause and I'll never be a saint. But Cooper loves me anyway. Fights for me anyway. Chooses me anyway.

Cooper loves me like I love Holden.

"I need to find who did this," I tell him. Cooper nods, knowing. Feeling the power in my words. The venom and the fight. "It's time for me to clear my son's name."

29

THREE MONTHS EARLIER

FINALLY COMING clean with Cooper about the truth of Betsy both helped and hurt me.

Now, when I think of Mark, I feel a deep well of shame and of betrayal. I keep replaying that night in my mind. The wool blanket spread over the sand, Cooper's hands running over my bare skin, taking me. Me, giving myself over to him.

It has to stop -- my incessant fantasy.

Mark sits up in the bed, and I turn to him. He came in so late last night I was already asleep. His phone in his hand, his eyes scanning the screen.

"What time is it?"

"Nearly seven. I'm running late." He pulls back the duvet and gets out of bed, his firm body as tense as his words.

"I'm in a summer time warp," I tell him. "The days are a blur."

"Lucky you. I have a busy day. Fucking Rosencraft wants me to revise the bill. Again."

"Sorry," I say, sitting up, adjusting the grey tank top I wore to bed. I only have on panties -- no shorts. Part of me hoped that he'd want to sleep with me last night. That maybe if we had sex, we could push past this uncomfortable divide that is growing between us. Maybe my affair would seem less permanent. Irreversible.

"It's fine. Just, please do me a favor and don't text me a hundred times today complaining about Holden. Fucking deal with him on your own. You're the one who wanted him."

"God, Mark." I grab my robe, tie it to my waist. "Can you just try to not be such an ass for one day? I'm doing the best I can."

"Yeah? Could have fooled me."

I open my mouth, ready to keep this fight going, but then I hear Betsy at the door, pushing it open.

"Don't fight. Please." Her blue eyes are written with worry and I exhale, shoulders falling, and leave the room. Coffee. That is what we need. Won't fix everything but it will take the edge off.

Ever since he returned from Orcas with Betsy, he has been more and more removed from our daily life. Well, not entirely. He is carving out plenty of daddy-daughter time. Which I appreciate. So much. But maybe he could try just a little bit with Holden. Instead, I'm the one trying to entertain him all day, every day.

I add grounds to the filter, starting the pot. Then I take the cream from the fridge and set out pancake mix on the counter, a whisk and a stick of butter. If I sit on the stool, drinking coffee, I feel okay with Holden manning the stove now.

He likes it, being in control of something. Especially food. The more therapy he has had, the better picture I have of my son. Food has always been a massive issue for him. Mostly because when he was little there was never enough.

The rotten food I find in his room still makes me recoil, but it also makes me see with clarity that he is in pain. And that kind of trauma can't be erased in a month. A year. Sometimes not for a lifetime.

Holden joins us in the kitchen and he looks extra tired. I know he's been lying about when he goes to bed at night. I need to take the video game console from his bedroom -- putting it in there was a bad, desperate idea. The reason I haven't done it yet is that I'm not up for the fight.

I'm a shitty parent. I'll let my tween stay up until all hours of the night, only to suffer the next day -- just so I don't have to set a few boundaries.

The truth is hard to admit -- but it's the truth all right.

When Mark comes into the kitchen I give myself a pep talk. Tell myself to start over, smile bright. Be nice. He looks handsome, as ever. In his suit and tie, clean-shaven, smooth jaw. White teeth. A politician who won me over. Then he gives Betsy a kiss on the head, a nod to Holden, a scowl at me. Great. Just what I always imagined for myself. A dysfunctional family that can't even eat breakfast in peace.

"Will you be home for dinner, Daddy?" Betsy asks.

Mark pours his coffee in a travel mug, shaking his head. "Sorry, sweetheart, but I've got so much on my plate today. This weekend though, I'll make it up to you. Promise."

"What do you have, besides the Rosencraft issue?" I ask, watching as Holden measures the pancake mix, stirring in water.

"I want to be a Congressman, Emery. Don't you ever listen? I won't get there if I don't put in the hours, make the connections."

I look up at the ceiling refusing to yell in front of the kids. "I do listen, Mark. I just didn't realize this was your priority right now."

He scoffs, looking at me with so much resentment it feels like his hands are on my wrists, squeezing hard, until I bruise, trying to make me feel what he feels. Trapped.

"It has always been my priority, Emery. Since day one. I was clear about what I wanted, where I wanted to go. You? It seems like every day you have a new idea of what it means to be married to you."

"Jesus, Mark!" I'm shocked, that he would talk so flippantly in front of the kids like this.

Mark kneels in front of Betsy. Taking her hands in his. "I love you, sweetheart. And I'm sorry for fighting with Mom. I'll make it up to you, I promise." He kisses her cheek, then leaves as quickly as he came.

Holden's eyes meet Betsy's. Tears have filled her eyes and he steps closer, giving her a hug. I press my knuckles to my mouth.

"It's going to be okay, Bets. I promise," he tells her. "I'll make sure you're okay."

I sit, frozen, watching the exchange. Not understanding it. Them. Their connection. But it's mesmerizing. My marriage may be a lost cause, but this -- this love between brother and sister -- it's thicker than water.

30

PRESENT

AFTER HOLDEN'S PSYCH EVALUATION, I drive him to Tom's office. Mark is meeting us there to go over Holden's case -- to retrace his steps after he left the trail.

I want Holden to tell me the details first, before Mark and Tom, and decide that sweetening the pot by driving through Starbucks is my best chance of getting him to talk – especially since he spent ninety minutes hashing out the inner workings of his heart to a doctor.

I order him a peppermint hot cocoa, myself an extra large latte. "And two slices of gingerbread," I add.

At the window, the barista gives us our drinks, his mouth falling open when he sees us. Recognizes us. Our family's story -- the one the reporter wrote from the steps of Seattle Courthouse -- has been circulating pretty heavily. I saw it on the front page of the *Port Windwick Tribune* while I was in the hospital waiting room. But it wasn't the original story. The new headline asked a question that had me running to the bathroom to throw up. Acid burning my throat, the words seared into my mind. MURDERED BY HER BROTHER?

"I'm so sorry," he says, handing us our gingerbread and my debit card. "It's awful." His eyes linger on Holden a beat too long. Wanting to protect my son from prying eyes, I press the gas, not even replying to the man.

But once I'm out of the parking lot, I drive slowly to Tom's office. I want to ask Holden about it, but when I open my mouth and turn to look at him, I see he's closed his eyes, snoring softly. It's a familiar sound.

So, instead of asking questions, I turn the music down low, and drive in circles, thinking about it myself. Trying to understand just what could have gotten my life to spiral so fast. Who could have been the root cause of it all?

Yes, I know I play a big role. I cheated on Mark. It pushed him away.

But he was pulling back before then. I know he was. One week he was all in with Holden, the next, after Cabo -- it was like he was done. Finished. As if his son was a chore. Worse: a bad decision he wishes he could take back.

What changed?

As I am nearing the office, Mark calls. I answer my phone, tethered to the car. "Hey," I say. "We're almost there."

"You can turn around, Tom had to cancel."

"Oh." I frown. "Everything okay?"

"Yeah, it's fine. I'll be home in fifteen minutes."

"Okay, see you soon."

As I drive back home, I pass Royal Chinese and my eyes roam left, to the motel. I take a right-hand turn and pull into the parking lot. A vision of Mark outside the hotel. He had a good excuse, that he was with Ryan, his manager -- but why would he be meeting this week, the week Betsy died? That was two days ago.

Without censoring myself, I dial Ryan's cell number. Mark gave it to me years ago because he can be hard to contact when he is in Olympia.

"Hello?" Ryan asks. Holden is still asleep which I'm grateful for. "Emery?"

"Hey Ryan," I say. "I know this is out of the blue but I just had a quick question for you."

"Of course, anything, Emery."

"Were you in town this week. In Port Windwick, two days ago?"

Ryan answers immediately. "No, I considered it. Mark and I discussed it but decided it would be best to wait until the case --"

I cut him off. "So you didn't come?"

"No, why, is there--"

"No. I have to go. Thank you, Ryan. Truly." I don't care if it comes off as rude. Right now I care about answers. Truth. He gave that to me and now I need to go find some more. My husband lied to me.

But why? There has to be another reason for Mark to be at this motel.

What has happened since I saw Mark outside this seedy motel? Marcie Devon's son was cleared, as were all the other kids out on Halloween. My desperate attempt to blame something on Caroline was dismissed. I have no other leads. No other ideas that I can follow.

But this is something. This is tangible. I need to go there, alone. Pulling out of the parking lot I try to take steady, deep breaths. I don't know why Mark was there... but there has to be a reason.

When we get home I jostle Holden awake. "Hey, we're home, the appointment was canceled." He wipes his eyes, looking like such a little boy, not someone who could hurt a fly. But I know that's just wishful thinking "Hey, just use the key code on the garage and let yourself in, alright? I have to run an errand. Dad will be home in ten minutes."

He frowns, hand on the door. "You'll let me stay here alone?"

I swallow. We've never left Holden home alone, never trusted him without supervision.

"I trust you, Holden," I tell him. Meaning it with all that I am.

I know he can hurt people. He's hurt me. I know he can lash out in anger, in spite, in pain.

The truth is, I don't know what Holden is capable of.

Still, I do know this: he would never hurt Betsy. He loved her.

So, if he didn't, who did?

————

I GET out of my car, wondering if the pain in my stomach is a warning. Looking around, the lot is nearly empty. It's the middle of the day, middle of the week, and there are only six cars here. I grab my phone and slide it into the pocket of my coat. As I walk toward the motel room where Mark stood, I lock my car and shove the keys into my purse. I don't know what I'm going to say when I knock on the door -- but I suppose I can start by asking whoever is inside this room how the hell they know my husband.

I knock, no answer. I knock harder, louder, finally banging my fists on the door. There's no way I'm leaving without some shred of information. A housekeeper is smoking, her back against the stucco of the motel. She looks over. "You okay?" she asks, flicking her cigarette, walking toward me.

"I just. I need to get in there."

"Yeah? Where's your key?" She has dirty blonde hair, tips pale pink. Last night's mascara caked on her lashes and her eyes are dilated. Charged.

"I um. I was looking for my sister," I improvise. "She was supposed to meet me an hour ago and she hasn't showed. I was nervous she had uh, gone too hard last night."

The housekeeper lifts her chin, eyeing me. My Hermes purse. Tailored wool coat over Lululemon leggings and two hundred dollar glorified slippers called Uggs.

"The woman staying in this room is your sister?" she asks, frowning.

"Uh, my husband's sister. Sister-in-law." Smile tightly. "Look, could you open her room for me? It's kind of important."

The housekeeper runs her tongue over her teeth, considering.

"I have money. Here." I reach into my purse, fish out all the cash I have on me. I count it out for her, one hundred and forty-six dollars.

"Sure," she says, shrugging, grabbing the cash and sticking it in her pocket. She uses a key hanging on the lanyard around her neck to unlock the door. "Just don't mention it, okay? And don't do anything stupid."

"Of course," I rush with gratitude. "I'll just be a second."

"I don't care how long you'll be." She pulls out another cigarette, lighting it as she walks away. Not looking back.

"Right. Okay then." I give her a tight wave and step into the motel room, shutting the door behind me, locking the door. My back falls against it as I collect my breath. Basically, breaking and entering on a hunch.

But what else have I got at this point?

I reach for the light switch, the musty reek of the room reaching my nostrils. Light filters through the curtains and I see empty bottles of Smirnoff and Beefeater. An empty pizza box on the bed.

I flick on the light.

My eyes go wide. I fall back, my hands gripping the curtains, catching me. No. This can't. This isn't. A primal scream escapes my mouth before I can slap my hand over my mouth, knowing I need to stay quiet or that housekeeper will be back.

My skin is clammy as I crawl on the floor to the wall

opposite the bed. Rasping breaths keeping me from passing out at what I see.

My daughter.

Everywhere.

I stand, my hands wrapped around the legs of the flimsy table, as I push myself up.

Her face, photos of her blanket on the wall. Tacked one on top of the other. At the playground. The park. School. The front yard.

My palms press against her life-size cheeks, her face blown up to a disturbing proportion.

The more I look, though, the more I see -- it's not just her.

It's all of us.

Holden. Mark. Betsy. Me.

Our entire family, caught on camera, over and repeatedly.

I look around, behind me, scared that someone might be waiting in the shadows. I spin, but no one is there. It feels like time is spinning, the memories of the last few months pinned to the wall, tacked in place. But why? Why was Mark here?

I look around, trying to gather my thoughts but it's hard. My head is dizzy, crowded. Overwhelmed. The table is covered in photos. But other things too. Newspaper clippings are spread all over it. The biggest one being our family at the courthouse the day of the adoption. The other ones are of Mark, political pieces referencing him. The work he does. *State Senator Wins Support! On the Road To Congress! Mark Gable: Hometown Hero. More Than A Father Figure!*

I keep sifting through the piles, trying to understand what this woman has to do with my family. I keep looking, reaching. What does this woman want with us?

And then, the next thought ... Did she kill my daughter?

Gasping as if pained, I see the photo that changes everything. That sets everything into place.

It's her -- the woman I'm looking for.

But in this image, she isn't with my husband.

She is with my son.

31

TWO MONTHS EARLIER

IT HAD BEEN the longest summer of my life, but finally, school is back in session. I pack lunches, cheese sandwiches, and applesauce and zipper them into Betsy and Holden's backpacks.

"We have to go, now," I holler up the stairs.

"Coming," Betsy says, a journal in hand. She takes her backpack from me and shoves the journal in. Holden is at her heels, and I smile. He looks so handsome in the school uniform. I had to order him bigger sizes when I purchased their back-to-school clothes. He's put on several inches over the last few months.

"I'm grabbing my coffee," I tell them, returning to the kitchen to get my Thermos as they head to the car.

Holden takes over the playlist for the drive, putting on Pet Sounds, and we roll down the windows, breathing in the salty air as we drive past the bend that showcases the gorgeous Puget Sound. I've always thought September would be a better month to have off than June. The kids are always sitting at desks during the best weather. So, we are soaking it in where we can.

When we pull into the drop-off line at the school-house, I ask if the kids have everything.

"We're good," Holden says.

"I wish I didn't have to go here," Betsy says, unbuckling.

"What do you mean?" I ask, eyeing Jenna and Arie in the distance. I want to get off this property before they ask me about volunteering for the school auction.

"She means this school sucks," Holden says, pushing open the door.

"What?" I frown; I hadn't expected this. "Since when?"

"Since forever, Mom." Betsy gives me a look that surprises me. She looks so much older than eleven. She has grown the last few months too. The pair of them will be in middle school next year, and right now I see that as fifth graders they are already morphing into older versions of themselves.

"Do you need me to talk to someone, help--"

Betsy jumps out of the car, and stepping to my open window, she kisses my cheek. "We're fine, Mom. You don't need to rescue us."

"But it's my job, I'm your mother."

She smiles, pulling her backpack on. "Sure, but we're not little kids anymore."

"I know."

"And we can handle the kids at this school. Holden and I can handle anything."

I give them a small wave as they run off toward the

building, not stopping to say hello to any other kids. A twinge of sadness burns my belly. Betsy really is growing up, finding her own voice, her own views. They both are.

I just hope those views don't hurt them in the long run. I want them to believe the world is for them, not against them.

Driving home, I think about this, how quickly things can change. Betsy's never been in the center of any social circle. When she was little she was quieter than other kids -- only feeling free to express herself in the safety of her own home, often with tears. Lots of them. She is friendly, sure, but she has always been so willing to see the glass half full, never empty. She chooses to believe in best intentions -- it's why she never gave up on Holden. But it's also made other girls think of her as immature, overly naive.

It wasn't character traits I wanted to course correct, and maybe my intuition on that was right. In her own time, she has found the armor she wants to wear to battle. Having a brother helps. A good book. A journal to draw in. And she isn't so precious as she was -- she said she doesn't need rescuing, she knows she is growing up.

And as I park the car in the driveway, a smile forms, taking up the space where there had been a frown. Betsy is going to be okay; strong. She'll never be like Jenna's daughter Julia -- loud and bossy. No, Betsy is gentle but equally wise. She can see past the bullshit, she can see the broken.

She's like her father.

Not Mark -- but the man who shares her DNA. She's like Cooper, fair-haired and bright-eyed. She is good. Pure.

Inside, I grab the *Port Windwick Tribune* and stop at the mailbox, grabbing the package that sticks out from it. I set down the paper on the countertop in the kitchen and turn over the manila-enveloped package in my hand.

It's addressed to Holden Gable in unfamiliar handwriting. There is no return address and it's been taped shut. Twisting my lips, I consider the contents. Soft. Bigger than my hand, but not by much.

It's definitely not from Mark's parents in Vermont. His mother's handwriting is distinct and she'd never send Holden anything, anyway. She'd been distraught beyond belief over our choice to adopt him in the first place. It's another thing I never knew about Mark's family. How fucking judgmental they can be.

"We just hate how this affects poor Betsy," Vera would say to me on the phone. "And it's ruined the birth order. She was an only child and now she's a little sister."

"They are one month apart," I'd say through gritted teeth. Eventually, I just stopped replying to messages, to calls. I figured it was Mark's family, he could deal with them. And so he has. I haven't spoken to them since before the adoption was final. So no, this package wasn't from her.

But who?

Not interested in handing over an unidentified package to my eleven-year-old, I pull a pair of scissors from the kitchen drawer and cut open the package with precision.

Inside there is a sheet of lined notebook paper, folded into fourths and a small beanie baby--one of those weighted stuffed animals.

It's a bear in a basketball jersey, an orange ball sewed to the bear's paw. He has on a black sweatband and shorts.

I open the note.

Dear Holden,

It's Mommy. I want you to remember I love you the way only a mother can.

You are in my heart, always and I won't ever leave you. Ever.

Love, Your One and Only Mom

THE WORDS themselves don't bother me -- I can only imagine what it would feel like to lose your child. I remember going through the file at the social worker's office. Linda had told me I could stay as long as I like, read as much as I wanted but it was painful. Seeing how many ways Holden's birth mother Tamara had been offered help, and yet didn't have the capacity to accept it, broke my heart. Still breaks it. She had custody of Holden for the first five years of his life.

So, it isn't the letter or the stuffed animal that has me shaking.

It's that she sent it to our home address.

We never gave her that.

When the adoption was finalized we decided to extend to her our P.O. box number where she could always reach us. She wasn't even given our names.

Yet, she sent something to Holden Gable at our home.

She knows more than she should.

32

PRESENT

As I STAND in the motel room, I know something is horribly wrong. My bones seem to shake and my mind spins. What did Tamara want with Betsy?

And why was she keeping such close tabs on our family? I try to think, looking again at the photos she has taken over the last few months. It's like she became obsessed with us.

On one of the images of me, she has written in sharpie, *She'll pay.*

My gut twists, thinking of Tamara getting her vengeance out on me by taking my daughter's life. It sounds so psychotic and it's hard to imagine any mother doing such a heinous thing to another mother.

But she had neglected Holden for years. To the extent that he was removed from her home and her parental rights had been terminated. It wasn't an adoption where she decided to relinquish her son to another in hopes of him receiving the best chance at life. She had no say in it. He was taken from her because she wasn't feeding him, bathing him. Wasn't looking after him. She'd leave her toddler alone for entire nights. He'd often wake up and knock on the neighbors' door asking if they'd seen his mommy.

As I remember the letter she sent Holden a few months ago, my blood goes cold. My heart pounds as I grab photos and the newspaper clippings from the table, shoving them into my purse. My hands shake as I reach for the photo of mother and son. I stare at it; Holden's dark eyes are so familiar. Doubt clouds my mind, could he have been an accomplice to Betsy's death?

No.

No. I said I would fight for him and I will. He's just a little boy. A boy who has been the victim so many times. If Tamara did something to convince Holden to hurt Betsy... Well, we will deal with that when we get to it. Right now, I need to tell Cooper.

I need to tell him I know who killed our daughter.

———

As soon as I leave the motel, I get in my car and call Cooper. He doesn't answer, so I decide to just drive directly to the police station. The November air is frigid, but I drive with the window down. Holden often wants to ride this way and as the air whips around my hair I can't help but think that maybe he does it so he can keep his mind sharp. Ready. Clear.

I wind my way through my familiar town. Before this year, it was a place I always saw as my home, my beginning and my end. But now Port Windwick seems to have closed in around me, not a cocoon but a cage.

After I park at the station, I pull out my phone and I see I've missed a call from Tom.

Frowning, I listen to the voicemail he must have left while I was in the motel.

"Emery, I need to speak with you. I've recently found some information that frankly, I find disturbing. And I am hoping you can clarify some things with me. I need to go to the police with this but I want to speak with you first. Please call me as soon as you can. It's urgent."

Disturbing is right. I wonder just how much he knows about Tamara. I return the call, but it goes to voicemail and so I hang up, frustrated, but knowing that I will be inside the station myself in a matter of minutes.

I should call Mark, tell him what I've discovered, see how much he knows. He was there -- at Tamara's motel. Why? I need to know and only he can tell me. But as I open my messages on my phone I see the last messages we sent to one another. They were brief and direct. When I talk to him about the person who killed Betsy, I want to look in his eyes, I want him to see the emotion swelling in mine. I want him to know that despite my affair, I never meant to hurt him. And that right now, I need to understand him.

But here I am, shoving my phone back in my pocket and walking toward the man who I turned to in my weakest moment. The man whose strength I really crave.

I'm a shitty wife, but a damn good mother.

And right now I can't let my mess with Mark get in the way of getting justice for Betsy's death. My head is clear from the drive. My words are ready.

I ask to see Cooper Dawson and the officer at the front desk calls him right away. "Emery Gable, sir, to see you. Yes, she's here right now."

He hangs up and looks at me as if he knows something. More than I do. "What?" I ask, not liking his stares.

"Nothing, ma'am, just, I'm so sorry for everything."

But I don't want his pity, his apology. I want Tamara in handcuffs, behind bars. I want her at the bottom of a ravine with her head bashed in. I want her to pay for this. For all of it. It's time to bury my daughter.

Moments later, Cooper is walking toward me, reading me without me having to say a word. He knows something has changed, he feels it in my vibrations. Silently, he leads me into his office.

"Emery," he says, closing the door. "Did someone call you?"

I shake my head. "No, why, did something happen?"

My immediate thought is that someone got to Holden. That Tamara got to Holden.

"Shit, Emery," he starts. Before he says anything more, there's a knock on the door. Margot steps inside the office and suddenly it feels that they understand why I'm here.

"I think I know who did this," I start the same time Margot clears her throat.

"Have you told her?" she asks Cooper. He shakes his

head. "I'm so sorry, Emery," Margot continues. "We are filing for an arrest warrant."

"It's her, right?" I ask, eyes widening. My stomach is twisting; my daughter's murderer will be held account- able. "Tamara?"

They exchange a look, frowning. "No, Emery. The warrant is for Holden."

"What?" I gasp. "No. No. It's not Holden. He didn't do this. He's a little boy. He's a child. Not a killer," I say, my muscles tight, my feet planted in a wide stance.

"Emery," Margot says in a calm manner that doesn't match my horror in this moment. "We just received the first of the DNA. The lab is faxing over all the results, but the first one was a match. Holden's skin--"

"No!" I step back, unwilling to listen. The room spins as everyone's assumption about my son is being fulfilled. I refuse to believe it. "It wasn't him. It was Tamara."

"Who's Tamara?" Cooper asks, his voice pained. Maybe he should have left this case, maybe this was a bad idea. He can't see the forest for the trees.

I reach in my purse, pulling out the papers, the photos. But they aren't of her -- they are all of my family. "Holden's birth mom has been stalking us; look." I thrust a photo in Cooper's face. "I found her hotel room, across from Royal Chinese. She's been staying there, casing our family. All of us. She wanted to make me pay for taking her son. For taking Holden."

I'm crying, but they aren't tears of relief, it's despera- tion. I need them to see what I see.

Cooper and Margot pick up the photos, trying to catch up. "I don't know who Tamara is, Emery."

I reach into my pocket, pulling out the photo of mother and son. Pushing it in Cooper's face I force him to look. "See, this woman... This is what she's done."

Cooper's face falls, and he takes the photograph, turning it to face Margot. Something shifts in the room and she steps closer, taking in Tamara and Holden. A pair that match in so many ways. Same skin, same hair, same nose. But not the same eyes. His are brown. Hers are dark green, the shade of the woods, the trail where Betsy was dragged against her will and murdered in cold blood.

"Emery, this woman, she --"

I cut him off. "She did it," I cry, grabbing the articles and family photos, shoving them at Cooper's solid chest. The man who knows me best needs to believe me now.

"Emery," he says, his voice so even it makes me pause, look up at him. "This woman was a Jane Doe. We found her in an alley two days ago, a needle in her arm. Overdosed."

"No. It's Holden's birth mom. And she... she killed Bets..."

"Em," Cooper says gently, his hand on my back.

"What do you mean she's a Jane Doe? It's Tamara. She..." I step away, heart pounding in confusion. "I was just at her motel. She was... She was stalking my family. She wanted..." I shake my head, angry with them for not seeing what I see.

"Emery," Margot says, trying to calm me but I move

for the door, needing to see Holden. "If his DNA matches Tamara... Maybe he... Maybe she told him to do this? Maybe..."

I start moving toward the entrance. There are too many maybes right now. I just need the truth.

"Where are you going?" Coopers calls. "Emery, don't leave like this. Just wait, okay--" But he's interrupted. Another officer comes toward him telling him it's urgent.

"Dawson," the officer says. "Tom, the boy's lawyer -- he's dead."

"Dead?" My mind reels. "No. Tom isn't dead. He can't be... he just called me."

"He was found at his office, held a gun to his own head."

I cover my mouth, handing Cooper my phone, and pressing play, my fingers trembling. "He said he was coming to the police with information ...."

I grab my phone, running out of the building. I need to see my husband. Find out what led him to the motel room. I need to see my son. Find out why his DNA matches the traces left on my daughter.

I need to piece this together. I'm the only one who can.

A mother's intuition is stronger than anything else on Earth.

I need to go save my son before Cooper charges him with murder.

33

ONE MONTH EARLIER

TRISTA IS HERE, splitting a bottle of wine with me when Mark walks in the door. He wasn't supposed to be back tonight. He glances around the kitchen, eyeing the half-empty glasses, taking in our hushed voices.

We were talking about him.

"Where is Betsy?" he asks, tugging at his tie. He doesn't lean in for a kiss, doesn't even say hello.

"She's upstairs with Holden. They're playing Minecraft."

"I told you, Emery, I don't like it when they spend hours alone together."

I suppress my urge to roll my eyes and take a sip of wine to avoid saying something I might regret.

"Maybe I should get going?" Trista says, looking between Mark and me.

I shake my head, my hand on her elbow. "Stay. We can go outside."

Mark snorts. "And leave the kids in the house alone?"

"They're eleven, Mark, and besides, you're here, aren't you?"

Mark's jaw tightens. "Yes, I am, but you didn't know I'd be here. You thought I was staying in Olympia. Is this what you do when I'm gone? Get drunk and let the kids run loose?"

"God," I sigh, standing up from the barstool. "I'm not drunk. I've had a glass of wine and the kids are happy. Go up there and see for yourself. You're being so--"

"What am I being, Emery? Why don't you tell me, exactly what I am?"

"I'm not doing this, Mark. The kids are fine, but I'm not." I grab the bottle of wine and the cheese board I prepared to share with my friend. "We're going to the patio."

I open the door leading outside to the veranda and Trista follows me. She closes the door and looks at me with wide eyes. I shrug. I am so tired of pretending but being honest is terrifying. Trista will never look at me the same way again.

"What the fuck was that, Em?"

I set down the cheese platter and uncork the wine, topping off our glasses. "*That* was your state senator, Trista." I give her an exaggerated smile. "And he's running for Congress, isn't that just super?"

She lifts her brows, sitting in a chair at the patio table. "I need more than a charade. Give it to me straight."

I groan, plucking a red grape and popping it in my mouth. "That is what happens when your husband resents you for adopting a child you both said you wanted."

"That's it?" She purses her lips.

"It? Tris, that's fucking huge."

"Yeah, but I've known Mark for six years. He can be a douche sometimes, sure. And borderline OCD. But he isn't mean just to be mean. It's something else."

"Did you hear how he was talking? He *is* being mean to be mean."

"Does he talk like that to Holden?"

I cut off a wedge of Beecher's Flagship cheddar. Nibbling on it, I think. He's been really hard on me ever since I started pulling away. We haven't had sex in ages -- not since Cabo and that was three months ago.

"He isn't outright rude with Holden -- more like, he's ambivalent," I tell her, processing as I do. "He always says he doesn't want Betsy and Holden alone together. Maybe he only says it to make my life more difficult. If Bets and Holden aren't hanging out alone playing a game or whatever, it means I have to entertain them." I pause, knowing that sounds bad. "Which... look, I love that part of being a mom. But I also love drinking wine with my friend without the kids asking for a snack."

"So, he's taking it all out on you, not Holden."

I nod. "Yeah, I think so."

Trista swirls her red wine, her eyes fixed as if she's working out a problem. "So what did you do?"

I huff in protest. "God, what kind of friend are you? Shouldn't you assume the best in me?"

She smirks. "I know you, Em. You aren't in the

mommy tribe for a reason. You're a fighter. You mask it well, to most people. But I'm not most people."

"So you're saying I started this?"

"You tell me."

This is the thing about letting someone in. Really in. They can see through the bullshit, the lies. The secrets. They can see the truth.

I've known my day of reckoning was coming. But I thought it would be with Mark before anyone else.

But now Trista is waiting for me to speak, to lay it out there. And maybe it's better to talk it through with a friend before I tell my husband I'm having an affair.

Maybe.

"That bad, huh?" She leans back in the chair, the sun has set and it's dark out here. I'm glad. I don't want her to see my face. I want the shadows right now. I want to hide.

"I slept with Cooper," I tell her. "A year after we broke up, he came into town and we slept together. A few days before Mark and I hooked up for the first time. This was twelve years ago. I hadn't seen Cooper after that until he moved back to town this year. And I never told Mark. But..." I bite my lip, wondering why I've started here.

"Em, what are you saying?"

Tris is smart. The smartest woman I know. She is exact and perceptive and way too good for me in a lot of ways. She's a woman who loves hard and deep. Will she still love me, after I tell her the truth?

"I found out I was pregnant three weeks later. I didn't know who the father was until I saw her. It was obvious to me. She was Cooper's. Same fair hair, blue eyes, and her heart on her sleeve the same as her father. That's why we broke up after my dad died. He fell apart, I needed a rock and he was a river of tears. And I was already married. Mark gave me a perfect life and Cooper was out of the picture and so I lied."

Trista sets down her wine, my story shocking her silent.

"Look," I say. "Coop figured it out, saw photos on Instagram and did the math and I mean, just look at her. She's his clone. That's why he moved back to town. But Cooper doesn't want to ruin Betsy's childhood by opening this can of worms. Not yet. He wants her to think the world is safe and secure. He doesn't want her to know."

"But let me guess, Mark found out and now he's pissed?"

I swallow. "No. God no. He doesn't know that. But I do think he wonders if I'm cheating on him though."

"Are you?

"Yes."

"With Cooper?"

"Yes."

"Shit, Em."

"I know."

We sit in silence, finishing our wine, pouring more. My hands shake as I drink. Trista's silence the blanket that I'm using to wrap around me. What words would give me solace? My life is falling apart. I'm losing my husband just as I gained a son.

"Do you love him?"

"Yes," I say without hesitation, tears pooling in my eyes. "I love Holden so much."

"Oh, Em." Trista reaches over and squeezes my hand. "I meant Coop."

I wipe my eyes. "Well shit, I love him too."

"And Mark?"

"I mean, how do we recover from this?"

"Are you going to tell him?"

"Not yet. Holden is doing well right now." I lift my hands in defense. "I mean, relatively speaking. I know he's suspended right now, but it's only for a week. And he didn't start that fight on the playground."

Trista nods. "Jasper is a little fuckhead."

I laugh, tears spilling down my cheeks. Her allegiance to us is too pure. She may have a hard-ass shell, but she's as pure of heart as Betsy.

"I'm a week late."

"Oh Em."

"I know, and Mark and I haven't slept together all summer." I blink back the onslaught of tears. "It's a fucking disaster."

"Did you take a test?"

I shake my head. "Maybe I'll start tomorrow. Maybe I'm being insane."

"Maybe."

The silence hangs between us again. This time though, everything is out in the open. I've bared my soul. She isn't running away.

"What am I gonna do?" I ask in a small voice that sounds nothing like me.

She sighs. "You're going to take a pregnancy test,

first off. And you'll keep this on the down low until Holden and Betsy are stable enough to deal with their parents' divorce and their mother's pregnancy -- if you're even pregnant. And until Holden's therapist has a clear understanding of the situation. Until you're ready to seriously blow up your life."

"I think I already did, Tris. When Holden came home."

She clucks her tongue. "I think you lit the match twelve years ago when you got knocked up, it's just that this bomb happens to have a long-ass fuse."

"My kids are going to hate me."

I can see Trista shake her head, the moonlight shining down on us. "No. Your kids love you, Emery. And the good news is, you love them too."

34

PRESENT

As I drive home my stomach is in knots. It's been twisting all day but now it's more painful. It's like my body knows this is bad... that my life is on the precipice of falling apart for good. Forever.

The pain, though, is unbearable. The worst cramping I've ever experienced, like a Charlie horse in my gut. I need to get home, to Holden and Mark.

Mark. Why was he talking to Tamara outside the motel? How is he involved with her at all? I reach for my phone, wanting to call Cooper and tell him that part -- but it falls to my feet. I couldn't place a call anyways, I have to keep my hands on the wheel as I drive, the pain so excruciating.

When I finally get home I feel light headed and woozy. I put the car in park and reach for my phone that's at my feet.

That's when I see it.

The blood.

So much blood.

I squeeze my eyes shut not wanting to admit that the pain is contractions. That I'm losing the baby.

I can't lose another one, not now. Not when I just lost Bets. I press my hand to my womb, tears streaming down my cheeks. No. No. This can't be my story. Can't be Cooper's story.

I was going to tell him. I took the test as Trista ordered me to do. I made an appointment with my OBGYN who said I needed to wait until ten weeks to come in.

I'm only 8 weeks along.

Never heard the heartbeat.

Haven't even told Cooper.

I had a plan. After Halloween, I was going to go to his house and tell him the news. But then everything changed.

Betsy died and my world came to a screeching halt and now it's too late. Now it's going to end before it ever began.

I get out of the car, forgetting the purse, the keys. I need to get to the hospital. Mark can drive me. He will be furious, but he won't want me to suffer.

Not after everything we've been through. Right?

God, I'm still so selfish, so ugly. So fucked up.

I get to the door, my breath shaking, blood dripping down my legs, soaking my jeans. It hurts so bad.

Pushing open the door, I enter the foyer hearing the screams. The shouts. I grip the wall, forcing my feet to take one step in front of the next. In the kitchen, I see

Mark, his fingers around Holden's neck. A phone on the ground beside them.

"What are you doing?" I scream. "Let him go!" My words are shaky, same as my legs and I try to focus, scared I might pass out. Mark turns to me and Holden uses the moment of hesitation to push Mark away.

But Mark is stronger. Bigger. And at this moment, terrifying.

"Mark, what are you doing?" I ask, falling to the ground, my knees giving out, my heart pounding too damn fast. "Why are you..."

My fall to the ground gets his attention, and he shoves Holden away, leaning in close to me. "I need to get to the hospital," I moan. "Now, Mark."

Holden's neck is red, Mark's hands were wrapped around him so tightly as if trying to kill him.

"Why?" I cry as Mark leans in close.

"What happened?" he asks me.

For a moment, I think it's Mark. My Mark. The Mark who held my hand when Betsy was born. The Mark who picked me up from the ground the night my daughter died.

I think, maybe I've got it wrong. Maybe Holden has done something, maybe he is the killer Cooper thinks he is. Maybe Mark is trying to protect himself, protect me.

But then I look deeper in his eyes, the rich dark brown so familiar. So familiar it's eerie.

I look at Holden, remember the first time I saw his photo in the newspaper. I knew he was family before we ever met. One look and I knew.

What did I know?

I blink, the pain is so unbearable. I writhe on the floor, trying to pull myself up, reaching out for Mark... But Mark doesn't try to help. To offer me his hand. His gaze is piercing, hard. Cruel.

"I'm losing my baby," I whimper, my skin cold, clammy, my heart slowing, my mind still racing. Desperate to keep up.

Holden is shouting, "Mom, it's going to be okay, Mom. I promise. Where's your phone?"

"My car," I manage to say.

Holden steps closer, but Mark pushes him away. "You little slut," Mark snarls at me. It's not my Mark. This man is unhinged. Broken. "Pregnant?" He bites his lip, shaking his head. Then he grabs my wrists and begins to drag me out of the kitchen.

"Let her go," Holden shouts. "Let her go!"

But Mark doesn't stop, refuses to listen. My blood a trail on the hardwood floor.

"Call Cooper," I pant. "Holden. Call Coop."

Mark kicks open the bathroom door. "Cooper? You want to call Cooper? Now?"

I nod, trembling. "Yes, he... Mark... I'm so sorry."

He isn't listening. "You can stay in here and lose the baby. I don't want you to have that bastard child. Not after everything."

He's lost it. Grief does wild things to a person. Is this what it's done to Mark? Sent him over the edge?

"I'm so sorry. You're right," I say trying to ease him back to me. "I don't need the hospital. I just need... I need..."

I try to pull myself onto the toilet. There is so much blood.

"What do you need, you little whore?" he asks.

"What happened at Tom's?" I ask, hoping Holden has gotten to the car. Found my phone.

"Tom?" Mark laughs sharply. "That little fucker thinks he figured it all out."

The shock of the words hurls through my chest. At the station, they said Tom held a gun to his head... that... Oh, god. "What did you do?"

"I did what needed to be done. He knew too much."

"What have you done, Mark? What did you do?"

"I'm saving our asses, Emery."

I clutch the basin of the toilet, wishing I'd told Cooper we were having another baby. This could all be so different right now.

I silently pray Holden has reached my phone. Why the hell don't I have a landline? This is why parents give their kids smartphones and data plans. So they can call 9-1-1 when their mother is being pushed into a bathroom, bleeding out. I've done everything wrong.

Except I know, even at this moment, as Mark screams and I shake, I know that I didn't. I didn't do everything wrong. I was a good mom. Am a good mom. I love my children. And I will love them until my dying breath.

"Why did you kill Tom?" I ask, my head falling back. I'm so tired but I have to know.

"You want to know why I killed that little snake?" Mark snarls. My mind catches on the word snake. It doesn't let go.

"Why don't you watch this? Maybe then you'll understand why I killed Tom. He found this little gem."

He turns, reaching for the phone that skittered across the floor. He shoves it into my face before pressing play. "This is why I have to kill Holden."

35

TWO WEEKS EARLIER

I HAVE my laptop open with a YouTube video playing. I've rewatched it half a dozen times. But this fabric glue is not working on this felt, no matter how many times I try.

"Maybe use a little stitch," Betsy says, threading a needle and handing it to me.

"Or maybe you could?" I say, smiling. I hand her the orange feather and felt.

Betsy laughs. "Mom, you're so funny. You're the one who taught me to sew."

"I've never tried to sew feathers to a costume, though."

Holden comes into the kitchen through the back door with a basketball under his arm. He looks over the piles of fabric and lifts his eyebrows. "Monica just took us to Wal-Mart to get costumes."

"Mom always makes mine. When she was little her best friend's mom always made her one. So now Mom makes mine, too. Isn't she good at it?"

"Those sewing classes at art college helped," I say smiling at the good memory of Cooper's mom making our costumes every year.

"You went to college for art?" Holden asks. It's not strange that it hasn't come up. My degree in fine arts isn't exactly relevant to my current life. I glance over at the table where my art supplies have been taken over by Betsy's.

"I thought I'd have a famous comic strip one day. Instead, I got even luckier and became a mother."

"That's why Betsy is so good at drawing, huh?"

I smile, liking that thought. "Maybe."

"It's in my DNA," Betsy says proudly, but then her smile slips. "Sorry, Holden. I didn't mean anything by that."

Holden shrugs, turning toward the kitchen sink to help himself to a glass of water.

"Sorry, Mom," she mumbles. "You think I hurt his feelings?"

I shake my head. "Holden knows you would never mean to hurt him."

Holden walks back to the table and sits next to Betsy. "I don't know anything about my DNA. I never knew my dad," he says. "And my mom..." His eyes flit up to mine. "I mean, my um, birth mom, well, she wasn't really good with details. Like, she never could tell me who my grandparents were, or if I had any aunts."

"We still don't have any aunts," Betsy says. "Mom and Dad are both only children."

"We're lucky," Holden says. "We'll always have each other."

Heat radiates through my chest at his words. I think of the baby I'm carrying, they will always have this little bean too. A big brother and big sister.

I took the test -- well six of them -- and they were all positive. I'll see my doctor in four weeks and I plan to tell Cooper before then. I want him to be with me. Especially after holding back from him when I was pregnant with Betsy. This time around, I'll be more open.

"Let's see how this fits, Holden," I say, holding up the black costume made of felt and sequined fabric meant to resemble scales.

"This is so cool," he says, pulling it over his head. It completely covers him, head to toe. The hood covers all of his face, and a snake's tongue hangs from the mouth. "I look just like Nagini."

"Coolest snake ever," I agree, happy the sequins aren't too bright. I wanted it to look both powerful and spooky.

"We can trade if you want, Bets. On Halloween, half-way through the night."

Betsy looks over at her brother and smiles. "Maybe." Then she adds, "If you go in the haunted house you'll shock everyone, no matter what you're wearing."

"What haunted house?" I ask, watching as she attaches another feather to the wings on her phoenix costume.

"The Becken house, on the top of the hill. Everyone dared Holden to go there on Halloween."

"Why?"

Betsy and Holden share a look. "They don't think he's brave enough."

"You don't have to prove your bravery with dares," I say. Holden takes off his costume and carefully folds it and sets it on the table.

"How else would I?" he asks. "Because the kids at school, they think..." He stops talking, looking at Bets.

"What, what do they think?"

"They say this dare will prove whether or not they will be my... friend."

"You want to be their friend?"

Holden shrugs. I glance at Betsy; she's teasing her lip between her teeth.

"If he does this, it will show them that he's the best. That he can be one of them," Betsy says.

"You want to be one of them?"

He doesn't answer, so I don't press. I know enough about Holden by now to know if you try to get him somewhere he doesn't want to go, he shuts down.

Betsy sews in silence and I make fringe on the hem of her costume. Holden watches.

"How else can people prove they are brave?" Holden finally asks.

"Lots of people think bravery means being strong, big, powerful," I say, leaning into this moment of sharing parts of my heart with my kids. This right here is why I am thankful to be a mother. These are the moments I treasure -- too precious to Instagram. "But the bravest people I know are the ones who love deep and wide. Who fight for happiness. Who choose to hold on tight when everyone else lets go? Bravery doesn't have to be a big show. A haunted house. A dare. It can be a lot of little things. And when you add them up, you are whole."

Betsy sets down her feathers. "Who is like that?" she asks. "Who is that brave?"

"My friend Trista. She's that kind of brave. She loves fiercely. And my friend Coop, he never gives up on people. And Holden, you're a special kind of brave. You keep fighting for your happily ever after. The kind that isn't in fairy tales. The kind that is right here, at this kitchen table."

Holden's chin trembles, and I know he hears me. Really hears me. And my shoulders fall, grateful for this moment. For my family. The last week at home was rough. He got mad that I wouldn't make him chicken nuggets and he filled the dishwasher and washing machine with dish soap. The floors in the kitchen need to be replaced and the washer is completely ruined. He refused to apologize, shouting at me that I should have made the food he wanted.

He can be such a monster; a menace. Some days, I wonder if I'll always have to walk on eggshells. But the other times, like right now, I think that all Holden needs is more time. More trust. More love.

It's exhausting, though, being that much for someone.

"And you, Betsy. You're that kind of brave too," I tell

her. "You hold on tight. You love deep and wide. Forever."

Betsy reaches for my hand, holds it. And I memorize her heart-shaped face. Her clear blue eyes and long, fair hair and rosy cheeks and her smile. A smile that could make anyone on Earth feel better.

"You're that kind of brave too, Mom." She nods. "You're fearless."

I twist my lips. "You think I'm fearless?"

Betsy laughs. "Mom, you're not scared of anything."

I tilt my head. Because I never see myself like that. But she sees me with childlike eyes. A pure heart. She believes I'm the best version of myself, not the flawed one. The one I always try to come to terms with. The version I can barely look at in the mirror.

She sees me as I wish I could see myself.

"I love you, Betsy," I tell her. "And you're going to be the most beautiful phoenix in the whole wide world."

She beams back at me, the colorful feathers strewn over the kitchen table, a rainbow. I look at my daughter and know that she's going to be okay. She's had setbacks and stumbles with her classmates, had to learn to share her parents with a new sibling. It's been hard at times for her to find her footing.

But maybe Betsy never needed to walk in a straight line.

Maybe my daughter was always meant to fly.

36

ONE WEEK EARLIER
HALLOWEEN NIGHT

Betsy

"JUST IGNORE THEM," he tells me. "They're stupid."

"Easy for you to say. They don't call you a baby."

"They call me worse things, Bets."

He's right. The kids at school are awful to Holden but he holds his head high, doesn't let it get to him. He is strong in ways that make me feel safe.

But I'm so sick of all of them. Of Cory and Pete and Sam. Of Jasper. But mostly of Julia. Every chance she gets, she tries to make me feel small. I'm so sick of it. Being the weird one. The different one. The girl who is called Baby Betsy. Cory asked if I had on a diaper under my costume and I wish I was stronger. Like Holden. Then I would have punched Cory. I would have stolen his candy and thrown it in Julia's face.

Instead, I walk in silence, my fists balled tightly and my mouth in a firm line. I'm so tired of keeping my mouth shut. I'm a bad sister, letting Holden always fight my battles for me. Tonight, I will tell those kids what I really think.

I'll show them what I'm made of.

Holden keeps leaning in and whispering to me but I don't want to hear it.

MAYBE HE'S RIGHT, fighting back will cause more problems. I turn toward the right at the end of the street. I don't want to trick or treat anymore. I want to go home, curl up in my bed with Mom. Tonight I'll tell her the truth about the kids at school. I'll show her my journal. I know she and dad are going to get a divorce, I know it. But it's too hard keeping this all to myself. Holden says being brave means being honest.

I never tell the truth. I don't want to hurt the people I love. If Mom knew about the kids at school, she'd be so sad. She'd feel like it was her fault.

"You want to go back home?" I ask Holden. He looks so cool in his snake costume, and I wonder what it would be like to wear it, to pretend to be someone else. To shed my skin and put on his.

What would it be like to be Holden? My brother never backs down. Not even when he's wrong. Cory called me a *diaper baby* and I didn't even reply. I hung my head and bit back tears and silently thanked my mom for making the phoenix costume with a hood so no one would see my eyes.

"We can go back," Holden says. "I think it's going to start raining anyways."

We get to the end of the cul-de-sac, where the trail we cut through begins when Jasper calls out to us.

"Are you going home because you're scared, little babies? Is it past your bedtime, Betsy?" Jasper asks cackling. Cory has his phone out and Julia tells him to put it away. But Cory just laughs and points it at us.

"We're going home because we want to. Just leave us alone," Holden tells them.

"Or what?" Pete asks. "You gonna make us pay?"

Sam, laughs. "Yeah, right. He's poor trash. He doesn't have any money. He'd have to steal it."

Holden steps toward him, raising his fists like he always does. He says he will fight all my battles. That the last thing he wants is for me to be as broken as he is.

I pull him back. "Don't, Holden. Mom said if you did one more thing you'd be grounded for a month."

Instead, I move toward Sam, pushing him, angry over his words. How dare he talk like that about my brother.

"Whoa, the baby is having a tantrum," Julia laughs. "Do you need a time out?"

"I hate you," I tell them. "All of you. I'm telling my mom and dad about how mean you are."

They laugh at this, cackling at the thought. "Oh, you're going to go tattle-tale?" Julia laughs. "Sounds about right for a little baby."

She has always hated me. Ever since first grade when I won the school art competition and my drawing of an orca whale got me a blue ribbon and her drawing of a horse got her nothing. She's always held a grudge and I'm tired of it. Of letting her make me feel small.

"You're an awful person, Julia," I shout, pointing at her. "I'm brave, what are you?"

She smirks, crossing her arms. "If you're so brave, go to the Becken house. It's haunted. Steal something inside with their name on it."

"Something like what?" I ask, wanting a way to prove myself to the people who have always looked down on me.

"Like a house number, or isn't there a weird sign in their yard? That says BEWARE?" Her eyes light up under the light of the moon.

"Yeah," Jasper says. "There is that sign there, by the door. Get that and we'll know you're not a little kid anymore."

"That's stupid," Holden shouts. "She doesn't have to prove anything to you."

"Fine, then we will know she's the big baby we always knew she was." Julia crosses her arms smugly.

"I'll get that sign," I shout, my voice bigger than it ever is.

"Alone," Jasper says. "You have to go alone."

I swallow, hard. Going alone is a hundred times worse than going with Holden. "Fine," I say with as much fire as I can muster. "I'll bring you the sign tomorrow."

I tug on my brother's arm dragging him toward the woods. Mom hates us coming through this trail, but Holden and I always do anyway. It takes half the time to get home.

Deep down I know it's a bad idea, me going to the Becken house alone. The place gives me the creeps, and their dog is terrifying. Julia and Jasper know that -- everyone knows that house is haunted. No one ever comes out of it, yet there is always a dog pacing the front yard.

"Betsy," Holden says, pushing my hand away. "What are you doing?"

"I'm going to the haunted house," I tell him. We're standing at the trailhead and I can tell Holden doesn't like this. Neither do I.

"No, we need to go home. It's gonna start raining and you hate walking in the dark alone. Plus." He stops.

"Plus what?"

"Plus I'm scared you're going to get freaked out."

"I don't care," I say sharply, looking over my shoulder I see the kids still in a circle, watching us. "I want this to be over. They've been bullying me for so long. I want to prove to them I'm--"

Holden cuts me off, shakes my shoulders. "Listen to me, Bets. You don't have to prove anything. Remember what Mom said? Bravery doesn't have to be a big show."

Tears prick my eyes, I hate that the kids are watching us. Holden tugs on my arm, pulling me away from their watchful eyes. He knows me so well.

We run into the woods, the ground covered in pine needles, the damp air hanging heavy in the branches. It's dark and familiar. The Becken house isn't familiar at all. How can I be thinking of going there alone?

"Betsy," Holden says. "Don't do this. You're already shaking."

"They will be even worse if I don't."

"We could go home, tell our parents about how awful they are. They will hear you and make it stop."

I shake my head. "That's the problem. Then Julia and Jasper will know that I am the big wuss they already think I am. I just want to fix this on my own. Mom and Dad don't need any more problems."

"They would never think of you as a problem."

I exhale, wondering if he's right. But then I picture Mom and Dad's faces, as they yelled in the kitchen last night. The way they argued about us kids. They don't need any more stress right now. Dad keeps saying he's running for Congress. The last thing he needs is a problem child.

"I want Julia to think I'm brave -- but Holden, I don't think I can go alone. I'm scared."

Holden pulls off his snake costume, the sequins glittering under the moon. "Here," he says. "Let's trade. I'll go and get the sign dressed as a phoenix. You put on the snake costume and go home. I'll bring back the sign and tomorrow you can show them how tough you are."

"You mean how tough you are?"

Holden grins. "If they are watching us, they will think it's you running across the street, up the hill. They will never think it's me. I'll be the phoenix."

"You'd really do that for me?" Relief fills my lungs and it's like I can breathe for the first time all night.

"Bets," Holden says, helping me out of the phoenix costume. "You're my sister, I'd do anything for you."

Holden gives me his lopsided grin and I thank him over and over again as I get dressed as the snake. "You think it will work?" I ask, helping adjust the wings on his back. The costumes completely cover us head to toe, and no one could tell us apart, not even Mom.

"I think you are the scariest snake this trail has ever seen." Holden flaps his wings, taking my jack-o-lantern bucket, and I take his skeleton sack. "Be safe going home. It's really dark."

"I've been on it a hundred times. It's way less scary than the Becken house."

"We are going to prove those idiots wrong," Holden says. "Just wait till they see the sign tomorrow."

"You have to go get it first," I say laughing.

"Maybe when I get home we can trade candy?" he asks, walking away.

"No way. I totally owe you after this. You can have any of my candy that you like."

We run in opposite directions, and I try not to think about the fact that I'm alone in the woods. Instead, I think about the fact that Holden has my back. Always has my back.

My foot snaps a branch, and an owl hoots in a tree, but besides that, it's silent.

Until it's not.

Until I feel someone lunge for me, punching me to the ground.

Covering my mouth with their hands. "Don't scream, Holden," he says.

37

PRESENT

THE VIDEO IS grainy but there is fluorescent lighting shining on the people in the footage. Blood pools around my feet as I sit on the tiles of the bathroom floor, but I watch, holding my breath, even though I already feel so faint.

It's clear who it is, what it is.

Mark and Tamara, in a bathroom, not so different than the one I am in now. He's younger -- much younger -- with the same floppy hair, he had when we met. His white dress shirt is unbuttoned down his chest, his eyes bloodshot and glazed. They have a white line of cocaine on the counter, using a credit card with his name to form a long, straight line.

Tamara laughs, grabbing a card from her purse, teasing him that she can make a better line than him. Their hands shake, their pupils dilated.

They both take a line. Then another. Another woman joins them, only she looks younger than Tamara. She pulls out a needle, and the three of them shoot up, laughing about how they are fucking out of their minds, and Tamara keeps filming, telling Mark he looks so hot. So, fucking good. His veins are popping and he shouts, clapping his hands, triumphant.

They begin peeling off their clothes, and bile begins rising in my throat. I know what's going to happen before it begins and my body shakes, recoils. I don't want to see anymore. I drop the phone, it clatters, and Mark lunges for it, pointing it at me as the three of them begin having sex. The phone is propped on the counter, catching each detail.

"Tamara had this -- all this time. Sent it to Tom after Betsy died. She saw our fucking picture in the *Seattle Times*. She'd been blackmailing me since the fucking adoption was a statewide headline. This is your fault. Do you understand now? Understand that I could never be a congressman if this got out?"

"I don't understand," I moan, clutching my stomach. "What does this have to do with Holden? With Betsy? With... You?"

"You're so fucking dumb. You always were. That is why I married you. Because you were so broken I knew you'd never be strong enough to fight back. I just never knew that you were a slut, too."

"What did she want?"

"She wanted Holden. Her son. I knew you'd never let that happen, never give him over willingly. So, I decided to take care of it myself. Make that little problem disappear. Kill him and have him cremated and no one would ever be able to prove a single fucking thing."

I need to move. To get away from him. On my hands and knees, I try to move past him, but Mark won't let me.

"If we hadn't had that picture taken, she would never have found us. And I would never have known I had a son. That I was his father. It's your fault this happened."

"Son?" Holden is here, back. My phone is in his hand. His face is written in shock. So is mine. Mark is Holden's biological father?

Mark stands, snarling at Holden. "Yes, I'm your father. Emery said she saw your photo and knew you were ours -- we just never realized how right she was."

"You knew he was yours when we brought him home?"

Mark drops down to me, slapping me hard across the cheek. "Of course not. I never knew that little drugged up whore was pregnant." He turns to Holden. "But here you are, part of the family."

Holden's eyes burn with hatred and when Mark has his back to me, I grab for his ankles, slamming my elbow into the back of his knees. He grabs the doorframe, to keep standing, but Holden seizes the moment to come at him, Mark moves faster, grabbing Holden's arms and pushing him against the wall in the foyer.

"You were supposed to die on Halloween. I wanted to kill you. Not Betsy. It's your fucking fault."

His words send a rush of horror over me. All this time, I've been married to a monster.

I can't take anymore, watch any more. So, I lunge

for the vase on the table in the hall and smash it over Mark's head.

He falls back, screaming, blood pouring from his forehead. And Holden reaches for the mirror on the wall, smashing it over Mark's face.

Sirens blare down the street and my chest tightens. Maybe I will get Holden out of here in one piece. Maybe I can stitch my son back together.

He stumbles toward the door, clinging to the door handle as if running now will make him free. It's too late.

He's already caught.

Cooper barges through the door as Mark falls to the floor. Holden stands shaking, my feet are covered in blood. Mark is shaking, ruined. Destroyed.

Cooper lifts me into his arms, a SWAT team swarms us from behind him, they barge into my home, guns pointed at Mark.

I reach for Holden's hand; I don't let go.

Cooper carries me from the house, blaring sirens and bright lights swirling around me.

"I'm losing our baby," I tell him, tears falling down my cheeks.

"I'm right here, Em," he tells me. And that's the thing about Cooper Dawson, he is right by my side. When I don't deserve it -- his love -- he gives me strength. We've never given up on one another.

As I'm placed on a stretcher, loaded into an ambulance, a medic talks to me but I can't hear their words.

The pounding in my chest is so devastatingly loud. The ache in my belly metallic, screeching to a halt.

Cooper's hands cup my face. Holding me. "Oh, my God," I pant, breathless with fear and shaking. I press my palms to my belly, praying this miracle holds on a little longer.

The ambulance careens away from the house and just like that, we're driving away, from the horror -- Holden, Cooper, and me.

"You did good," Cooper tells Holden. "Calling me saved your mom's life, your life too."

I blink, watching Cooper pull Holden in a hug. My son's shoulders shake as his sister's father's arms envelop him.

Holden looks down at me, his dark eyes the same as his father's. Fate brought us together. I saw this photograph and I knew where he belonged. Here. With his family.

I just didn't know that it was his own father who would try to take his life.

No one did.

"I love you, Mom," he tells me, eyes swimming with tears.

He has never said words like this to me. I didn't think I needed them -- that my love for him would be enough to see us through. But words have power, and his will give me the strength I need.

Barreling toward the hospital, I look to Holden, to Cooper. My twisted family tree. Our roots are mangled and looking for a stronghold anywhere they can find one.

Even in darkness, seeds can grow. And we've been

planted right here, in this messy marrow. Our bones are not broken and we will not wither.

My marriage is over. Holden's father will be in prison for the rest of his life. Cooper and I may lose this baby. All these things will require strength.

Burying Betsy will require a different kind of strength.

A kind of strength I didn't think I possessed.

"I love you, too, Holden," I tell him.

Love doesn't solve every problem, and sometimes love is not enough.

But sometimes it is.

Sometimes it's more than enough. Sometimes it is everything.

38

ONE WEEK EARLIER
HALLOWEEN NIGHT

Betsy

IT'S DAD. It's Dad's voice. "It's time for me to take care of you once and for all."

I need to scream, to tell Dad I'm not Holden. That it's me, Betsy, but before I can, I'm pinned to the forest floor. And he's slammed something against my head. Blood runs down my forehead, into my eyes, and I see white lights, blinking.

Bright.

I close my eyes. It's hard to breathe as something bashes into my head. Over and over again.

"I knew I'd find you out tonight. Eventually. You just made it easy for me," he hisses.

I kick, try to open my eyes. Want him to stop.

"You didn't even make it hard. Here, all alone. Didn't even make me follow you home from the Becken house."

No. This isn't right. I try to think, to understand

what's happening. I grab at the costume, trying to rip it off.

"Daddy!" I try to scream, but my voice is muffled. Lost.

Finally, his hand stops. He pulls back, ripping off my hood himself. His hand is raised, his eyes so hard to see. "Betsy?" he chokes out. "What... why are you," he garbles, shaking. The rock in his hand falls to the forest floor. "Shit. Shit!"

"Daddy, I can't... My head. I'm bleeding Daddy," I tell him, not understanding what is happening. Why is Dad hurting me? Trying to hurt Holden? I feel dizzy like my world is spinning. It's so bright.

"It was supposed to be him," Dad moans, clutching his hair.

"Help me, Daddy," I whimper. He doesn't. So, I grab my hands over his face, my nails digging into his skin, my final plea for him to help me. "Daddy, I can't see. You hurt me. My head..."

He pulls my hands from his face, not wanting me to fight back. He picks me up, and I sink against his chest.

"Oh God, I'm so sorry," he cries. "I'm so sorry, Betsy," he moans.

And I close my eyes, knowing I'll be okay. My daddy is holding me, and he'll carry me home. Make sure I get help. He'll fix this. Fix me.

"I love you, Daddy," I whisper, tears splashing down my cheeks. I'm scared but also, safe in his arms.

"I'm so sorry," he repeats, and I sink against him. "It will be all over soon," he tells me.

I whimper, wanting the pain to go away.

"I'm so sorry," he says again and then just like that, I'm no longer nestled against him.

"I never meant to hurt you," he moans.

And then he lets me go.

I don't fall to the forest floor. I don't fall into my mother's arms.

One blink, and I know -- this is the ravine.

I think of Mom. Of Holden. I want to cry but I'm too scared.

I'm just glad it's me here, in his place. That Daddy is killing me, not Holden.

My brother who no one understands, who deserves to be loved the way Mom has always loved me.

I want Holden to live. To be happy. To be free.

My body catches the air, and I close my eyes, knowing it's over.

But before I die, I get a chance to fly.

39

PRESENT

WHEN I COME TO, I kick. I scream. "Help," I bawl, needing someone. Anyone. I'm in a hospital bed, alone. I need someone familiar. Cooper.

I press my hand to my belly, not knowing what happened. Last thing I remember, I was in the ambulance careening toward the hospital. And now here I am. Hooked up to an IV and wearing a hospital gown.

A nurse rushes in, seeing my panic. "Oh, Emery," she says. Light pink scrubs and soft blond hair. A marshmallow. She's the least intimidating person ever. "You're okay," she assures me. "You're okay."

"And the baby?" I ask, my cheeks wet with tears.

The nurse rests her hand on my arm. "The baby is fine. A heartbeat is nice and strong. A miracle with all the blood you lost."

"Truly," I cry, my face splitting. How is this possible?

"Yes, truly. I'll get the doctor and your family."

Family. I blink on the words. Choke on them. The

truth clawing at me. Mark killed Tom. Killed Tamara. Killed my daughter. Tried to kill my son.

I lean over, vomiting on the floor. This isn't my life. Yet here are Cooper and Holden, walking into the room, real. Tangible. Here.

"Oh, Em," Cooper growls, coming to my side, cupping my face in his hands. "Look at you."

I grip his wrist, not wanting him to pull away, wanting to anchor him here, to my side. For always.

Holden stands on the other side of me, and I turn, looking at the boy who shares his DNA with the man who adopted him. No wonder he always felt like family -- he was family before we ever met.

The doctor joins us, tells me I hemorrhaged badly, but that the baby is strong. A fighter. Wasn't going to back down.

"And Mark?" I ask. "Where is he?"

"He's going to prison," Cooper says. "For a very long time. Holden had us on the line for the entire time until we arrived. His confession will put him where he belongs."

I cover my mouth in shock. "You saved me," I tell Holden, reaching out for him. I pull him to me, hugging my boy. My son.

"It's my fault Betsy died," he says, his face pressed against my body. "It should have been me."

He tells Cooper, the doctor, and me about the dare for the sign. How they switched costumes so it would seem like it was Betsy who was doing the big brave thing. How in the end, it cost her everything.

"Do not blame yourself," I tell him, looking into his

sorrowful eyes. "You did nothing except try and stick up for your sister. You were so strong for her."

"But what if I hadn't..."

I shake my head. "Holden, in life there will be so many what-ifs. You can't hang your heart on what is already done. You loved her, you were willing to do anything for her."

"I would take her place if I could." Tears fall down his cheeks.

"Oh, Holden," I say. "So would I."

Holden's therapist Dana pops into the room. "I'm so sorry, to be intruding, but I'd love to speak with you, Holden, if that's alright?"

Holden looks to Cooper, who gives him a nod. "Go on, tell her what she needs to know."

The doctor follows Holden and Dana out of the room and when they are gone, Cooper clears his throat. "Margot requested that Dana be here while she takes Holden's testimony. It will help him, don't you think? To have her there?"

I nod, my chin trembling. "It's been a week since Betsy died, Cooper. All this happened in a week... My entire life fell apart."

Cooper runs his hand over my belly. "And yet, in part, it's come back together."

"I was going to tell you, before the first doctor appointment," I say, guilt wreaking havoc on my conscience. "I was waiting for the right moment."

"I don't need perfect moments, Em. I don't need the right time. I just need now. You. Us."

I set my hand on his, resting on the baby we nearly

lost. "He meant to kill his own son," I say, my breath shaky, the words so raw.

"He will pay for this."

"We all will, Cooper."

We sit in silence, the events washing over us. I keep thinking that I should have known sooner, seen the signs. But Mark was the perfect husband, politician. I was always so focused on my own flaws that I never paused to see them in him.

"Trista is here for you. She's a mess," Cooper says.

I nod. "She can wait. Right now, I just need this. Cooper, I need you."

He kisses my forehead. "Do you have any idea how long I've been waiting to hear you say that?"

Tears fall down my face as I nod. "I'm so sorry, Cooper."

"I love you," he says.

And for once I don't correct the words, I don't add a disclaimer or a caveat. I accept them. Cooper loves me. All of me.

For the first time since I lost Betsy, I fall asleep. When I wake, I see Cooper has fallen asleep too. I bet he's run himself as ragged as me trying to find the killer. The whole time I was sharing his bed.

Holden is here, and when he sees me, he sits up straighter.

"Oh, I was so scared," he says when I reach out and touch his arm.

"Scared of what?" I ask.

"Scared you might not wake up." His eyes reach mine.

"I'm wide awake, Holden."

Awake for the first time in my life. Things are clearer now. Sharp. And what I see is this: A mother's love is a complicated thing.

Flawed, surely. Hopeful too. Irreverent. Pure.

And beneath that, there is a battle cry. A warriors' song.

I will fight for my children; I will draw blood. I won't quit.

And the blood that spills in that war, the carnage we carry -- its bonds are thicker than the water that fills a mother's womb.

I may not have brought Holden into this world -- but I will bleed for him.

He is my son and I am his mother.

And I will never stop believing in him.

SEVEN YEARS LATER

Being Holden's mother has taught me that everyone deserves a second chance. Sometimes a third. A fifth. A fiftieth. People don't change overnight. Sometimes they never change at all.

Just because we promise to love someone, doesn't mean it will be easy. I may have been wearing rose-colored glasses all those years ago, when I stood before a judge and promised to love and protect my son -- but not anymore. I threw them to the ground a long time past, smashed the lenses with my foot, the frames cracking under my weight.

I'm not bitter -- at least, not most days. Now I'm able to see through bullshit faster than most mothers I know. And sweet Sparrow is just learning that now. She's six -- born eight months after Betsy's death. Four months after my ex-husband was sentenced to life without parole. Two months after Cooper and I stood before a justice of the peace and made the vows I should have made a decade ago.

Or maybe not. Life isn't built on even steps one after the next, a straight line. Not mine, not anyones. If life is built on anything it's built on a slippery slope. The angle isn't aware of our good intentions or our bad. There are lots of loose rocks. Lots of muddy paths. Lots of places to make a mistake and fall. It's bound to happen. Your knees will get scraped and you'll break some bones. You're lucky if there is someone beside you, offering you their hand. Helping you back up.

Trista is behind me, sitting in the pavilion at the fairgrounds where the alternative high school graduation is taking place. Jeff is next to her. Cooper is next to me, Sparrow tucked under his arm. His wing.

Betsy died on the night she was a phoenix, and I like to think she took her last breath flying. I don't want Sparrow to be scared to take flight. I want her to soar.

"He's next," Coop says, squeezing my hand. "There he goes."

"Holden Dawson," Principal Sheldon announces from the podium. Sheldon has been through the wringer with Holden -- and the fact that my son walks across the stage now is a miracle in and of itself. Sheldon grins as he shakes Holden's hand and tears fill my eyes.

For so long, I wanted this moment for him. There were nights I wondered if it would happen.

But it has. He accepts his diploma and his cheering section claps for him, hollering, filming everything. Cooper pulls me to him, kissing my cheek. Pride blossoms in my belly. I'm so proud of him.

We sit back down, Holden sheepishly smiling as he

joins the other graduates. But he looks up at me, and he smiles. He knows. He knows that my heart pounds with relief that this day finally came. That he is here, a future spread out before him.

Afterward, Sparrow gives her big brother his bouquet of balloons. A candy lei she helped me make. Trista gives him a bouquet of roses. Pink ones. Betsy's favorite. It's not lost on him.

"Thanks, Aunt Trista," he says hugging my best friend. They say you can't choose your family, but whoever they are -- they are wrong. We've chosen ours. It's messy, but I wouldn't have it any other way.

We leave the pavilion, and everyone is smiling, on our way to the parking lot his best friend Lucia runs over, gives him a hug.

"We did it, Holden! We really did it!" She throws back her head, her bleached blonde hair swishing, her short denim skirt barely covering her ass as Holden grabs her by the waist, swinging her around. They both laugh with incredulity. Her mom, Tabitha walks over, waving hello.

"I swear, these two can't get in any messes tonight," she says with a shake of the head, a weary smile. "I have a night shift and can't be worrying about bailing them out." She's a single mom, holding on by a thread, and she loves her daughter the way I love mine. With all that I am.

"They won't," I say loudly. "Will you?"

Lucia and Holden bite their lips, stand up straight, as if toy soldiers. "We promise to be good," Holden says.

"Lucia has to walk the straight and narrow, boot camp won't take any delinquents."

Cooper chuckles. "The school grad-party will be the best place for you two tonight."

"It's gonna be super fun." Lucia gives us a fake smile, and I know her idea of fun is similar to Holden's.

Lucia and Holden became friends the first day of their sophomore year when they got in trouble for smoking pot behind the dumpsters. They've been inseparable since.

Now though, they have futures on the line -- Lucia joined the Marines and Holden is enrolled at the tech school to become an EMT. His dream is to be a fire-fighter. To save someone who can't save themselves.

Lucia and Tabitha, Trista and Jeff, and our family, all get in our cars, headed to a waterfront restaurant to celebrate this special day.

As we're walking to our table on the patio, the water of Port Windwick before us, Trista pulls me aside.

"You did it, Mom," she says, pointing to our family as they are seated. "Look at your boy, he's all grown up."

"You paved the way," I squeezed her hand. Last year, Levi went off to Stanford on a basketball scholarship. "But thankfully, Holden isn't moving away yet." The tech school is only twenty miles from our home. "Sparrow would be a mess without him. He's the sun to her moon."

"So, is she still obsessed with Arlo?" Trista asks as we head to the table. Sparrow and Arlo became friends this spring when I signed my daughter up for swim lessons. Of course, the first person she came home talking about was Arlo, Caro's daughter.

I lift my eyebrows. "They have a play date planned for next week. I swear, when Caro texted making the plans, I was shocked. But I mean, I'm not going to tell Sparrow no. It's ancient history, right?"

Trista nods. "You haven't seen her in how long?"

"Since Betsy's funeral. Seven years ago."

Trista shakes her head. "Girl, you're going to need happy hour after that play date. You better text me where to meet you. Gin martinis, on me."

"Arlo goes to the Montessori Schoolhouse," I say.

"I wonder if the Mommy Tribe is still in full force," she says. After the fall Betsy died, Trista and I pulled our kids from the program. We moved across town to a public school -- and turns out, it gave Levi a wonderful education. He's Ivy League for Chrissakes.

"I wouldn't know," I say. Then I smirk, adding, "Maybe I'll ask Caro next week."

I have no idea what happened to Jenna's twins, the Middleton boys, Marcie Devon's son. I deleted all social media after everything went down and haven't looked back. I can't, not when I have so much in front of me.

We get to the table and Cooper pulls out my seat, kisses me before I sit down.

"You ladies plotting something?" he asks.

I laugh. "Always."

We order drinks, and when they arrive, I look to Cooper, to make a toast, but Holden pushes back from the table, raises his glass.

"I wanted to say a few things. Uh, first, thanks for

being here. All of you. For all of it. I know I didn't exactly make it easy for you those eight years."

We all smile, eyes meeting, memories swirling around us all.

"I wish Betsy was here today. She taught me what it meant to be a friend -- which works well for you, Lucia." His dark eyes fixed on her.

She shakes her head. "You're gonna make me cry!"

"Betsy also taught me how to be a brother," he says. "And good thing, because Sparrow, being your big brother is an important job."

Sparrow smiles up at Holden, savoring his every word. I swallow, tears filling my eyes. Cooper reaches for my hand, and beside me, Sparrow rests her cheek on my arm.

"She also taught me what it meant to be someone's child," he says, his voice cracking. "Which is a good thing for Mom and Dad, because even though I've made a lot of mistakes, there would have been a hell of a lot more if she hadn't modeled for me what it meant to let someone take care of me."

Cooper runs a hand over his beard, his emotion spilling out from his eyes. Being a father to Holden and Sparrow has made him the best version of himself. That I have the privilege of being his partner, through thick and thin, is one of life's greatest honors.

"And the last thing," Holden says, clearing his throat. "Before I came home, I never knew what love was. Betsy started to teach me before anyone else, and Mom, you finished after she was gone."

Everyone's eyes are glassy, and I push back from the table, stepping toward him.

Holden is taller than me -- taller than Coop! He's grown. His depth knows no bounds.

I wrap my arms around him. He doesn't flinch. Doesn't pull away. With all the love in the world, my son hugs me back.

ALSO BY:

THE WIFE LIE

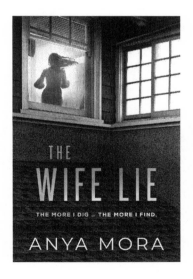

My husband is missing.
And his wife is on my doorstep.
The wife I never knew he had.

Does that mean my husband's out looking for wife number three?

The more I dig... the more I find.

Ledger Stone is not the man I thought I knew.

What I'd thought was a whirlwind romance has turned out to be a hurricane laced with lies.

It started with one.

Will it end with another?

The Wife Lie is a domestic suspense novel where secrets are buried deep.

Penny Stone gave up everything for the husband she thought she knew -- and now she must uncover the truth: just how much of her marriage was a lie?

And is their love worth fighting for?

DOWNLOAD NOW: **On Amazon**

ACKNOWLEDGMENTS

Eryn Scott, G.L. Snodgrass, and Kristi Rose – thank you for believing in me even when I didn't believe in myself. It's been a long road and I'm eternally grateful that we've travelled it together.

Many thanks to Myra Scott, Pamela Kelly, and Kim Lorraine for your feedback. The story is better for it.

Thank you, Jeremy, for loving me so hard even if the book broke your heart.

And to my children, you make me want to be the bravest mother in the world. I'm yours, always; and you are mine.

ABOUT THE AUTHOR

Anya Mora relies on her experience as a wife and mother to form her creative expression. Mora grew her family through birth and older child adoption and her writing captures a unique view on relationships and motherhood. Her novels, while leaning toward the dark, ultimately reflect light, courage, and her innate belief that love rewards the brave.

To learn about sales and new releases, sign up for Mora's mailing list here: https://anyamora.com/newsletter/